Painting the Lake:
A Murder on the North Shore

JODY WENNER

Cover design by Scott Wenner
Cover photograph by Michael Lindquist
Author photograph by J.J. Killins

ISBN: 1523957085
ISBN-13: 978-1523957088

DEDICATION

To my mom and dad. They say write what you know so I gave George my dad's quiet strength because he really did sacrifice for his family and always did it without complaint. Unlike Melinda, thankfully, my mom continues to be a fighter, beating her cancer one day at a time.

ACKNOWLEDGMENTS

I need to thank retired St. Paul Police Sergeant Richard Klein for reading an early draft and for giving me several thorough and thoughtfully produced notes to help make sure I was accurate with my police work. I hope I did justice to the final pages in that regard. I was truly humbled to be able to sit down with him as he shared some of his personal knowledge and experiences with me.

To Robert Hansen for graciously offering to read my work and for giving me such kind and encouraging feedback. I hope I was able to capture some of the mood of his own experiences as a cabin owner on Lake Superior. Your insight regarding weather and the science behind it was priceless, so thank you.

Thank you, Susan Sey, for so generously sharing the coffee shop with me as I attempted to absorb your writing abilities from across the table. And on days when I wasn't confident the magic was happening on its own, thank you for being patient with me as I interrupted your workflow so you could help me work out a plot point or two. They were often crucial to this story's success, so I appreciate it.

To all of my early readers, friends and family, who helped me shape the story in one way or another. I know you are all sick to death of my constant begging for another pair of eyes. Without your feedback and encouragement, I'm sure I'd have given up by now, so thank you. You all know who you are.

Lastly, to my daughter and husband, who mean more to me than all of the success in the world, but without them, there would be none. Olivia, I hope you will at least wait until you are older to read this story, even though you've already gleaned too much of it hunched over my shoulder as I clicked away at the keyboard. I also hope you continue to snoop your way through many more books in the future. Scott, you have had to endure my emotional hills and valleys as I traverse this creative landscape, which has been tiring and mostly uphill. Luckily for me, you understand the creative journey well and have been more or less patient with me as I find my footing. There's no one else I'd want to make the trek with but you. Love you always and forever.

Chapter 1

Nancy absolutely hated her job. Actually, that wasn't true. She loved her job, she just hated doing it in Duluth. As if it wasn't already bad enough being a woman in a predominantly male job, being a detective in a small, northern-Minnesota town was probably even tougher. To make matters worse, Nancy was the new kid on the squad. She could admit she never wanted to come to Minnesota. There were plenty of things to be mad at Roger for, but this one was unforgivable, as far as she was concerned. Even she had a preconceived idea of what "up north" was going to be like. Most people thought of it as pristine lake country, but Nancy didn't see that side of things. This was no vacation destination, as far as she could tell. Her experience was that of the real Duluth, the working class area, or Duluth proper, which didn't feel like a cozy cabin nestled in the north woods— quite the opposite, really. Besides that, she wasn't born yesterday. She'd seen Fargo. She was somewhat relieved once she got here to realize the Coen Brothers had taken some liberties with their character portrayal of northern cops, though she could also admit she'd met a few who weren't far off from the bumbling idiots in that film.

Today, Nancy sat at her desk near the back of the station filing some paperwork, contemplating what to have for lunch. Usually she packed a lunch because going outside in March was often more dangerous than being a detective in Duluth, but this morning she'd avoided the kitchen because her husband was in there making coffee. She'd rather fight the cold weather than deal with Roger some days. Most of the time she tried to pretend everything was fine, but they'd had another argument last night, and this morning she was tired. It felt easier to avoid the whole thing altogether.

The fight was trivial. Roger had forgotten to put the trash can out again. It irritated Nancy that she had to tell him every single Tuesday that Wednesday was trash day. Part of their problem was the simple fact that both of them considered themselves to be the alpha in the relationship; neither of them would back down, even if it was just a fight about trash. Roger could be so stubborn, he actually had the nerve to tell Nancy he thought she liked putting the can out because she did it every week. Nancy knew she could be difficult too, but it was the job that made her have to fight for everything. She didn't mean to be so headstrong.

Last night's argument was just another notch in the long frayed belt that comprised their marriage, which was beginning to cinch so tightly around Nancy she felt like she was suffocating. It'd been riddled with problems since early last year, beginning with Roger moving her here from the West Coast to take a sales job for one of the big steel distributors that ran out of the Great Lakes. Nancy liked warmth more than anything else. She missed tall buildings and palm trees. So to add to her list of disadvantages of being a relatively new detective in Duluth, she wasn't actually from Duluth. She was a big city outsider. She knew the entire force called her "California" behind her back, like it was a terminal disease. She wasn't sure she'd ever understand Midwesterners.

"Detective Simmons," an officer said, snapping her out of her beach-laden daydream.

She looked up at Anderson who was standing in front of her desk, waving a piece of paper. "A call just came in. A possible body's been washed up near Canal Park."

"Okay. Thanks."

Nancy grabbed her trench coat, which was way too thin for this ridiculous weather, but she hadn't gotten around to getting a real winter coat yet because that would mean she was staying, which was something she still didn't want to admit, even though this was the second full Minnesota winter she'd endured. But really, how could people take a detective seriously wearing one of those ridiculous puffy jackets? She sucked it up and put the coat on. She wrapped her wool scarf around her neck several times, grabbed her leather bag, slung it over her shoulder, and headed out. Her bag held everything she needed: a small recording device, a crime kit, a digital camera, and a little pad of paper for notes. She also kept her gun in there. Most cops would laugh at that, especially her colleagues in California, but in the time she'd been in Minnesota, she'd never needed it. Not once. That was definitely one thing this state had going for it. Sure, there were bad guys here too, but shootings were too rare to warrant her need to keep her weapon holstered.

On the drive down the steep hill on Lake Street she thought more about lunch. At least there were some decent places to eat in Canal Park. She wasn't trying to be glib about a possible death, but she'd been on a bunch of these calls. They usually just ended up being a tire or a drowned raccoon, maybe something that had fallen overboard from a cargo ship making its way into the narrow port. By the time she got down there, it would probably already be pulled to shore and the call canceled, making her freed up in time for lunch. Maybe she'd try that new microbrewery everybody at the station kept saying had great burgers.

Nancy was part of the Investigations Unit in Duluth. Her area of expertise was homicide. She had fifteen years as head of the homicide unit in San Diego, and it was the area she had the most knowledge and passion for, so when a call came in, she was usually the first to volunteer. She was comfortable solving murders. She never wished for a homicide, but it had been a while since she'd actually worked a case, and she liked to keep her skills sharp. So if she had to postpone lunch, and dinner, and most all food for the next few days, she would. She just wouldn't believe it was a homicide until she saw it.

When she arrived, yellow crime scene tape already secured the area. As Nancy weaved her way closer, she made out the dark spot wedged between the ice ridge and a jagged rock about eighteen to twenty feet off shore. She said hello to the officer blocking off the area from the public, to which he replied, "Nice day for a trip to the beach, eh Simmons?"

She scowled. "Minnesotans have a weird understanding of the term beach." He chuckled, and she headed past the tape to the other officers huddled on the shoreline.

"What have we got?" she asked Balton. He was an old-school cop whom she particularly loathed, but she had a job to do, and she wouldn't be pushed around by a bigot like Balton. Besides, as she stood next to him now, she practically towered over him. Her height often intimidated men, and she didn't mind using it to her advantage in certain situations.

"Spotted by a jogger about a half an hour ago," he said, eyeballing the dark spot a ways off from where they stood along the bluff. The breeze coming strong off the water shot loose snow toward them, making visibility temporarily poor. Nancy pulled her scarf around her face a little tighter and squinted to try to get a better view of the scene.

"What's the best option for retrieval? Can we get a boat in that close or do we need a diver?" she asked.

"That's what we were just discussing," Balton said, turning back toward the guy from Rescue.

"Coast Guard is just a few minutes away," the young man from Rescue said, having the decency to look at Nancy when he said it.

"Great. Let's start there then. Can you radio them?"

He nodded.

She pulled her notepad from her bag and jotted the time down as well as some other general notes about the location, though she was still too far away to get much detail. She snapped a couple of photos of the ground and the dark spot bobbing out in the water. She would save the rest of the details for the CSIU if the object turned out to be a body. She walked toward the water to a rocky area just off the shore and picked a large boulder to stand atop for a better view. Where she stood, Lake Superior was roughly to her east. The shoreline ran in this location for miles, more or less from northeast to southwest, and was covered in several feet of hard-packed snow this time of year. Just off the rocky shore, layers of massive ice sheets collided together as they battled each other and the beach to form sharp, snarling ridges that reminded Nancy of broken glass shards. She couldn't help but think they added an element of brutality to an already harsh environment.

Surveying the landscape leading out to the water, she saw no discernible prints on the ground. The snow here took a major beating from the powerful wind, known as the lake-effect in these parts, causing not light and fluffy drifts, but a smooth, icy surface to form. The ground in the other direction, back toward the beach, wasn't giving Nancy much to go on either, but for a different reason entirely. The Lakewalk, a paved walking path running adjacent to the shoreline, was one of high traffic even in the dead of winter, much to Nancy's bewilderment. The snow on and around the path had been trampled so much, it was impossible to isolate anything unusual in the way of clues.

Widening her view, she looked toward the town's crown jewel: the aerial lift bridge, a massive hulk of steel that hovered above the shipping canal on South Lake Avenue. Canal Park, the area of town surrounding it, was a popular tourist destination because of the iconic bridge, and the ships making their way in and out of the harbor, and therefore had several eateries, hotels, gift shops, and even a maritime museum within walking distance.

Nancy's toes were starting to tingle, and she definitely wished she had worn a thicker sweater today. She closed her notebook and jumped from the rock, heading back toward Balton, who was now talking with a few more officers who'd recently arrived on the scene. She was sure she could hear the word California blowing in the frigid breeze, but she tried not to let it bother her as she joined them to wait. A huddle was the warmest option she had at the moment.

Before long the Coast Guard boat had its winch out and was hoisting the unidentified object out of the water. Someone handed Nancy a pair of binoculars. The wind died down just in time for her to see black leather knee-high boots flopping as the object was lifted high, dangling over Lake Superior, before being brought on board the search and rescue boat. The boots were obviously attached to a body, which could only mean one thing. It was a woman. Nancy called for the medical examiner and crime scene investigators to join her on the scene.

"Hey, Erickson," she said to one of the officers when she returned to the huddle, "I'd like someone to talk with the lift bridge operators. Find out if they saw any jumpers."

He nodded.

In Nancy's time in Duluth, though short, there had actually been a few jumpers. That lift bridge seemed to call to people in the middle of winter like the beacon on the Split Rock Lighthouse up in Two Harbors. Hell, Nancy could admit she'd even contemplated climbing that steel monster a few times in order to plunge into the icy water, especially since she and Roger had been in such a bad place, and especially in March when it felt like the cold was never going to abate. So yeah, a jumper was a very real possibility. But Nancy had a gut feeling about this one and she knew she should trust it. She didn't think this was a suicide.

She looked back longingly at the microbrewery. She wondered if her gut was right, or if she was simply hungry. She was probably not going to get that burger if she was right. She'd be lucky to eat much at all over the course of the next crucial forty-eight hours.

Chapter 2
Several Months Prior

George felt his retirement coming at him like he was about to crash into a brick wall. Time was moving too fast, and he couldn't stop it. He slipped his time card into the rusted stamper for what would be one of the final times. How had this many years passed? All spent at the same company, no less. He still recalled answering the ad in the paper; he was no more than a kid himself, with his own on the way. Now it was his last week of work. His child was grown. He still felt the same way he'd felt every day clocking in and out. Nothing had changed in his mind except the surreal notion that he'd somehow become an old man overnight.

He remembered his very first day on the job like it was last week. He wore khaki pants, a turtleneck, steel-toed work boots, and he carried a big black lunch box with a green, metal Stanley thermos. He'd grown out a scruffy beard so he would appear a little older and maybe slightly more intimidating to the rest of the factory workers. Now he was a man of sixty-five, wearing a thick flannel shirt and dirty jeans. He still had the beard but it was fuller and weaved with silver threads that stuck out like a coarse reminder he was about to retire.

He threw on his coat as he made his way to the parking lot filled with pick-ups and over-sized SUVs. There was a crisp nip in the air; some moisture too. An early snowfall was on the way. George got in his little silver Toyota Prius. As he pulled away from the dank warehouse, there was nothing but dread tied to the thought of leaving Bronze. He'd been with the company for forty-five years. It was hard to jump from such a moving train. Most people didn't think of retirement as coming up against the wall; they looked forward to the day. Why he didn't was beyond even his own comprehension. Yet, he knew it was time to go. The problem was, when he boiled it right down, George wasn't a man who settled into change easily. He wasn't a creature of habit necessarily, but he liked predictability. He liked the slow drive on a Sunday in the country. He liked knowing exactly what up ahead. But given his current situation, he felt like he was driving blind. So there was definitely some apprehension, but he was sixty-five, and at sixty-five you collected your retirement package, no matter how meager, and you moved on, let someone else take the driver's seat while you found some other way to spend your days.

Before heading home, George had an appointment with a realtor. His wife had set the whole thing up and was supposed to meet him there, but she'd texted him during the day to say she wasn't feeling up to it. It worried him enough to called her back right away. Melinda reassured him she just had a little headache, so he went to meet the realtor alone.

He found Olson and Sons Realty in a strip mall on Lexington Avenue, only a few miles from his house. Mel had been referred to them by a neighbor. George glanced at his wife's text one last time in the parking lot, taking in the details. He was scheduled to meet with Michael Olson, one of the sons of Olson and Sons.

"Okay," the agent said once George was seated behind the desk, "what type of place are you looking for, Mr. Altman?"

"A cabin where we can spend some time with our daughter near Ely. My wife would like something right in Ely, but I would prefer something on Lake Superior, so maybe closer to Silver Bay or Two Harbors. I'd like a view of the lake if at all possible. Something modest is fine. Two bedrooms. Oh, and maybe something that can work as a studio space where I can paint," George said.

As Michael typed the requirements into his computer, George examined him. He was a younger guy with an expensive suit and tie on, probably in his mid-thirties with slicked back hair and a flashy watch—much too conservative looking for George's taste. Maybe it was all the time he'd spent in a factory, but suits always felt stifling to him. Fake. He knew it was proper attire for the profession, but it still somehow turned George immediately off to the realtor.

"So, you're a painter?" Michael asked, waiting for his computer to search the MLS database for appropriate home listings.

"Well, I studied art in college. Now that I'm retiring I figure I'll need a hobby."

Michael nodded and focused back on his computer screen.

After Melinda got pregnant in their sophomore year, he dropped out of college. He had no discernible skills, so he took the first job he'd stumbled across in the classified ads. He'd planned to be a painter; he figured factory work was probably slightly more profitable. Instead of painting canvases, he spent the last four decades in a factory painting miscellaneous parts for just about every gadget known to man: car parts, game pieces, scale models, furniture, and the list went on and on. He was a patient man and that was all you really needed to be in order to have marginal success in a blue-collar profession. While the other employees came and went, in search of something bigger and better paying, he remained and worked his way up the ranks to floor manager. It was an oddly satisfying job to George, who assumed from a young age he would be a farmer. Perhaps it was because he was raised in the country that he had an immediate fascination for the gritty, mechanical feel of the St. Paul factory: the dirty floors, the paint sprayers puffing out hues of every color in the palette; but mostly, he liked the simple routine of seeing the pieces all come together as the belts and motors churned out a finished product.

Finally, the computer sounded off, alerting them to the fact that the search was completed. The young realtor said to George while still peering at the screen, "Unfortunately, there's not much in your price range available on the lake. Those places tend to go for about a hundred thousand more than the numbers we discussed. But I do have a possibility for you while you wait for something to come up." He wheeled his office chair slightly away from the computer to face George now. "I do a little property management on the side and I've actually got a rental available in Duluth right now, just a bit north of town. It's right on the lake, only a one bedroom though. But this way, if you decide you hate it up there, you'd only be locked into a year lease."

"Hmm. It could work. I don't know if the wife will go for it. Let me talk it over with her."

"Sounds good. I'll email the information to you. In the meantime, I'll keep checking the listings in case something else pops up."

"Okay. Thanks."

"Oh, let me give you my card." He handed him a business card and they shook hands.

"Have a good one," George said, reading the card as he walked out.

"Your company gonna throw a big retirement party for ya?" Michael asked suddenly, causing George to stop at the threshold and take in what this young professional had asked. He obviously knew nothing about factory workers. Probably hadn't had to do a single day of hard labor in his life. They didn't buy cake and balloons each time someone left a company like Bronze. If they did, it would be like one long birthday party. It was a rather strange question thrown out of left field, but George realized this kid was still trying to connect with him in order to clench the sale. George knew he'd been rather cold, as was his way with sales people, but he had no reason to distrust this guy. He was just a go-getter, George decided. He turned and tried to smile. "A cabin where I can paint is enough for me, uh, Mr. Olson," he said, looking back down at the business card in his hand.

"I'm sure I can arrange that for ya." Michael Olson produced a wide grin and sat straight in his chair, exuding confidence.

"I appreciate it." With that, George turned and headed for home.

***

Melinda had dinner ready on the table when George arrived, just as she had most every weeknight George could remember, even when she was working. His wife had retired from teaching elementary school when she'd been diagnosed with breast cancer last year. It was a scary time, these past several months, but Melinda was now in remission.

"You didn't have to make dinner," George said, kissing her on the cheek when he entered the kitchen, setting his lunch box down on the counter.

"I'm fine. Just a little headache."

"Did you take something?"

"I will, after we eat."

They sat down at the dining room table to roast beef and mashed potatoes.

Melinda said, "Only a few more days to go and Bronze will be a thing of the past."

"You don't have to tell me." He smiled at her from across the table. She was a little heavier from the chemo and hormone therapy she'd gone through, but he didn't care about that.

"Hey, how did the meeting go with the realtor?" she asked.

"There's not much on the market right now within our price range."

"Do we need to bump it up a little?"

"Not if you still want to take all of the trips we've discussed, but I think I have a good alternative. The realtor said he has a property for rent right now in Duluth. I don't know how nice it is, but it would put us closer to Ella, and it's right on the lake. He's going to send me the details and some photos."

"A rental? When's it available?"

"Beginning of February."

"But I had my heart set on traveling first. What would you rather do? A freezing cabin in Duluth or a tropical getaway?"

George didn't have to think about it. "A cabin."

"Seriously, George!"

He shrugged his shoulders. "Forty-six years and I think we're having our first disagreement."

Melinda laughed. "You wish."

"I just feel like I've put my art on hold for such a long time and now I'm anxious to see if I even remember how to paint."

"You've waited this long, I think you should save it for when we're too old to get around and too numb to notice the cold."

"I thought you wanted to be closer to Ella?"

"I do. I worry about her, and she never visits anymore, but she's an adult, and we could use some relaxation after the year we've had."

"Fine. We'll do it your way," George relented, even though he didn't love the idea of traveling.

His wife smiled at him. "And that's why we've lasted forty-six years."

"I know when I've been outmatched, that's all," George said looking at his wife lovingly. Even if he was feeling unsure of what was to come, at least he wasn't doing it alone. That was maybe the one takeaway from the cancer. He didn't really care what they did, he was just happy Melinda was still there to do it with him.

Chapter 3

Nancy got a preliminary look at the body as the Crime Scene Unit processed it. She pulled her scarf up around her nose because even outside on a thirteen degree day with wind whipping, the smell of the corpse permeated the air.

Now that it was laid out in front of her, as was Nancy's way, she said a silent pledge, a sort of promise to the deceased, that if she turned out to be a victim, Nancy would do everything in her power to work for her, find who had committed the heinous act, and bring some justice. That was the code she had taken when she signed up for this job, and that really was the part of her job she loved, helping those who could not help themselves.

As she listened to the examiner inform her of his initial impressions, Nancy visually noted the large discolored contusions covering the body, but it was not evident at this point if they were caused by the violent actions occurring in the water as the body slammed against the rocks, or if it was produced by another human being. According to the examiner, there appeared to be no initial evidence of gunshot wounds to the body. Nor were there any distinct identifying markings or features that would help make a post-mortem ID easier—no tattoos, no unusual moles, birthmarks, scars, nothing of that nature. She was a petite woman measuring five feet, one inch long. She had long brown hair. Nancy cursed to herself knowing that just finding out who this person was could prove to be a more difficult task than she wanted. It was even hard to pinpoint an age given the condition of the waterlogged body.

"Can you check the coat pockets for a wallet?" Nancy asked.

"I got a very wet smartphone. That's it."

The phone was bagged. No wallet, no purse, no ID.

Once the hearse arrived and the body was taken back for a full autopsy, Nancy went back to the office. Frozen, she sat at her desk trying to thaw out while she ran some searches for missing person reports filed and checked the call logs for domestic abuse that might match the very vague description she had. She found nothing for either of these initial attempts at identifying her potential victim.

That night, after a few more calls with the medical examiner and the beat cops who were doing the initial inquiries, she still had no identification, and therefore she was at a standstill. She'd created a case file for Jane Doe and sat at her desk, bouncing her pencil eraser into the cheap wood veneer, thinking about her next steps. It was frustrating knowing time was slipping away. She checked her watch. It was close to nine o'clock already.

She'd hounded the medical examiner several times since the body had come in. She didn't want to pester but these were crucial minutes. A loud ticking noise had been sounding off in Nancy's skull since she saw the woman come out of the lake. Just as she was about to dial the examiner's office again, her phone rang.

"Finally got something for ya, Detective Simmons."

"I'm ready, Bill."

"Got a full set of clear prints. The cold water preserved them fairly well. We just sent them to the crime lab. Someone will call ya if they get a match on them. Could take a few hours for the run."

"Great. That's good news. Thanks, Bill."

"No problem."

"Anything else?"

"Not yet. Still working. Will let you know."

It was something. A possible lead. A start. By the time Nancy hung up the phone and finished making her notes, the station was mostly quiet and fairly dark. She stood and stretched her back, letting a loud yawn escape. She decided to head home and get cleaned up while she waited.

***

She sat in her living room eating cold pizza, adding information to the new case file by the light of the lamp next to the couch when Roger came in.

"How was your day?" he asked, cracking open a can and plopping down into the recliner.

"Pulled a body from the lake," she said, keeping her gaze on the paperwork in front of her.

"Oh, I bet you're excited about that."

"Yeah, I'm thrilled a young girl has died," Nancy said dryly, finally facing her husband. He looked ridiculous drinking a cheap beer in an expensive suit, even if it was wrinkled. He yanked his tie off and Nancy noticed his thick head of hair beginning to thin.

"You know what I mean," Roger said. "You just mentioned recently how it's been a long time since you've worked a case, that's all."

"Having beer for dinner? You really have become a Duluthian."

He shrugged. "I had a late lunch."

She nodded and looked back down.

"So, this is bad timing. I just found out I've got to be in Cali for a couple of days. I was hoping you might come along, but now...I suppose you'll be busy with work."

Nancy closed the file in her lap. "Why are you going to California?"

"I'm meeting with some potential investors. Thought you might want to get out of the cold."

"That would be nice, and I've been meaning to visit my mom, but you're right. I can't."

Roger nodded. "All right. I need to pack. I have an early morning flight." He got up and headed for the bedroom. Nancy felt his hand lightly make contact with her shoulder as he brushed past her.

When he was gone, she grabbed the remote off the coffee table and turned the TV on. She checked her phone for any calls she might have missed while Roger babbled at her. Still nothing. She yanked the blanket perched atop the couch and pulled it down around her, trying to get comfortable. She closed her eyes. She needed rest if she was going to solve a murder.

Chapter 4

In bed, George tossed and turned. He looked over at Melinda, who seemed to be sleeping off her headache soundly. Eventually, he surrendered and got up to get a drink of water. Sitting at the kitchen table, George continued to ponder the uncertainty he was feeling. It likely had to do with the fact that every time he thought of being retired, he couldn't help but connect it to aging. After this week, he wasn't going to be a regular working guy anymore; he was going to be an old guy in the final hurdle of his life.

He could never have guessed retiring would be a source of so much anxiety. It should've been the exact opposite, in fact. He'd worked hard for a very long time, for very little money. Yet, he'd still managed to save enough so he wouldn't have to concern himself with financial woes. Slow and steady. That was George. He'd done the math, and he and Melinda would be just fine with what they had. So, why couldn't he just relax now and be happy? Instead he felt a nagging foreboding. He couldn't say why, only that it was a change and with change came stress. It was probably normal, he decided, though he still wished he could somehow avoid it.

After setting his glass in the sink, George stood for a long time just staring out the kitchen window. The moon's light reflected off the snow just beginning to fall. It reminded him how a Minnesota winter could have so much beauty to it. He'd always loved the winter months. Most people hated the cold and snow, but he'd grown up in this state and actually wouldn't have it any other way. He loved the extreme

changes of seasons and the familiar yet nostalgic air
the winter brought with it. Something about being
bundled up in layers, feeling cozy while just feet away,
on the other side of the wall, Mother Nature was
trying to do whatever she could to take you out. He
couldn't really explain it, he just liked the feeling, like
being swaddled in a warm blanket while being
submerged in icy water—weird, yet comforting.
Something only true Minnesotans understood. But he
knew Melinda wasn't a fan of the long dark winters.
She'd been through so much this year, and he knew
she deserved some warmth and relaxation, even if it
wasn't his desire. Maybe escaping the brunt of the
cold wasn't the worst idea. He'd probably experienced
enough long winters to last him a lifetime.

Besides, the art would still be there when he
was ready to try his hand at it again. He'd waited this
long, what was a little bit longer? There had just never
been time or space previously to fully commit himself
to it. Or maybe he'd just always found excuses
because he lacked the confidence to open up on the
canvas. There was a vulnerability to it all that he
didn't like to show. But now that he was an old guy
with little purpose and little time left, he was feeling
ready to do something bigger than factory work, to
put himself out there before it was too late.

Whether or not he could accomplish what he
had swimming around his head was yet to be seen,
but it was something to look forward to—a plan.
Once he and Mel took a few vacations, he would
tackle the canvas.

Feeling mildly better, thinking he now knew
what was to come, George crept into bed and
managed to get a few good hours of sleep until it was

time to get up and continue with the grind for a few more days.

**

That next evening, George walked in through the garage door after work and felt immediately that something wasn't right. There were no smells of a home-cooked meal wafting from the kitchen, no Melinda there to greet him. One quick glance toward the dark dining room with an unset table proved him right. He picked up his pace, calling, "Mel! Are you here?"

He tried to tell himself he was being ridiculous and hypersensitive but she hadn't texted him at all today, which was a little unusual. She'd been bored during her recovery months and had been extra chatty with him during the workday. He should have checked up on her. Since she'd gotten sick, he couldn't help but feel like Melinda was still somehow fragile, even if the doctor had said she was in the clear. He climbed the stairs two at a time and opened their bedroom door.

Melinda was in bed. Her eyes were closed. *Thank God*, he thought. She was fine. She was just napping, something she was doing a lot more these days. Before the cancer, she wasn't one to sleep much. Maybe her headache from yesterday returned and she was just sleeping it off. That was probably it. He let out his breath and took the opportunity to just watch his wife in such a peaceful state. He pulled the covers back just a bit and that was when he saw her face. Something about it didn't look quite right. Was her color a bit off?

"Mel," he said softly. He touched her shoulder. She didn't respond. He bent closer to her then he shook her a little harder. "Melinda!" he hollered. Still no response. She wasn't dead, he was certain of that, but something was definitely not right. He fumbled for the cell phone in his pocket and dialed 911. As it rang, he felt her neck for a pulse. There was a very weak thumping, but he definitely felt it.

"911. What's your emergency?" a woman asked.

"I don't know! Something's wrong with my wife. I think she's unconscious. Please hurry!"

***

At the hospital, George watched helplessly as the EMTs rolled his wife away, telling him they'd do everything they could for her. He paced the floor of the lobby for a few minutes then took out his phone and dialed Ella's number.

"Hey, Dad. What's up?"

"El. It's Mom—I came home from work and she was unconscious in bed. She had a headache yesterday, but I don't know. We're at the hospital now."

"Oh, God. Okay. I'm coming," Ella said.

"Are you sure you want to drive all this way? The roads aren't totally clear from the snow yesterday. Maybe you should wait. I haven't spoken with anyone yet. Maybe they'll come out and tell me she's fine." God, he hoped so. He really did.

"Okay. Call me back when you know more."

"I will. I'll let you know as soon as I talk to a doctor."

When George hung up he went to the desk and they gave him a pile of paperwork to fill out while he waited. Normally he would have loathed the idea, but it was exactly what he needed to keep his mind off of what was happening in the room where they'd wheeled his wife. Except as he finished up with the forms, there was still no news. He returned the clipboard to the desk.

"Can you tell me anything about what's going on?" he inquired. His voice was shaky but he didn't care.

The receptionist barely looked at him. "A doctor will be out to talk to you when they're ready."

He sat back down, tapped his foot on the ground to match the rhythm of his beating heart, got up again, walked the length of the hall, and sat down again. He looked at his watch. It had been nearly an hour since they'd arrived. It was also now close to eight o'clock and he hadn't eaten anything since lunch. He was exhausted too, having not slept well the previous night, but he had so much adrenaline coursing through him, he felt more light-headed than tired. He got up slowly to get something from the vending machine to see if it might help.

He selected a bag of chips and a bottle of water and headed back to his chair near the reception desk. When he approached he saw a man in scrubs standing propped up against the desk. George quickened his steps.

"Mr. Altman?" the doctor said, extending his arm.

"Yes." George shifted the chips to shake the doctor's hand.

"Why don't you sit down?" the doctor said, pointing to the chair George had been sitting in earlier.

George's stomach felt hollow and he was suddenly very dizzy. He sat and somehow managed to squeak out, "How is she?"

"Mr. Altman, your wife suffered a major stroke. I understand from reviewing her chart that she was recovering from cancer?"

"Yes."

"Strokes are not uncommon in people who've just undergone extensive radiation and chemotherapy treatment. They can affect the blood vessels and cause clotting to occur. Unfortunately, Mr. Altman, we did everything we could, but we weren't able to save her. I'm sorry."

Chapter 5

Nancy stayed on the couch pretending to sleep as Roger slipped out at roughly four-thirty the next morning. She felt guilt and relief. Guilt that she was actually relieved he was gone and she could give her undivided attention to this new case. It was exactly what she wanted to do—be distracted. She'd deal with Roger later.

Once she was sure he was gone, she quickly got herself up off the couch and stretched her sore back. She had only herself to blame for her discomfort. She checked her phone again and saw there were no messages. She headed for the bathroom. She was anxious to get moving so she skipped the shower and pulled her hair into a tight bun, washed her face, and called it acceptable. There was nothing she could do about the bags under her eyes. She was in her mid forties—they were just a part of her now.

Just as she was walking out the door at almost five a.m. her phone buzzed. They had an ID. Nancy didn't even bother dragging the garbage can back to the side of the house before she left. She wondered how many days the can would sit near the road before Roger would notice it. She wasn't sure if it bothered her that Roger had always put his job before her career, or if it was that he might actually put his job before Nancy altogether. Either way, she couldn't worry about it now. A murder investigation had priority over steel. Seemed pretty straightforward to her, anyway.

Nancy didn't bother with breakfast either. She headed straight for her desk at the back of the station and found the information waiting for her. The database had hit on a match. She brought up the record on her computer. It was for one Mona Clark. Caucasian. Female. Twenty-six. Present Address: 1472 Main Street, Apt. 2. Duluth, Minnesota.

Her police record was pretty clean. She had three speeding tickets. But the one saving grace for Nancy, the thing that got her fingerprinted, was an underage drug misdemeanor for marijuana use at a party several years ago. They'd brought all of the kids in and processed them to give them a little scare while they waited for the parents to come and retrieve them; at least that's what the notes stated from the incident report Nancy read next.

She jotted Clark's info into her notepad. She hadn't taken her coat off yet so she grabbed her bag and headed out again. It only took her five minutes to arrive at 1472 Main, which was literally blocks from the department. It was an older, brown brick, stand-alone building in the central area of downtown, a coffee shop on street level with a few apartments overhead. Nancy stepped into the foyer and hit the buzzer for #2. She wasn't expecting an older woman's voice to come over the crackling speaker. Her victim was twenty-six. Nancy had anticipated a boyfriend, or perhaps a roommate, but not a parent.

"Hello," the woman said.

"Hi. I'm here about Mona Clark. I'm with the Duluth Police Department."

"What about her?"

"Do you know her?"

"I...Who?"

"Mona Clark. Are you…her mother?"

"Mona? Yes."

"Could I come up and speak with you, Ma'am?"

"Mona's not here."

"I'd like to talk with you about that."

"About what?"

Nancy wondered if she was an elderly woman. Maybe she was simply hard of hearing. She considered yelling louder into the squawk box but then, just like that, the intercom cut out and the door buzzed. Nancy grabbed the handle and pulled. She climbed up the staircase filled with dread. She hated this part of the job. She wasn't a parent herself for this exact reason. She'd been on the receiving end of it before. It wasn't something she liked to think about. She stopped at the door and tried to compose herself before she knocked.

Usually she didn't even have to knock because the person was often waiting for her when she got to the door. Nobody liked to hear a police officer asking to speak with you, especially about a child. So this was odd. The door was still closed. Nancy got closer and put her ear to it. She didn't hear any footfalls coming closer either. There was a TV playing loudly. Nancy was slightly befuddled but she'd seen lots of strange things in her line of work; stranger people even.

She rapped on the door lightly while she pulled her badge from her jacket pocket. Still just sounds of a television blasting. Nancy knocked louder. She was beginning to wonder if the elderly woman was perhaps bed-bound.

"Hello," she hollered into the door. Finally she heard light footsteps approaching.

"Who is it?" the person on the other side of the door called.

"My name is Nancy Simmons. Duluth PD."

"What's this about?"

"Your daughter."

The door opened slowly. A very slight woman of maybe seventy stood in front of Nancy. She was wearing a long nightie with a pastel floral print. "Can I help you?" she said.

Nancy was starting to realize this woman had something wrong with her. Physically she looked okay, but her eyes were searching.

"Could I come in and speak with you about your daughter?" Nancy asked gently.

"Okay."

They went into the living room and the woman sat down in a recliner that looked to be from the early eighties, beige with extra padding on the armrests and a towel over the headrest. Nancy sat down on the edge of a couch, facing her. "Do you mind if I turn the television down?"

"Okay."

After the volume of the TV was decreased, Nancy took out her notebook. "Can you tell me your first name?"

"Jan."

"Last name?"

"Clark."

"Jan, I have a few questions about your daughter, Mona."

"I don't know where she is," Jan said.

"When's the last time you saw her?"

Jan's eyes began to flutter. "I don't remember."

29

"Okay." Nancy nodded. She peered at the counter that separated the living space from the kitchen. It was lined with pill bottles. Nancy got up and picked up one. "Are these yours?"

"Mona handles all of that," she said.

Nancy read a few labels. These were medications with Jan's name on them. She was beginning to think she had some form of dementia based on her behavior. She wondered when Mrs. Clark had last taken the pills, understanding now her daughter was clearly her caregiver and she hadn't been there for some time. She knew now she couldn't deliver the news about her daughter under these circumstances.

"Mona's probably at work," Jan said. "When she's not here, that's where she is."

"Where does she work?" Nancy asked.

"Downstairs," Jan said confidently.

"The coffee shop?"

"Yes." Her head bobbed up and down.

"And no one else lives here with you?"

"Just John."

"Is that Mona's boyfriend?"

"Husband."

"Okay." Nancy scribbled it down. "Mona's married. And what's his name?"

"John Clark."

Nancy looked up from the paper. "That's your last name, Mrs. Clark."

Jan shook her head. "Yes."

"Is John Clark *your* husband?"

"Right."

"And where's he?"

"Gone."

"So John is no longer with us?"

Jan didn't respond but got up from her chair and went to the window near the desk and looked out. She walked back toward Nancy and then turned and headed for the window again. The question clearly agitated her.

"Okay, Mrs. Clark. We don't have to talk anymore about John. Please come and sit down again. I just have a few more questions about Mona, and then we're done."

Jan sat back down. Her eyes wandered back to the TV.

"Does Mona have a partner? A boyfriend, girlfriend, a significant other I may talk with?"

"Yes, but I don't remember his name just now. I want to say Ben," she paused. "Or is it Paul?"

"Ben or Paul?" Nancy wrote both names in her pad. "Okay. Great. Thank you, Jan." Nancy saw a phone sitting on a desk up against the living room wall. "Do you have a list of phone numbers around in case of emergencies? Any other children I could call?"

"No. Just Mona."

"Maybe a doctor?"

"Over there," Jan said, pointing toward the small desk. Nancy went over and jotted a few names and phone numbers down. Jan's attention was still held by the television featuring a popular daytime game show. Nancy decided to take advantage of the distraction.

"Which bedroom is your daughter's?" she asked.

"That one." Jan nodded toward the hall.

"Do you mind if I have a look in there?"

"Okay."

"Great. I'll be right back." She turned the volume of the television up again as she left the room.

Nancy opened the bedroom door and scanned the room. It was a fairly sparse, yet organized space, featuring a queen-sized bed, which was neatly made. There were several pieces of modern art lining the walls and two paintings on the dresser, propped up, as if waiting to be hung. There was a laundry basket filled with dirty clothes and a few books scattered on the nightstand. Nothing stood out to Nancy as unusual. No struggles appeared to have taken place, and she saw no blood anywhere.

She closed the door and went back to Jan. "Thank you for your time, Mrs. Clark."

Jan turned from the television briefly and looked at Nancy. "Who are you?" she asked.

"I'm Detective Simmons. I'm going to call your doctor and send someone to come see you today, okay?"

"That's just fine."

Chapter 6

George hated that it took an event as grave as this one in order for his daughter to come home. It had been over a year since Ella had been back to visit. She always complained she hated the cities, the urban landscape, but the truth was she was an environmental scientist who was married to her job; which was probably good considering she was a forty-six year old divorced woman with no children. George just wondered if there was more to it. Was there another reason she'd stayed away? She and Melinda talked on the phone often, but George usually just got updates from Mel from time to time. He loved his daughter but he knew she was an adult and had her own life to lead. He'd seen plenty of parents who smothered their children, but that had never been him. He was good knowing she was happy, at least he assumed she was happy based on Melinda's steady reports.

They sat in the living room drinking coffee. Ella had come in late the previous night, and this morning they were scheduled to go to the funeral home to go over all the details of Melinda's service, which would take place the following day. George felt like he was living outside of himself. Helpless. He'd hardly slept and no amount of coffee was going to help him, but he sipped it anyway, lacking a better plan for what to do with himself.

"What have you done about work?" Ella asked him.

"Nothing. The owner left a message sending his condolences. Said I could just come by and clean out my desk whenever. He said I didn't need to finish my last two days. I guess I'm officially retired."

"It's so weird. It feels like one of those stories where the guy gets hit by a bus the day after the doctor tells him he's not dying after all or something." She sniffled and quickly wiped her nose.

"I know what you mean. I can't help but feel like I let my guard down too soon. Like I was blind to the fact that there were all of these possible side effects because all we were thinking about was how lucky we'd been that she beat the cancer."

"It's not fair." Ella's bubble finally burst and the tears flowed. George went and sat down next to her on the couch and put his arm around her.

"It's not," he said, trying to hold back tears himself, knowing if he started, he'd likely never stop. He consoled his daughter with a dull numbness, putting himself somewhere else entirely.

"I wish I'd have come sooner but I was going to surprise you for the retirement party Mom was planning."

"She was planning a party? I should have known. Well, your mother would've loved to have seen you more often, but it's not your fault," George said.

"I guess. I just wish…I should have told her so much more." She covered her face with her hands and let several small noises escape that ripped at George's chest.

"She knew, honey."

When she came up for air, he handed her a tissue. They sat quietly then for a long time. George knew there was so much more to be said but it felt like the task was too immense to tackle. Where to

even start? He'd rather leave it alone and he knew
Ella would too. Even if he wanted to try to dig into
things with his daughter, he wasn't sure how to go
about it. She'd always been somewhat out of his
comfort wheelhouse. She carried his similar rational
disposition, which made her come across as slightly
standoffish. Verbalizing deep thoughts had never
come easy to him, so it was probably his fault that his
daughter also had, in his mind, an invisible force field
around her, preventing him from gaining access to
her inner thoughts. She kept her emotions in a vault
and he could relate to her in that way. He never
actually thought it necessary to try to unlock them,
until now. Melinda always complained that he was too
internalizing and that both he and Ella had always
been too comfortable with silence. His wife had been
the communicator of the family. George wished he
could say something more, something to comfort his
daughter now, but he just wasn't good at it. That was
Melinda's role, and now there was nobody there to
cut through the silence.

"Well," he finally said. "I guess we'd better get
over to the funeral home."

Ella nodded and they both got up to go.

***

The actual service was short and sweet, though the
day felt like it lasted two lifetimes to George.
Melinda's colleagues from the school were in
attendance, as well as her brother who now lived on
the East Coast. A few of George's buddies from the
factory made a brief appearance, which he had not
expected. At sixty-five, neither he nor his wife had
living parents and George was an only child. A couple
of neighbors showed, too. All this is to say that there

was a rather small turnout, but that didn't bother him. He knew his wife was an amazing woman. He could have done without a service entirely. He really despised the awkward small talk and the staring. It felt like he was being forced to perform on a stage at a time when he'd rather crumple up into a ball in a dark cave.

When the funeral home cleared out, Melinda's brother forced him to go out to dinner. Ella spent much of the time reacquainting herself with her cousins at the far end of the dining table. George would have preferred to sit near his daughter knowing they would both be good with the silence. Instead he had to endure Mel's sister-in-law making sad puppy dog faces at him across the table. She kept asking him how he was doing. He'd be doing better if his wife were still alive, he wanted to say. Instead he just nodded and remained quiet.

"So, George, what do you plan to do now?" Melinda's brother asked.

"We'd been talking about traveling, but I don't know if I want to do that now."

"Traveling would probably be good for you, though. Get your mind off of stuff. After everything, a vacation is exactly what you need."

"I don't know. It feels sort of wrong, I guess."

"You can always come out east and spend time with us," Mel's sister-in-law said.

"Thanks, Patty. I'll keep that in mind."

George caught Ella's eye, and she smiled at him from across the table. He forced himself to smile back. He was drained. All he really wanted to do was go home and sleep. Maybe when he woke up, the nightmare would be over.

***

Once everything was said and done and Ella returned to Ely, George allowed himself time to grieve. He didn't shower or even bother to get dressed. He lived off of what Melinda had stocked in the fridge and occasionally ordered take out. When he couldn't sleep, he watched TV.

When the fridge was finally mostly empty and he'd watched more television than he ever cared to watch, he decided it was time to clean himself up. He'd gotten another voicemail from his boss about clearing out his desk at the factory. He couldn't put it off any longer.

He got himself showered and dressed, threw on his boots and coat, and got in his Prius. He was about halfway there when he realized he'd forgotten a box to collect his things in. Contemplating whether or not to turn back for it, he realized he didn't have much in his desk that he really wanted to keep. In fact, the only personal effects he could even think of were a couple of photos of Melinda and Ella that sat on top of his desk. He didn't need a box for two small photos.

In truth, George had been putting this off because he was worried it would be awkward, but once he walked in, he realized not many people even noticed his being there. He sat down at his desk, which was not much more than a small table and chair sitting in the midst of clutter that made up the office for the handful of people who were privileged enough to have their own space in the factory. A few guys sat in the small room but besides giving him a quiet nod when he entered, they remained focused on their computer screens.

There was a 3M sticky note attached to the front of George's computer from the IT person that gave George explicit details on how to clear all of his passwords. Once he accomplished that, George opened his file cabinet one last time and flipped through it, making sure the files were organized and that he hadn't left any personal information. Then he looked around the rest of his space for anything else he might have forgotten about. There was nothing besides the two photographs. He picked them both up and stood again, taking one final look around the place where he had spent a good portion of his life. Next week someone else would be sitting at this desk doing the job he'd done for over forty years, and he'd be forgotten. In fact, it seemed he already had been. It struck George how it might have all been different last week, but now it had a very existential feel to it. He felt like a ghost walking out of Bronze; like he wasn't sure if he had really ever actually worked there. He certainly felt like a different person. Everything was changed, just like that. It snuck up on him and the fact that he hadn't left his mark was just now settling in, invading his already unsettled mind like an unwanted visitor.

Once home, he parked the car back in the garage and walked to the end of the drive to collect the mail. He hadn't bothered with it while he'd holed himself up inside the house during his grieving period, so as a result the box was overflowing with letters and newspapers. He shuffled through a few pieces quickly on his walk back to the house and stopped on one that was stamped URGENT in red. Back inside, he threw the rest of the stack on the counter and peeled the envelope marked URGENT open.

> Dear Mr. Altman,
> On behalf of all of us here at First Mutual Insurance Group, we wanted to offer our condolences on your wife's passing. We have some paperwork that will need to be filed in order to collect on her life insurance policy. Please call us at your earliest convenience to schedule a meeting with an adviser.
> Sincerely,
> Jeanette Baker
> First Mutual Insurance

Life insurance? He'd never taken out a policy on his wife. This had to be some kind of a scam. He'd heard about people trying all sorts of shady business on widows, especially elderly ones. He probably would have dismissed the letter outright had this not come from his actual insurance company. There was probably no harm calling and seeing what they had to say about the matter.

"How can I help you today, sir?"

"My name is George Altman, and I received a letter from your office about my deceased wife's insurance policy."

"Okay. Let me put you on hold and connect you with the correct adviser."

"Thank you."

After a few minutes, the line clicked. "Hello, Mr. Altman. I'm Donald Carpenter. Did you want to set up that meeting to go over the paperwork?"

"Well, I guess I'm confused because I wasn't aware that my wife had a life insurance policy," George said.

"I'm looking at the file right now, and I see that it says she was a school teacher through the St. Paul School District, is that correct?"

"Yes."

"It looks like this policy was a rollover as part of her state pension plan. Something they worked into contract negotiations a few years back."

"Oh. So, it's legitimate?"

"Very. Once we've gone over the paperwork, you're entitled to a one hundred thousand dollar compensation as her primary beneficiary. Shall we schedule that appointment, Mr. Altman?"

"Uh. Okay."

***

A few days later, he returned from the meeting with his insurance agent where he'd completed the paperwork to receive a settlement check that would be processed and put in his bank account within eight to ten weeks.

George spent the holidays in isolation, avoiding everyone and everything, except his daughter, who called to check up on him but not uncharacteristically made no attempt at another visit. This in some ways concerned George and in others relieved him. He certainly wasn't up for any sort of celebration, and he knew Ella just needed time to heal in her own way, as well. So, when he turned his computer on sometime in mid-January and saw the email from the realtor about the property in Duluth, he thought it might finally be a good time to attempt to close the distance gap with his daughter, physically and emotionally.

The message from Michael Olson said the following:

> Mr. Altman,
> Attached is a link to the rental property I mentioned to you. It's a modest cabin, only one bedroom, but it's right on the big lake and in good condition. It's available beginning February 1st. Let me know if you're interested.
> Sincerely,
> Michael Olson
> Olson and Sons Realty, St. Paul, MN

George viewed the sparse listing information then clicked through the photos. There were only three pictures attached to the property details. The first was of the exterior of the cabin. It was plain and rather uninspiring, the yellow paint faded and worn from the weather, but that didn't bother George. The second picture was of the interior of the cabin, which was all of a few hundred square feet. It was outdated but clean. He clicked on the last picture. It was a breath-stealing view of the lake, taken in midsummer. It made up for anything else the little cabin offered in spades, and it was all George needed to make up his mind.

The date of the email was months prior, before everything happened with his wife. He hoped the cabin was still available. February was just a few weeks away. He replied to the message immediately and let the realtor know that he wanted to rent the property if it was still an option.

Fortunately, he got a response not long after hitting send.

"Not a lot of people looking for a rental in Duluth starting in February," the young realtor said when they spoke on the phone the next day.

"I imagine that's true."

"So this works out great for both of us. Why don't we meet here at my office for you to sign the lease agreement?"

"Sounds good," George said. And it did. It sounded like the exact right thing.

***

He met Michael Olson again at his office just a few days later. Even though he knew he could easily afford something else now, he didn't ask Michael about searching the database for any more properties. He still liked the little rental on the lake in Duluth. He had a good feeling about it.

"Okay. We're signing a year lease on the one bedroom in Duluth, correct?"

"Yes," George said.

Michael grinned. "Great. I know you're gonna enjoy this property."

"I'm sure I will."

Michael sifted through the papers on his desk. "How would you like to pay? I'd prefer first and last month's rent, as well as a five hundred dollar security deposit up front. You can mail rent checks to me by the first of each month."

"Uh. Would it work if I paid for the year in full all at once?"

"Certainly."

"Great. Then I don't have to bother with finding a mailbox and all of that while I'm there."

"No problem. I completely understand. And I hope the wife finds the accommodations okay. I know women can be picky, but if you have any issues once you get up there, just let me know."

"Oh, it's just me actually."

The realtor raised his brows. "Divorce?"

"My wife passed recently."

"I'm sorry to hear that."

George nodded. "Anyway, I'm sure the cabin will be fine. I don't need much."

"All right. If you can just sign this last one for me, it will be yours. I'll have someone meet you up there with the key. Here's the total amount." He tapped a number on the bottom line of the receipt he'd printed out.

"Who do I make the check out to?"

"ORC. Olson Realty Corp," he said.

"Okay." George wrote out the check and they shook hands again, one last time.

Chapter 7

As Nancy walked down the stairs, she pulled out her cell and made a few calls to the station to get Mrs. Clark squared away, then she entered The Grind. She looked around at the art lining the walls. It had a familiar feel to her, and she realized it was because it looked a little like the walls of Mona's bedroom.

There was a young blonde woman behind the counter wearing a baseball hat with a ponytail pulled through the loop in the back. She was chewing gum rapidly but she somehow managed to smile at Nancy while she did it. "Good morning. Would you like to try a white chocolate mocha? It's our special this week!"

"Sure," Nancy said.

The barista's smile widened. She had very white teeth. "Really? Nobody ever says that."

"Just a medium though, please."

"Okay."

"Can I ask you a couple of questions while you make it?"

"Go for it. This one will take me a little while."

"Do you know Mona Clark?"

"Yeah. She works here, or used to work here. I dunno. She hasn't been in for a while."

"When was the last time she worked, do you know?"

"Um, I guess her last shift was Monday."

"She was here Monday? You saw her?"

"Yeah."

"When did she leave here? About what time?"

"She worked the morning, I was on the evening shift, so she probably left at around two o'clock."

"And you didn't see or talk to her at all after Monday?"

"No."

"Does she have a significant other that you're aware of?"

She shrugged her shoulders. Nancy noticed her smile turn off, if just a tiny bit. "She has a lot of friends."

"Are you included among them?" Nancy asked, eyeing her nametag. "Jenny?"

"Sure." Jenny's jaws started chomping fast and furious again. "I mean, we're work friends. I don't hang with her much outside of The Grind. Why? What's going on with Mona?"

"She's…missing. I'm with the Duluth Police."

"Whoa! You're kidding me, right?"

"No. Do you remember anything weird about that last time you saw her?"

She shook her head, smacked her gum a few times, then set Nancy's drink down on the counter near the cash register. "One mocha. It's four and a quarter."

"Okay. One more question. Who curates this art you have on display?"

"That's Mona's deal."

"Is she an artist herself? Or associate with any of the artists on display?"

"Oh, yeah. She was hanging out with this one artist guy. She introduced me to him a few weeks back."

"Do you know his name?" Nancy asked, scrabbling to juggle her coffee and grab her notepad out of her bag.

More gum smacking preceded her answer. "I dunno. Old dude."

"Do you know where she met him?"

"No. That's one of his paintings there though." She pointed to an abstract with bold colors along the west wall of the shop.

"Thank you, Jenny. You've been a big help." Nancy swapped her notepad with her wallet and handed Jenny a ten. "Keep the change."

She cradled the coffee with both hands, trying to steal all of its warmth as she moved toward the painting on the wall of the coffee shop. It wasn't too bad, she thought, not that she knew much about art. Her mind worked more in concretes, but she could still appreciate something that was pleasing to the eye, and this piece was nice-looking. It felt warm and even somewhat calming. She'd hang it on her wall. There was a little piece of white paper stuck to the canvas stating the price of two hundred and fifty dollars, but there was no name, nor was there a signature scrawled directly onto the canvas, at least not on the front. Nancy looked back towards Jenny, who was stocking cups along the back wall of the shop. There were only a few customers in the place, and they were either reading, chatting, or staring at screens.

Nancy reached up and gently pulled the canvas from the wall. She flipped it over. In pencil on the bottom right-hand corner of the backside of the canvas was a name.

George Altman.

Chapter 8

February in Duluth could only be described as akin to what the dinosaurs must have experienced as the ice age settled in around them. Yet, George maneuvered up the snowy drive full of optimism for what was probably the first time since he lost his wife. This place felt perfect. It was a small yellow cabin with brown trim sitting on a slight elevation, surrounded by nothing but some tall white spruce trees, a mountain of snow, and one giant lake practically engulfing the whole eastern portion of landscape. George barely noticed that the paint was peeling on the trim and the driveway wasn't cleared. He did see a rusty pickup truck parked at the end of the drive, which he assumed belonged to the caretaker scheduled to meet him with the key.

"Howdy," a slight girl said, emerging from the rust-bucket. He wasn't expecting a woman at all, much less a petite young woman. She was wearing skin-tight leggings, impractical knee-high boots, and an oversized parka with a faux fur collar that nearly hid her entire face.

"Good morning," George said.

"I'm Mona." She extended her hand.

"George."

She fished in her small handbag and handed him the key. "Can I help you unload your boxes?" she asked, peering in the window of his packed Prius.

"That's nice of you, but you don't have to do that. I bet most of these boxes weigh more than you."

"I'm stronger than I look," she argued.

"I didn't mean it as an insult."

47

"Maybe not but you still don't believe I can do it."

He didn't quite know how to respond to the feisty ball of faux fur in front of him. He wasn't sure if it was a millennial characteristic or just the attitude of a true northerner. Either way, he'd survived a forty-six year marriage for a reason. He said, "Okay. I'd appreciate the help." She smiled through the fur lining at him.

He opened the trunk of the car, and together they began to trudge the boxes through the snow and set them in the small entryway of the cabin. When they finished, George thanked her, adding, "You proved me wrong."

She shrugged. "Common mistake. Anyway, there's a shed just behind the house with a supply of wood for the fireplace. Garbage pickup is on Wednesdays. I think that's it. I work up in town at The Grind if you need anything else."

"The Grind?"

"Coffee shop. Clever, right?" she said dryly.

"You have more than one job?"

"Believe it or not, being a barista in a small town coffee shop doesn't really pay the bills."

George laughed. "How many bills can a girl your age have?"

"Not only am I stronger than I look, I'm also older."

"Well, I know it's not polite to ask a woman her age, so…"

"I'm twenty-six," she said.

He nodded uncomfortably. Mona started toward her truck then stopped. She turned back to him and added, "You should come hang out at the coffee shop if you need company. It gets pretty quiet up here this time of year."

"Maybe I'll do that," George said, watching as Mona crunched down the snow-packed drive in her stylish boots. She hoisted herself with ease into the pickup and peeled down the drive, throwing loose snow in her wake.

***

Once alone, he began to unpack the boxes and get familiar with the cottage. After he informed his daughter of his plan, she said she worried about him living all alone in a little cabin on Lake Superior. The thought of it was depressing, even to her. George assured her he'd be fine, and it actually wasn't all that different from how she lived. Besides, it was just temporary, and he was going to use the time to finally dive into his art.

"You never know," he said chuckling, "I could be the oldest man on record to create his first masterpiece."

"Well, just remember, I'll be closer now if you need any company."

"I'd like that. I'll give you a call after I get settled."

Now he had two options for company if he really needed it. Not that he really planned to take up the twenty-something on what was just a polite gesture, but he liked knowing there was someone close by. Honestly, he was really looking forward to the isolation and quiet. He'd always loved Duluth in the summer, and in winter it was only intensified. It made him feel alive.

As the days passed, George definitely got what he bargained for in the way of solitude. The only other sounds he heard that first week were the strong southerly winds pounding the little cabin at all hours of the day. But the place provided that snug feeling George had been searching out, and it was only compounded by the view outside, which was sometimes angry and sometimes incredibly calming. He kept the wood-burning stove going around the clock to combat the cold drafts that found their way in, seeping through the cracks and crevices of the aging structure. Being a stubborn, hearty Minnesotan, he embraced the conditions but kept his long johns and wool socks on at all times, day and night.

There was knotty pine throughout the place, which was typical of a north woods cabin. This one also boasted higher than average ceilings for such a tiny cabin. The furnishings were less desirable, being outdated, and they contrasted starkly with the woodsy atmosphere. They reminded George of his parents' house growing up. The living room featured a harvest gold loveseat, and the kitchenette along the north wall had cheap stained cabinets with a very orange-tinted finish. There was a small stove and fridge that looked to be from the seventies. A laminate counter divided the living space from the kitchenette, and a round oak table with two mismatched chairs was wedged between the countertop and the living room.

Unpacking didn't take long. George had only brought the basics with him. No television or computer. The only piece of electronics, besides his cellphone, was a small radio, which he plugged into the wall near the counter and set to MPR: Minnesota Public Radio.

As soon as he could, George set up his easel and paints near the small, half-frosted over front window in the living room, which offered a clear and spectacular view of Lake Superior. He found a folding chair in the closet and set it in front of his easel. He sat down and stared at his canvas and then back out the window for hours those first few days. His plan wasn't to paint the lake, because he didn't have the confidence to tackle such an intimidating undertaking, never mind the fact that given the particularly bitter and snowy winter, she was currently ensconced in a blanket of white, with only a few pockets of open water scattered around.

It was hard not to be moved by the eerie power of such a beautiful thing though, no matter what her state, but instead of attempting to capture the lake exactly, George used the mood to create an abstract piece, his first work of art in many years. He began by putting several shades of blue oil paints onto his palette, then he loaded his brush and started applying the colors gradually and deliberately to the square canvas, converting it from snow white to an array of blues. It didn't come easy, though he never wanted it to. He piled on layer after layer with the palette knife, covered up corrections with fresh color, used a fine brush to inject his feelings and emotions into some of the detailed line and stroke work, and after several false starts he got into a groove, which felt familiar but also therapeutic.

He'd kept up with art trends by subscribing to magazines, and though he knew he wasn't hip, he felt he had a good sense about what was classic and what was passé. Mostly, he tried to pour his heart out onto the canvas, and in doing so, he felt a purging of so much emotion he'd kept bottled within him. It was cleansing, and before he knew it, the painting was shaping up to be what he'd envisioned.

By the time he was finished with it, almost a full week had passed, and he was pleased with how it had come out. His concentration and focus was spent, and he felt exhausted but exhilarated with what he'd accomplished, and that's how he finally knew the painting was done. Now he was in need of a break. He made his first trek into town to do a little exploring and restock his supplies.

Duluth was more sleepy than he expected it to be, given the nature of the town. The people who lived this far north were a rugged breed. They didn't hide out when it was cold or snowing. If they did, they wouldn't see the light of day for three quarters of the year. They didn't let Mother Nature guide their actions. From George's limited experience, it was just the opposite actually—they often acted as though snow and ice was a challenge and fought winter with bold force, embracing the conditions head-on, like a matador in a bullfight.

So, he was a little surprised by how quiet the main street felt today, but he found what he needed at a small shop that doubled as a grocery and hardware store; a hilarious, yet functional, combination, but a necessity for up there. He loaded his car with the groceries and other supplies. As he did, he noticed a shabby-chic chalkboard sign dangling from one of the storefront windows less than a block down and knew it must be The Grind. On a whim, he decided to stop in and patronize the independent coffee shop. He could use a cup anyway, and thinking about his daughter's concern in their last phone conversation, he knew it was probably a good idea to at least attempt some social interaction with another human as long as he was in town.

It didn't surprise him to see Mona behind the counter, but what was slightly startling was seeing her face since it had been fairly covered during his last, brief encounter with her. She definitely still looked young. Twenty-six was young, he reminded himself. Now that he could really see her, he could tell she wasn't as rough or callous as he'd initially pegged her. Her eyes were popping with a charismatic spunk that sort of reminded him of Melinda during their early days of dating. He was equally impressed with her style, which wasn't the cliché bohemian coffee shop look. She was dressed fashionably, maybe a bit more mature and understated than he'd expect of a twenty-six year old, but it felt classy and polished—a simple gray sweater, black slacks, and tall black boots. Her dark, loose curls looked like they'd been done in a salon that morning.

"Hey, you're still alive," she said when he approached the counter. "I'd been thinking I should drop in on you and make sure you weren't a frozen ice block."

"Nope, still thawed for the most part."

"Good. Well, what can I get for ya? Would you like to try our double caramel latte? It's the drink of the week," she said with a sarcastic edge, shifting her body toward a sign on the counter. There was nobody else in the shop to hear, so when they both laughed it filled the boxy cafe.

"I think I'll just take a large dark roast," George said.

"Good choice. I definitely had you pegged for a dark roast kind of guy." As she filled the cup, she said, "So, what could you possibly be doing in that little cabin all by yourself, if you don't mind me asking?"

"Painting," George said, getting out his wallet.

"Oh yeah? What do you paint? Modern Abstract? Impressionism? Realism?"

He arched an eyebrow at her. "Oh, you know something about art?"

"Only what I've learned from what we consign here." She did a wave of her arm like the girls on The Price is Right to show him the paintings lining three of the four walls of The Grind. "We have a bunch of local artists around, so I started doing it as a little project."

"Some of these are pretty good," George said.

Mona slid his coffee toward him. "It's on the house. A little welcome-to-the-neighborhood gift."

"Oh, you don't have to do that. I…" He still had his wallet in his hand, so he fumbled with it awkwardly.

"You can just leave a tip." She eyed the little jar on the counter, which sat empty.

"Oh. Sure." He put a five in. "Thank you."

"So, you never answered my question."

"What was it?"

"What do you paint?"

"Oh, right. Well, I guess it's abstract but I don't know how modern it is considering I haven't painted in years and well, I'm no spring chicken myself."

"I'd love to see it. We'll have some space available next week if you want to consign a few pieces. I like to rotate stuff out a lot so I don't drop dead from boredom while I'm working."

"Oh. I don't know. Like I said, I'm rusty, and my stuff is nowhere near as good as what you've got hanging up in here now."

"Frankly, I'm sick of looking at these pieces. I could use something new. Besides, art is subjective. One man's trash and all that crap. But seriously, you should see some of the stuff I've sold."

"You actually sell stuff?"

She shook her head. "It happens."

"Really?"

"Well, obviously, we do better in the summer when the tourists flock in, but you never know until you try."

"Hmm. I'll think about it. Thanks again for the coffee."

"Are you leaving already?"

"Oh, I…"

"I'm joking." She smiled and waved him off. "But seriously, if you don't bring in some paintings, I'll come and peek through your windows. I know where you live."

"You do. That's true." He laughed. "Give me a little more time to work. I only have one canvas done."

"Can I see it?"

"I…suppose."

"How about I crash your place then? That way there will be no excuses. Next week?"

"You're very persistent," George said.

"I've been told that."

He looked at Mona for a moment before he relented. "Okay. Next week."

"Great. I'll be there on Thursday. It's my only day off."

"All right. I guess I'll see you then."
"Bye, George."

Chapter 9

Mid-February brought more snow and with it some record cold temperatures. Again, George hardly noticed. He embraced the quiet and took the time to reflect on his life and continue to mourn inwardly for his wife. Some days, if the weather was slightly less brutal, after he'd worked the canvas for hours, he would take a brisk and brief walk on the big lake and think about Melinda and the life they had together. He missed the simple things: talking about their day over dinner, and the meals themselves, which he definitely missed now that he was mostly eating cold sandwiches. He also thought about how passionate she was about teaching and how the worst part about getting cancer for her wasn't being sick but missing her students. He also thought about how she always wanted to drive because she hated being a backseat driver, and how she always brushed her teeth after him because she claimed it was just good manners, but George knew it was really because she wanted to wipe the sink down after he spit toothpaste in it and forgot to rinse.

George smiled at the memories as he walked along the shoreline of the frozen lake, though he did so without letting his guard down. The act of walking on the big lake wasn't something he took for granted. It wasn't like city lakes that froze solid after a few short weeks of winter. Most of the areas along the shores of Superior were safe enough to walk on but it hardly ever froze completely over, so there were still many spots of open water. If he was feeling particularly brave, he might walk out nearer to the areas where the local fishermen put up their ice shacks, or were huddled around holes, sitting on plastic buckets holding their reels and beers. George trusted that those guys must have known what they were doing. They waved at him as he passed by, like the good Minnesotans they were, and then they tucked back into their layers like turtles with just enough of their heads sticking out for them to stare back down into their fishing holes.

Ella called several times over the course of those first few weeks, though the conversations never lasted long. He knew his daughter was just checking up on him to make sure he hadn't offed himself or suffered a heart attack in his sleep. George tried to put an upbeat tone in his voice when she called so she wouldn't worry about him, but it wasn't easy for him because his normal disposition was that of a somber man. It was hard to sound peppy and excited when all he had to report to his daughter was regarding his painting. He had no idea how to talk about his work. He hoped the art would speak for itself. That was the point, after all.

By the time Thursday rolled around, he was well into his second painting, though he didn't think it was quite done yet. That was the problem with paintings—knowing when they were finished. He'd built up several layers of color and was trying to convey a strong emotion, but he thought it still felt flat. He took a break for lunch and leafed through the magazines he'd brought along with him. People always assumed that because he was an introvert he was a big reader, but that wasn't true. He was a visual person. He only liked to read things in short segments, and if pictures went with them, that was even better.

There was a knock at the door. He hadn't forgotten about his arranged visit with Mona, but he still jumped a little when the sound of rapping knuckles against the wood cut through the weeklong silence. He wasn't sure if she'd really show, so he hadn't built up any expectations. His experiences working at the factory had made him skeptical of most people who said they were going to do something on a given day, especially the younger ones. They were rarely reliable to their word.

He got up and went to the door. Mona was standing with two paper to-go cups of coffee in her hands.

"I brought drinks!" She handed him a cup.

"Thank you." He moved to let her in. Once she was inside the tiny cabin, the room suddenly felt very tight, and though George knew this was simply a young girl being nice to an old man, he couldn't help but feel out of sorts by the situation, even mildly guilty. He fiddled uncomfortably with the drink in his hand.

"I like what you've done to the place," she said, looking around. She was being sarcastic. George, of course, hadn't done anything to the place besides put up his easel. Everything else was here when he arrived.

"Do you do routine inspections for all of the occupants of the cabin?" he inquired. "Is it part of the job?"

"No. I just get the luxury of cleaning it when it switches hands. So I happen to know where everything goes, and I know that you've hardly touched anything."

"Would you like to sit down?" he asked.

"Thanks."

They both sat at the little oak table. George felt his mouth go dry. He took a sip of his coffee and nearly choked on it. "Is there Bailey's in this?"

"I thought it would warm you up. I hope you don't mind. I mean, you aren't in AA or anything, are you?"

"No. Haven't been to a meeting in years."

Mona's eyes widened. "Oh, God! Sorry!"

"No. It's fine. Really. That was a very long time ago." He took another sip. "It was just unexpected, that's all."

"I'm an idiot sometimes," Mona said.

"It's not a big deal. Don't worry about it."

Mona's eyes wandered to the easel. George stood quickly, feeling himself flush. "Oh. I won't keep you. You came to see the paintings. I don't know if I really have much to show you. I was hoping to have two works completed by now, but the second one is giving me some trouble. I have one in the bedroom that's done. I'll just grab it."

When George returned, Mona was standing next to the easel. He assumed she was looking at the lake.

"I like it. I think it just needs a little more orange in the top right corner," she said, pointing toward the area George had been fumbling with for several days.

He thought about it for a second. He nodded. "I think you might be right."

"Can I see the other one?"

"Sure." He held it out for her to see even though he was having second thoughts. His confidence was waning, and he remembered why he hadn't pursued art in such a long time.

"Yes. This one is done." She reached for it. "It's very good."

"I'm glad you think so," he said, feeling relieved.

"I want to put it up in The Grind."

"I don't know…"

"Come on, George." She said his name as if they were old friends.

George started to loosen up. Maybe it was the couple of sips he'd taken of the coffee, so as not to make Mona worried about the fact that she'd spiked the drink. He hadn't touched the stuff in years, but it shouldn't have had that strong of an effect on him. No, this was maybe just him being grateful she seemed to genuinely like the work he was doing. They were standing close now, and George felt warm. "Maybe."

Mona smiled wide. She held the painting close to her puffy coat. "Maybe is always a yes in my book."

"Really? Maybe is a yes, huh? I've never thought that to be the case before," he said.

"It's more than a no. That means you're almost there. What's holding you back, George?"

"That's a good question."

"You have nothing to lose. The painting gets displayed in a rinky-dink coffee shop in the wintry plains of the Midwest and is seen by like fifty people. There's not gonna be a write up in the New York Review if someone doesn't like it. But maybe…just maybe, someone sees it while enjoying their hot drink one day and says, 'You know what? I like this. It moves me. I'm gonna hang it in my living room right above my new couch.' The next thing you know, their friends are asking about it and want to know where they can get a George Altman original for their living room wall. Boom. You've made it." Mona smirked at him.

"You are really, very good at this," he said.

"I try. Now, how much would you like to sell it for?"

"Oh, I don't know. What do most people mark them?"

"I'd say at least two fifty."

"Really?"

"Absolutely."

"Okay. You're the expert."

"Great. Why don't you bring that one to me when you've finished it. I have two empty spaces to fill." She glanced at the easel again.

"If you really want it."

"I do."

"Do you paint, yourself?" he asked.

"Me? No."

"Why not? You seem to have an eye for it."

"That's about all I have."

"Have you tried?"

"No. I know my own strengths. Painting is not one of them."

"How do you know if you haven't tried?"

"You sound like my parents right now, George."

"Sorry. I'm probably old enough to be your grandparent so I can't really help it."

"You're much more attractive than my grandpa." Mona laughed, clearly conjuring a vision of her grandfather in her head.

George remained quiet.

Mona said, "Sorry. That was weird."

"No big deal."

"Okay. Well, I should get going."

"Thanks for the confidence boost," George said. "I was kinda working in a bubble, so this was very flattering, especially for someone my age."

"I don't discriminate. I know when a painting is good. You watch, this will sell."

George laughed. "I'm not holding my breath."

***

When Mona left he went straight to the canvas on the easel, loaded his brush with some rusty copper tones, and worked it along the top right edge per Mona's advice. Sure enough, when he stepped back to examine it, the piece felt much more balanced. He played around with it a little bit more then cleaned out his brush in the sink.

He sat down on the little folding chair and contemplated what he would do on the next blank canvas. He felt the creative juices flowing through him stronger than he had probably since he was a young man. He smiled to himself. He was feeling pretty good, happy even. He knew most people probably would've thought him nuts, but this was exactly where he wanted to be right now.

Chapter 10

On his next trip into town, he briefly contemplated stopping at The Grind, if for no other reason than to see his painting displayed on the wall, but he thought better of it. He didn't want Mona to think he was a weirdo stalker or something. He got a few groceries, and restocked his paints at a little art supply shop he'd found before returning to his peaceful solitude.

When he got back to the cabin, he called his daughter and invited her to come for dinner on Saturday night. Melinda had been the regular cook in their house, but he wasn't afraid to get his hands dirty in the kitchen either. He often prepared meals on the weekends, so he had a few decent recipes under his belt. He decided to make one of Ella's favorites, chicken cacciatore.

Halfway through the prep work, he realized he might have taken on too big of a challenge for this tiny, outdated kitchenette. He hadn't even actually turned the stove on since he'd been there. His appetite hadn't been much since Melinda's passing.

It was taking forever for the stove to heat, and he had only one pan, so things got complicated. He had his paint smock on for an apron, which was good considering he'd somehow managed to spatter the front of it with crushed tomato. Finally, he got the dish into the stove and was just about to tackle cleaning some of the mess he'd created, when he heard knocking.

George opened the door expecting to see Ella, so it was a surprise when he found Mona standing in front of him.

"Oh, hello."

"Have I interrupted a murder?" she asked casually.

He looked confused until she pointed down to his red-soaked apron. "Oh, no! I was cooking and, well, I don't know how I managed to do this."

"What's for dinner?" she asked, stepping inside.

George closed the door. "Cacciatore."

"Do you have a date?"

"No. I mean, yes. Sort of. My daughter is coming down from Ely."

"Ah. That's sweet. Anyway, I didn't mean to intrude. I just wanted to drop off your check."

"Check?"

She handed it to him. "I sold your painting. Just like I said I would."

"You're kidding me!"

"Nope. Can I take the other one? I was hoping you would have dropped it off by now…"

"That's just…wow! I'm still in shock." He went to the bedroom, and Mona followed him. "Who bought it?"

"A customer, one with good taste."

George handed Mona the completed second painting. She held it out. "You worked the orange in nicely. I think I like this one better than the first."

"I have you to thank for that."

Just as they were stepping out of the bedroom, the front door swung open, and Ella made her way in calling, "Dad, I'm…"

She froze and stood with the cold air blowing in behind her from the door she had yet to close.

"Hi, honey," George said, rushing to grab the door and close it behind her. He knew it looked bad, them coming from the bedroom. "This is Mona. She's taking one of my paintings. I'm selling them in town at the coffee shop where she works."

"Nice to meet you," Ella said coolly.

"You too. Well, I'll leave you to your chicken. I'll see you at the shop soon, right George?" Mona swooped past Ella and didn't wait for his answer before she was out the door.

After she'd gone, Ella continued to stand for a long time staring at George. He knew he was blushing and turned back into the kitchen, trying to busy himself with the dishes.

"Spill it," Ella said.

"There's nothing to spill. She's the caretaker of the property and brought the key when I moved in. When she found out I was painting, she mentioned this consignment thing at the coffee shop where she holds a second job." He picked up the check from the counter. "Look at this. I sold my very first painting!"

Ella took the check. "What? You've only been here for a few weeks. That's great! Uh, why is it for two hundred and thirty seven dollars? And why is it a corporate check?"

"Wow. You're more of a skeptic than I am." George laughed. "I suppose Mona probably gets a small cut, that's why she's so motivated to sell them. I imagine she funnels the money through the coffee shop to collect. Probably writes a new check with the coffee shop's business account."

"Huh. Well, that's still pretty cool."

"Yeah. I mean, it's not like I'm in it to get rich. I hadn't even considered what I'd do with the paintings, and definitely didn't think I would actually sell any. The money is just an unexpected bonus."

El looked around the space. "Are you sure you don't need the money? I can tell you certainly didn't splurge on this place."

"It's rustic," George said.

Ella laughed. "I'll say."

"I picked up some wine for you. Would you like a glass?" he asked, glad the Mona topic had passed.

"Sure. Whoa. What the place lacks in charm is made up for with this view," she said, looking out the front window.

"Now you get it. I've been mesmerized by it. Just imagine what it will look like come summer."

"Are you planning to stay here that long?" She turned and came back toward the kitchen.

"I don't know yet. I mean, I have a year lease, so probably."

They sat down at the little table. George put a glass of red wine in front of Ella.

She said, "Have you thought much about your long-term plan?"

"Long-term? I haven't got a long-term, dear. I'm sixty-five."

"Dad! I'm serious."

"Not really. I've never been a long-term thinker. How do you think I managed to work at a factory job all my life?"

"I'm just worried about you."

"Don't be. I'm fine."

"You always say that."

"Because it's true. Besides, what about you? I can say the same about you."

"What about me?"

"Well, I worry about you too. You're a single workaholic. I don't even really know what you do."

"I do water research. And I'm happy with being single. You didn't get a choice on the matter."

"I had always thought I would die before your mother so this is all very strange for me. I never thought about a future being…single. That's a weird thing to even say."

"I'd have been perfectly happy if Kevin would have died before me," Ella said dryly.

"That's harsh."

"Sorry. I'm just bitter."

"Just because he was a cheater doesn't mean every man is going to be. I never cheated on your mother in all of our years together."

"That doesn't mean I'm stupid enough to try again."

George got up to check on the chicken in the tiny oven. "You shouldn't be so closed off to the idea of a second try. You're still young."

"What about you? You could date too. You don't have to be alone either."

"It's very strange to hear your own child advising you to date," George said, bringing some bread and cheese to the table.

"It's just as strange saying it, but I'm serious. I'm just giving you my blessing if the option should arise."

"Thank you, sweetie. Maybe I'll check out the local bingo hall this week and see what those options are." They both laughed and began to nibble on the cheese.

The oven timer buzzed. "Time to eat," George said, pulling the pan from the oven.

"This is nice. A cozy Saturday night dinner with my dad. Just like when I was a kid. I don't even have to cook. We'll have to make it a regular thing while you're up here."

"I'd like that."

Chapter 11

The last week of February began a slight, and rather unusual, warming period. George was still slogging along with painting number three. He thought he had years of ideas stored up in his brain, but now after several days, he was still staring at a mostly blank canvas. Defeated, he decided to head to town while it was mild outside and the roads were clear.

He went to the small bookstore and found a few art magazines he hoped would give him a boost of inspiration. He took them to The Grind to peruse alongside some coffee. The place was much busier than the last time he'd been in. Perhaps it was the warmer temps, or maybe he'd just hit on a good day. There were two people working behind the counter today. He waited in Mona's line to get his drink. As he did, he had a direct sightline to his painting on the wall. When the customer in front of him pulled away suddenly, Mona caught him admiring it.

"It looks pretty good up there, don't ya think?" she said as he advanced to the counter.

"Not too bad," he admitted, though he felt foolish she'd noticed him checking out his own work.

"I've already had some people inquiring about it," she said. "Large dark roast, right?"

"Please. For here. I'm doing some reading today." He held up his small stack of magazines as proof.

"Great." As she moved toward the brew machine, she nudged the girl next to her. "Jen, this is my friend George."

Jen stopped what she was doing and turned to give him a full once-over. "Ah. So, this is George. Nice to meet you." She smiled at him.

George went a little red at the remark, realizing Mona had been talking to her co-worker about him, but he managed to get out a hello.

Mona slid the coffee toward him. "It's three twenty-five."

He handed her a five and waved away the change. He took one of the last open seats in the busy cafe and began his research. After about a half an hour, his coffee was gone and he was considering packing up and heading back when Mona slid into the seat across from him. "Break time. Mind if I sit here? It's one of the only open seats today."

"Sure. No problem," George said.

"Can I ask you a personal question?"

"Sure." He closed his magazine.

"Are you married?"

"Uh, yes. Well, I mean…I'm widowed. It's weird to say that out loud. I just lost my wife a few months ago."

"I'm sorry. I didn't mean to be nosy, I was just curious. You know, the daughter and all. Is she your only child?"

"Yep."

"I just like getting dirt on my customers. Keeps the job interesting, you know." She smiled at him. "You can ask me something personal now if you want."

"Oh, I…" George thought. He didn't want to be rude but prying wasn't his usual way. An awkward silence led him to blurt out the question that was really on his mind. "Okay. Are you a single gal?"

"Yes."

"That surprises me."

"Have you looked around this town? Most of the men are missing teeth, and they think beer is on the top of the food pyramid."

George smiled. "Why do you stay here then?"

"It's where I'm from, what I know. I mean Duluth isn't all that bad, but I've always thought I was meant to be a city girl."

"The city isn't as beautiful as this."

"That's what they tell me."

"You have family here?"

"My mom. It's why I stay. She's…not well. Dementia."

He nodded. "Sorry to hear that."

"When I save enough money, I plan to put her in one of those fancy nursing homes, and then I'll probably bust out."

"Sounds like a plan."

"I guess. Anyway, enough of my sad story. I've got to get back to work, but I was wondering if you'd like to come to a party with me."

"Um. No offense, but I don't think…"

"It's not a date or anything. It's an art opening, up at UMD. I thought you might like to see some of the work. You know, get inspiration. Isn't that what you're doing with the Art Today?" She eyed his magazine.

"Oh. Well, yes. I am having a bit of a slump, but…"

"Great. It's Friday night. 7:30. I'll pick you up."

***

After making some progress on the painting, before he knew it, it was Friday. He rinsed out his brushes at the end of the day, covered his palette of paint with plastic wrap and pulled his smock over his head. George looked down at his plaid flannel shirt and worn jeans and decided he should change his clothes before going to the art opening. He moved to the small bedroom and looked through his bag, only half unpacked still, even at a month into his stay. He decided on a brown wool sweater and some slightly cleaner jeans. That was the best he could do with what he'd brought. He hadn't anticipated any art gallery soirees in his future when he was picking out clothes to pack back home, that was for sure.

Mona arrived a few minutes before she said she would, and George was once again pleasantly surprised by her promptness. She was wearing a rather short skirt with nothing else covering her legs, along with the big parka she'd worn the first day he'd met her. She carried a stylish little handbag; he believed Melinda would have referred to it as a clutch.

"Aren't you going to freeze?" he asked, letting his dadness seep out.

"Why? It's a balmy thirty-seven degrees today."

"Right. I might be underdressed," he said, grabbing his coat. "I didn't bring anything very fancy."

"Trust me, you will look a thousand times better than most of the people in attendance. I promise."

When they got outside, George said, "I can drive."

"Really? Do you know how to get there?"

"Well, no. But everyone knows the campus is on top of the hill."

"Does that little car even have four wheel drive?"

"No."

"Right. We'll take mine."

George reluctantly hoisted his old bones into Mona's pickup. He felt foolish, though he wasn't sure why; Melinda often drove when they went places. He wasn't much of a car guy. He always let Mel take the new cars so he didn't worry about her breaking down, therefore when they went somewhere it was usually in her car, but this was different. Mona drove quite a bit faster than Mel for starters. Plus, she wasn't his wife. That was the main problem.

About halfway up the very steep incline, she turned to George and asked, "What did you do in St. Paul?"

George said, "How'd you know I live in St. Paul?"

"I haven't been stalking you or anything. I think it was printed on the rental agreement."

"Right. Sorry. I was a factory manager."

"Really? I never would have guessed that."

"No? What would you have guessed?"

"I assumed you were a retired professor or something. You have a very intellectual aura about you."

"I don't know about that."

"It's true. If you met me on the street, what would you think I did?"

"Uh. Is this one of those trick questions that females ask and then get mad about after?" George asked.

"No. It's just for fun. Come on!"

He thought. "I don't know, maybe a real estate agent."

"Seriously? Why?"

"I guess because you dress very professionally."

"Huh," Mona said.

"You said you weren't going to get mad."

"I'm not mad. At least, I don't think I'm mad. Although…realtors are pretty boring. Maybe I am mad!" Then she laughed, clearly as a means to let George know she was only teasing him. She parked the truck and jumped out and didn't waste any time charging through the parking lot in front of George. This was okay by him because it felt slightly more indicative that this was just two people heading to the same event. They weren't necessarily there to be together.

Inside the gallery, George followed Mona's lead still as she casually wandered around the space and looked at the art. Occasionally, she would stop and discuss the works with him in a way that surprised and impressed him. She also touched his arm several times while she pointed things out or commented on a piece. The first time she did it, his immediate instinct was to pull back, but he knew she couldn't possibly mean anything by it, so when it happened again, he let it.

Later, they joined a small crowd assembled in the lobby for a reception. They stood for a bit and made easy and pleasant small talk while Mona had a glass of wine. George realized he was enjoying himself very much. Mona asked him what his favorite piece was, when out of the corner of his eye, he saw a young man heading toward them with obvious intent. Just before he reached them, Mona pulled George close and looped her arm through his. This time, it was clearly quite intentional. George felt droplets of perspiration forming beneath his wool sweater.

"Hey, Mon," the man said. "Did you like the show?" He was referring to the local exhibit, the one the reception was for, which had pieces from several Duluth artists on display. George could only assume some of that work belonged to this man, with whom Mona clearly had some kind of a connection.

"A little overworked for my taste, but it wasn't the worst stuff I've ever seen," she said.

He smirked. "How about your dad. Did he like it?"

"He's not my dad. He's my date," Mona said.

The man's smirk disappeared, and he looked George in the eye. George stayed silent. The man shrugged and turned his attention back to Mona. "Anyway, nice to see you."

"Uh huh. Bye, Doug."

When Doug disappeared back through the crowd, Mona said, "Sorry about that. He's an arrogant jerk I dated once. Thought he was going to make it big in the art world then move to New York. Too bad his work is complete garbage. Anyway, I just wanted to make him jealous."

"Oh. I don't see how I would…" George started, but Mona just tugged on his arm with a hard jerk and pulled him through the people still mulling about the lobby and out the doors.

"Let's get out of here," she said.

She didn't release her grip from George's arm as they walked to the pickup. If anything, George thought, she held it even tighter.

As Mona drove George back down from the University of Minnesota campus perched high above the city, he marveled at the spectacular and expansive view. The lights near the waterfront businesses twinkled, illuminating the ice on the lake. Conversely, going down the steep road, coated in dirty snow and potholes, was harrowing, and George had to grip the door handle with white knuckles once or twice as Mona's old pickup fishtailed. She recovered from it quickly and calmly, like it was another day, and for someone driving in this town, it was. George was surprised how much worse the roads were here than in St. Paul. City driving in winter was nothing compared to this.

Back safely in the driveway of the cabin, George relaxed a little until Mona turned the key off.

"Thank you for inviting me," he said, opening the car door. "I had a nice time and I think I did get some inspiration."

"Aren't you going to invite me in?" she said. She was already unbuckling her seatbelt.

"Mona...I don't think that's a very good idea."

"Why not?"

"Because I'm old enough to be your grandfather."

"Actually, my grandparents have been dead for years. Anyway, so what?"

"It's just...people will talk."

She looked around dramatically. "I don't see any one else around, just some trees and water."

"The age isn't the only thing." He paused. "If I'm being honest, I'm just not ready."

"Oh." Mona's voice went softer. "I didn't mean to be presumptuous."

"It's okay. I'm flattered, really. More than flattered. Confused is maybe a better term."

"Well, you shouldn't be. You are a gentle, caring guy. I can tell. I've been waiting for someone like you to come around."

"I'll be dead soon, just like your grandparents," George said.

"I might be too. You never know. Besides, I'm not the naive teenager you keep making me out to be. I'm old enough to know what I want." She bit her lip and looked at him with an intensity he remembered Ella having when she was younger.

"Goodnight, Mona." He got out of the car and walked through the slushy snow to the cabin before he could change his mind.

Chapter 12

Inside, George put some hot water on the stove for tea. What a strange turn of events. He didn't know how to even process it. On the one hand, he felt incredibly guilty. He hadn't even thought about another woman besides his wife that way for as long as he could remember. The idea of starting now was crazy. It was beyond crazy, really. Given who he was thinking about, it was actually insane. Yet, here he was. He chalked it up to being lonely and feeling somewhat vulnerable. And then there was the fact that Ella had given her blessing, but she couldn't have thought he'd choose a twenty-six year old. He hadn't really been the one to do the choosing though, had he? It was more like she'd picked him.

The age factor was just not something he could get past. She was far too young, he knew. Yet they'd had a very good time together, and she really wasn't like the kids he'd worked with at Bronze. She seemed like a bit of an old soul—confident and punctual. Still, he just couldn't. Maybe he was being old-fashioned, but more than likely, he was just old.

***

The short February thaw had been Mother Nature's idea of a little tease because the first few days of March brought in a snowstorm that rivaled anything George had seen in the cities. Sitting at the easel, he felt like he was stuck in a snow globe; the white spun and blew and settled on the lake around him in clusters. The actions taking place outside of the little cottage's front window were comparable to the ones going on inside his head. With a goal to finish painting number three, thoughts of Mona blew around inside his brain, distracting him from accomplishing it. He wasn't thinking about her in a sexual way, per se, just in a way that filled the quiet spaces that had been there previously.

In what was probably the height of the storm, George heard a vehicle rumble down the driveway. He peered out the little kitchen window facing the drive and saw Mona's familiar truck parked next to his Prius, which currently looked white instead of silver. He opened the door and mother earth spit cold flakes into the cabin as George watched Mona sprinting her way toward him in her high-heeled boots.

When she was in and the cabin door blocked out the storm's continued rage, George said, "What are you doing out in this weather?"

She peeled her soaked parka off and handed it to him. He hung it on the hook and by the time he turned back toward her, she was already seated comfortably at the table.

Her eyes didn't have the vibrant strength they usually held. "I was lonely. I just needed someone to talk to. My mom's having a bad day."

George recalled caring for his own mother before she died. Though she'd actually had cancer, the heavy meds she was on at the end had made her confused often. He remembered it being the hardest thing he'd had to endure. And that was when he was already an older man. He couldn't imagine going through it when he was in his twenties and especially not alone. He'd always had Melinda there with him to ease the burden and sorrow that went along with losing a parent. "I'm sorry," he said. "Would you like some tea?"

"Thanks."

When he sat back down again, handing her a mug, he could see Mona's eyes had red rings around them and were slightly puffy. "I'm a good listener," he said.

"It's just hard, you know? Some days I hate taking care of her, which makes me feel like a horrible person. But why should I when she doesn't even know who I am? I know it's not her fault. I..." She stopped in what George assumed was an attempt to hold back more emotion.

"I'm sure you're doing the best you can," George said. He wished he had better advice, but he didn't. "You don't have any relatives that can help you?"

"Nope. That's why I need to save money, so I can afford to put her in a facility somewhere. I just can't do it anymore."

"The state won't help out at all?"

"Sure. They send a nurse once a week to bathe her and give her a check up."

"You live with her then?"

"In our apartment over The Grind."

He nodded.

"Anyway, I don't want to talk about it anymore." She got up and walked toward the front window. "How's the painting coming?"

"I'm not sure. What do you think?" George got up and followed her to the easel.

"Hmm."

"You can tell me the truth."

"Well, the colors are a little boring. It feels a bit flat. The composition looks a little more confused than the other two, if I'm being honest."

He stood behind her. "It is confused. You're right. Because that's how my brain has been lately. Very jumbled."

She turned and looked at him. "I like you George. Do you feel the same? It's really as simple as that." She moved her hand and placed it gently on his forearm.

He looked down at it. "Maybe."

When he looked back at her face, she said, "Please, don't overanalyze it. Just kiss me." That was exactly what Melinda had always said to him. He over-thought everything. How could he not do it now? He had so many concerns, but her touch felt so soft. Little pulses of heat shot up his arm where her fingers started gently rubbing him. He turned his mind off, closed his eyes, and he did as she asked. He kissed her, softly at first, but then he let her steer the ship, and she drove her boat a lot like she drove her rusty truck—fast and reckless.

When they moved toward the bedroom, George had another pang of regret and considered putting a stop to it, but Mona eagerly nudged him on and he obliged. Once they were on the bed, the confident, spunky girl continued to take the lead, while he continued to shove all of the emotions he was having out of his active mind. There was nothing wrong with what he was doing, he reminded himself. His wife was gone. At that point, he knew that even if he wanted to stop, he was powerless to do so. There were other forces far more active than his mind working, and as his desire overtook his brain, he relaxed and let it happen.

Chapter 13

The next morning, he made a small breakfast for the two of them, but Mona had only a few bites. George worried that now that it was all said and done she had regrets. Was she feeling the same concerns he'd felt prior to doing it? Where did they stand now? This was all so new and strange to him. He tried to discuss it with her, but she didn't want to go there. "I gotta get home to check on my mom before my shift starts."

"Are you sure you're okay?" he asked for a third time.

"I'm better than okay. I'm great. Thank you." She kissed him on the cheek and bolted toward the door, throwing her coat on. "Bring that painting to me at the coffee shop when you get it done. I want it."

"Okay."

When Mona left, George showered then put his paint clothes on and sat in the metal folding chair, staring out at the snow still falling. He drank his coffee and tried to reassure himself that he hadn't done anything wrong, yet he still felt uneasy with the whole thing. This wasn't something he'd sought out but what exactly was wrong with it? He was widowed and she was old enough to consent, which she had. He wished he wasn't such a worrier. Why couldn't he ever just let things be? He dipped his brush in the dark red and began to work the color around the canvas. He tried to focus on the painting in front of him so he didn't have to analyze what had occurred anymore. Besides, there was nothing he could do now. It happened. It was done. He couldn't change it.

He wasn't sure how much time had passed as he wrestled with the painting and his decisions, when his cell phone rang from the kitchen table.

"Hey, Dad. Are we still on for dinner this weekend?"

"Do you really think you should drive in this?"

"It'll be cleared by Saturday, I'm sure. Unless you're trying to ditch me. Hey, did you meet someone at the bingo hall already?"

"What? No!"

"I was joking. Are you okay?"

"I'm fine. Why?"

"You just sound kinda weird."

"Oh. I don't mean to sound weird."

"All right. Well, unless this turns into the storm of the century, I'll be there on Saturday."

"Okay."

"Sold any more paintings?"

"No. Have you…examined any more water?"

Ella laughed. "I have. In fact, I'm heading to the lab right now. I'll see you Saturday."

"Okay. Drive carefully."

"I know, Dad. I will."

When George hung up, he examined the painting on the easel. It looked better than it had yesterday. He wasn't sure if it was done yet, but he was nervous to touch it now. His mind was a mess again. Talking with Ella added a new layer of concern to his pile. He wasn't sure how to handle this situation regarding Mona with his daughter. It was probably best to keep it to himself. It wasn't likely to happen again anyway. Was it? He didn't think so. The idea that such a fascinating young woman would even contemplate more with an old man with a soft belly and gray beard was ludicrous.

He rinsed out his brushes and fixed himself a sandwich. He sat down to eat and paged through one of his art magazines. He looked outside again, bundled himself up, and went out to shovel the drive. The snow was still falling, but every Minnesotan knew better than to wait until it was done falling to get it all up, unless you had a snow blower, which George did not. No matter, the physical exertion was exactly what he needed to get his mind to calm down.

When he finished clearing the first pass of snow from the drive, he went in to warm up. He felt slightly better, but still not great. He decided to take a trip to the coffee shop and hash things out with Mona. He didn't like leaving everything so unsettled.

The painting was still a bit tacky when he loaded it into the car, but he wanted to have a legitimate reason for showing up there like this. He didn't want to seem too concerned or desperate. He draped a garbage bag loosely around the canvas to prevent the snow from ruining it.

He parked on a side street and walked to The Grind. He assumed the little place would be completely devoid of people, given the treacherous driving conditions, but this wasn't the cities and snow didn't stop Duluthians, so when he walked in, he found the place was packed.
He was glad he'd brought the painting along or he would have felt foolish showing up there unannounced, the very next day. And now it was clear

he wasn't going to be able to actually have a meaningful conversation with Mona. He could hardly get near her. He waited in a long line. When he reached the counter, he held up the painting.

"You finished it! I wish I could take a look, but obviously now isn't a good time." She took it and set it against the wall behind the counter.

"Why's it so crazy in here?"

"There's a poetry reading tonight. You want to stay?"

"No, I'll get out of your hair."

"You want coffee or anything?"

"Nah."

He turned to let the next person in line order. Mona grabbed his hand. "Wait," she said. She grabbed a napkin from a stack and wrote something on it. She folded it and handed it to him. George took it and shoved it in his pocket, hoping the person behind him didn't see him blushing.

As he weaved around the crowd to get out of the cafe, he looked over at the spot on the wall where a few days before his second painting had hung, but in the space a different piece of artwork was now displayed. He looked back at the line and decided it was too crazy in there at the moment to attempt to ask Mona about it.

He really wasn't ready to head straight back to the little cabin now that he was actually out for the first time in a while, so George decided to stop at a little bar a few blocks down called The Iron Ranger. It was Thursday night, a busy bar night in any small, working-class town. The Iron Ranger was no exception. George found an empty stool at the bar and ordered a coke.

He drank it slowly and tried to drown out the conversations happening around him. He was no stranger to rough talk, having been surrounded by it at the factory, but it wasn't something he was interested in himself. He blended in well enough that people in the bar left him alone for the most part besides a little probing by the bartender.

"Haven't seen you around here before."

"Renting a cabin on the lake."

"That right?"

"Retired from my job, lost my wife. Just taking some time away."

"Sorry to hear."

"Thanks."

"Seems like you could use something harder than a coke."

"Probably, but I better not."

"Understood. I'm Harry. Just give a holler if you change your mind."

George nodded as Harry went to help a couple of regulars at the far end of the bar. George knew better than to take Harry up on the offer, even if the idea seemed like a pretty good one. It was a slippery slope; one he didn't need to go down right now. After he finished the soda, he pulled the napkin Mona had given him out of his pocket and unfolded it. In pen she'd written, "Call me." Preceding the short message (or was it a direct order?) was a little heart and seven digits. He smiled to himself and stuck the napkin back in his pocket. That was enough of a message for him. She was okay.

George threw a couple of bucks down on the bar and called it a night.

Chapter 14

George sat at his easel the following evening looking at the accumulation of snow on the lake. The storm had finally fizzled out and now the sun was fading on the newly whitened blanket. It was still, and George thought there was probably a good foot and a half of fresh powder piled up.

He picked up his phone and dialed his daughter. He got her voicemail so he left her a message. "Hi, El. I was thinking, I'd kinda like a change of scenery. Maybe I'll drive up to you tomorrow. I could cook at your place. That way I won't worry about you driving. Give me a call back when you get this."

He was about to get up from his canvas to fix himself something for dinner when there was a knock at the door. He slipped his paint smock off before he answered it. Mona stood shaking the snow from her boots, her clutch tucked under the armpit of her parka.

"Hi," George said.

"You didn't call," she snapped.

"I…"

"I'm kidding. Can I come in?"

"Of course."

She slid her boots and coat off and they both stood in the middle of the room awkwardly. She dug her hand into her little purse and took out an envelope. "I brought you a check. It was so busy in the shop when you were there, I forgot to tell you that you sold another painting." She handed it to him.

"Thanks. I may have noticed it was gone. So, it wasn't a thief after all, huh? Amazing." He looked at the check like it wasn't real, then he tucked it into a little file folder he had sitting on the counter.

She giggled a little. "How's everything?" she said.

"Not bad."

"You don't talk much do you?"

"Not really."

"How about offering a girl a drink?"

"Oh! Sorry. What would you like?"

"Got any scotch?"

George moved to the kitchen counter. "No. I only have some wine on hand for when El visits."

"Wine is perfect."

He poured her a glass and set it on the table. Mona sat down. "This doesn't have to be so strange, you know."

"I don't mean for it to be."

"Maybe not. But it is."

"I apologize. Maybe it would help if we talked about everything?"

"Is that really necessary?" Mona groaned.

"I don't know. You tell me."

"It's not necessary for me, but if you feel the need…"

"I just want to make sure you're okay," George said.

"I am. I've already told you that," Mona sighed. "One thing you should know about me, George. I don't do things I don't want to do."

He nodded. "I believe that."

"If I have a problem, I'll let you know loud and clear. If I don't, then leave it be."

"Okay."

"Now that we've cleared that up, I only have one more thing to add."

"What's that?"

"Are you okay?" she asked.

"As long as you are, then I guess I am, too."

"Perfect. Now, what's for dinner? I'm starving."

***

George woke to the smell of coffee brewing. He stayed in bed listening to Mona moving around in the tiny outer rooms of the cabin, trying once again to not think too hard about what had transpired the night previous. Finally, he got up and pulled his robe on.

Mona handed him a cup when he came out of the bedroom. "You don't have to do that here," he told her.

"I can make coffee in my sleep." She kissed him. He was surprised how normal it felt. He assumed she would run off soon but instead she sat down on the ratty little loveseat in the living room with her mug and tucked her bare feet under her legs.

"No work today?" he asked, sitting on his folding chair.

"Day off, and I've got the nurse coming to care for Mom today, so…"

George sipped his coffee. "So, what kind of things do you typically do on your day off?"

She looked out the little front window. George turned and did the same. The sun was shining over the lake creating a bright, almost blinding, sheen. Several dots of dark contrasted with the glare and stuck out.

"How about some fishing?" Mona said.

"Are you serious?"

"Sure! What? You've never been fishing before?"

"No. I'm not much of a fisherman. Especially not the ice variety."

"There's some equipment in the storage shed out back," Mona said. "You're not a true northerner until you've fished the big lake."

"Okay. I'm game."

"Yeah? Great!"

They hauled two buckets out onto the frozen surface. After they'd walked for a little while, Mona stopped and stomped a boot down hard. "Right here. This is the spot."

"If you say so."

"You sit down. I'll be right back."

He sat on the cold, hard plastic bucket and watched Mona march toward a group of men not too far from them. He was stunned by her enthusiasm and youthful energy. A moment of guilt stuck him as he again wondered what the hell he was doing. It didn't last long though because he was enjoying himself too much. A minute later, Mona was heading back to him with one of the men following close behind with a gas powered ice auger flung over his shoulder. George didn't know much about ice fishing, but he knew they needed a hole drilled, and this guy was obviously the one selected to do it.

"This is Bud. He's gonna fix us up," Mona said.

"All right." He gave a nod toward Bud.

"Howdy. Gorgeous day, huh?" Bud said before he fired up the drill and punched two perfectly round holes in the surface of Lake Superior. "There ya go. Good luck."

"Thanks so much," Mona said as he walked off.

She popped the top off her bucket and pulled out two short poles, an ice scoop, and a jar of Salmon spawn sacks. Mona grabbed the scoop and scraped the ice fragments from the top of the holes, popped two pieces of the bait on the hooks and handed one of the poles to George.

"How'd you learn how to do this?" he asked, marveling at her.

"The only thing my dad ever taught me," she said, releasing her line into the oblivion.

George emulated her actions. "Where's he now?"

"He took the easy way out."

George looked at her but stayed quiet.

Mona wiggled her line a little. "Made a cowardly exit by way of the water when things got tough with Mom."

"I'm sorry."

"I'm not."

"It must have been hard for him."

Her voice rose up. "And you think it's not hard for me?"

George's eyes went wide. "I'm sure it is. I just mean, he must have known you were strong enough to handle it."

She shook her head. "I'm not. He was wrong. I'm still mad at him for leaving me to do it myself."

"But you are. You're doing it. He wasn't wrong."

"I don't know how well, but yeah...I guess I'm doing it." She paused and blew into her cupped gloves. "I'm sorry I yelled at you."

"It's fine." George felt a tap on his line. "I think I have a bite. What do I do now?"

"Give it a hard tug."

He did.

Mona jumped to her feet. "Now reel it in!"

Soon a small dark speck began to emerge and make its way to the surface. Mona's face was practically inside the hole by this point. "You got it. A little more," she said. Then she whipped her gloves off and reached down into the icy water to her elbow. When she pulled her bare hand out, she had a fish attached to the end of it. She held it up. "It's nice."

It was actually tiny. They both laughed. Still, George couldn't help but be impressed. He examined the fish. "Do you know what kind it is?"

"A steelhead. Good eating when they're larger, but since we don't have a license, we'll just catch and release." She unhooked it and set it back into the hole. It stayed still initially, as if literally frozen, until it finally gave a slight wiggle and then one fast and fierce bolt, disappearing into the murky depths.

Mona baited his hook again and he dropped his line back in.

"Can I ask you something?" George said. "Are you sure you're twenty-six?"

"You figured out my secret. I'm actually an old hick trapped in a young girl's body."

He laughed. "I don't mean the fishing. Well, that's also an interesting surprise, but I just…you seem mature beyond your years and so put together."

"I've always been told that I'm an old soul." She paused. "And you're old, so I guess that's why we get along so well."

George looked up from his fishing pole at her. Her eyes were wide and then she let out a snort that caused his laughter to come firing up from deep within his belly. The sound of it was so foreign, it almost startled him, but it felt good. He hadn't laughed this hard since well before Melinda had died.

When they finally went quiet, Mona said, "Anyway, I would hardly say I'm put together. I have baggage."

"I don't believe it."

"It's true."

"What's your baggage?"

She peered down her ice hole. "You mean besides my daddy issues? Oh, you know, just your typical variety. A few years back I had a serious boyfriend. He asked me to move in with him, and I told him I couldn't leave my mom. He knocked me around. I told him to go to hell. So one night he came in the coffee shop when I was closing up and waved a gun around like a lunatic. I wasn't worried, he could be a hothead but he was mostly just dramatic and spoiled. Except another employee was still in the stockroom and she called the police. So, yeah. The usual baggage."

"That doesn't sound very usual to me." George looked at her. "You clearly haven't let it damage you though."

"I'm not perfect. Trust me."

"Nobody's perfect. What happened to him?"

"Bobby? He went to jail for aggravated assault. I think he's been out a while now but he hasn't given me any trouble."

George's phone rang. He fumbled to remove his gloves and get it out of his pocket. By the time he'd reached it, it had stopped. He listened to the message.

"My daughter," he told her with his phone to his ear, "I almost forgot I'm going to her place for dinner tonight."

When they were well past cold but not quite frostbitten, they dragged their buckets back across the tundra. They'd managed to catch a few more small fish but had released them all.

George made them some tea, and they sat at the table warming up. "That was fun," he said, and he meant it.

"Thanks for indulging me."

He looked at his watch. "I probably need to get myself cleaned up and head out. It's a bit of a drive to Ely, and I have to stop for a few groceries."

"Okay. Do you mind if I stay for a while? I'd like to shower, and I hate being at my apartment when the home health aide is there."

"Sure. I can leave you the key to lock up."

"I've got one."

"Oh. Right."

"Is that weird? I'd never use it…"

"No. It's fine."

Chapter 15

George had time on the road to Ely, which was about a two hour drive, to juggle once again his decision to tell his daughter about Mona. No matter how he framed it, there was no way he could make it sound anything but wrong, so he tucked the idea away again.

He couldn't stop thinking about Mona saying she had "daddy issues" and he wondered what exactly she meant by that. And was he contributing to the issue by allowing her to essentially play out whatever it was she was conflicted about with him? The thought made his stomach sour. He was a father himself. What would he think if Ella ever brought home a much older man? He would worry, of course, but probably only internally.

Oddly enough, when he arrived at Ella's, she had a guest joining them for dinner.

"Dad, I took your advice. I want to introduce you to Jeff."

"Nice to know ya," Jeff said.

George reached to shake Jeff's hand. "Likewise." He was a little stunned but only because Ella had told him just the a few weekends prior she was happy being single.

Ella unloaded his grocery bag while he began to prep the salmon. He was in the mood for fish for some reason. Jeff sat at the counter drinking a beer. George no longer had to worry about his daughter dating a much older man because if he had to guess, he'd actually peg Jeff as quite a few years younger than El. He was wearing a plaid flannel button-down shirt, so he got some points right away for his good taste in clothes.

George put the fish in the oven and started working on the salad.

"So, what do you do, Jeff?" George asked.

"Um, I'm actually currently unemployed."

"Oh?"

"Well, I should say, I don't work a typical job. I'm an artist. I know most people don't think of that as a viable means of making a living, but I do okay. I mean, I've chosen a lifestyle that doesn't require a huge overhead. You know, so many people live outside their means these days."

"What kind of artist? I'm a painter myself," George said. Now that he'd actually sold a few pieces, he felt okay giving himself the title.

"It's kind of hard to explain. I collect animal sheds and then I mount them and turn them into something that reflects the true beauty the animal once possessed."

"Animal sheds?"

"Antlers. When you find them on the ground, they've been shed. They're called sheds at that point. Most people don't know that."

"I see. Well, that sounds interesting. And you sell enough pieces to make a living?"

He shrugged. "Sometimes. Sometimes I also just sell the sheds at a roadside stand. You'd be surprised how many tourists want to buy them."

"Where do you get them from?"

"I spend a lot of time wandering through the woods."

George gave his daughter a sideways glance. "Where did you two meet?" he asked her.

"I was at a collection site and ran into him on a hike. When he told me what he did, I asked if I could see his work sometime. He gave me his card and I called him. When I went to see his art, he asked me on a date."

"Huh," George said. "Well, I'd love to see it sometime, as well."

"That'd be cool," Jeff said.

"Minus the date," George added.

Jeff didn't laugh. He lost a few points from George for that.

***

After dinner, Ella convinced George to stay the night. He felt a little torn by it because it was apparent to him that Jeff would also be staying the night, but George was tired and this shouldn't be weird. His daughter had been married before, and he had stayed in their home tons of times, but somehow this felt a little different. They stood at the sink washing dishes while Jeff conveniently escaped to the living room.

"Are you sure you're okay?" she asked.

"I'm fine."

"Do you not like Jeff?"

"No, he's…interesting."

"I thought you'd like him. You have the whole art thing in common."

"He's not anything like Kevin. Kevin was a lot more buttoned down."

"That's the point," she said.

"I see."

"So, you don't like him?"

"No, I do. How long have you been seeing him?"

"Not long. Don't worry. It's not serious. Jeff wants to keep it casual, which is perfect for me."

"Mm." He wanted to say more, but didn't.

"Why don't you go sit down? I'll finish up here and bring dessert to the living room."

While Ella plated the chocolate cake George had picked up on the way, he sat down on the couch opposite Jeff. He said, "So, have you ever done any painting, or do you stick with the shed antler thing?"

"I find traditional art to be pretentious garbage."

"Why's that?"

"It just doesn't have a message, you know. I mean, where's the expressionism? It still follows the standard rules set up by our society. I work outside the system."

"So, what message do you express with dead animal carcasses?"

"Nature is the truest form of art there is, not synthetic colors strewn on a board in a manner taught by conventional methods."

"I thought art was anything the artist decides to create," George said.

"Hey, I don't mean to criticize your methods. They're just not current or relevant."

"Well, I guess someone should tell that to the two people who purchased my paintings recently."

Ella came in and distributed the plates. "Did I just hear you say you sold another piece?"

"I did."

"That's great, Dad!"

"Thanks, honey." He looked over at Jeff and gave him a patronizing smile.

George didn't care for his smug, closed-minded philosophy, but a lot of people had strong opinions on art, especially when they were passionate about it. He wondered what Ella saw in him though. They didn't seem to have much in common, or at least, Ella had never expressed any interest in art before; she was more science-minded, like Melinda had been, but George held his tongue and tried to be polite. He was a patient man who loved his daughter, and if that meant putting up with arrogant, unemployed shed hunters for another hour to stay in his daughter's good graces, that's what he'd do. That was just the kind of man he was.

After the coffee and cake, George took the dishes to the kitchen and cleaned up. When he was done, he feigned exhaustion and excused himself for the night, leaving Ella and Jeff on the couch. From the guest bedroom, he heard the television in the living room click on. He tried not to judge Jeff so quickly, but he still worried about his daughter. She met a random stranger on a hiking trail then went to his home. That was dangerous. He also didn't care for the way she'd thrown out the term "casual" as a way to indicate it wasn't serious, yet this guy sure seemed to be making himself comfortable here. Maybe George just wasn't comfortable with the term casual, in general. He knew Ella was too old for him to keep protecting her like a child, but he thought they'd raised her better. This was the exact scenario in which Melinda would've helped to calm him down, tell him he was being crazy, but he wasn't sure he was. Ella barely knew this guy.

As he drifted off to sleep, he couldn't help but compare his own situation with that of his daughter's.

They were obviously both sleeping with people much younger than themselves, whom they barely knew. She justified it to George by saying he and Jeff had things in common. And that's when something disturbing occurred to George. Did Ella have daddy issues?

Chapter 16

The days and weeks that followed were slow and drawn out. It was too quiet, and the painting was going nowhere. The little cabin started to feel stifling to George, and an uneasy air moved in around him. He spent more time contemplating this sudden notion that perhaps he and Ella had some work to do. He always knew there was distance there but he didn't think it was anything more than that. Was that in and of itself enough to cause damage to Ella? What could he do to break the barrier between them? He didn't even know for sure if he understood what might have caused it, or if it was something he was inventing in his head. Maybe he should just leave it alone? Experience taught him that forcing things with Ella only resulted in more pullback. Perhaps these dinners were enough for them to slowly start closing the gap.

George fluctuated his thoughts between this new concern about his daughter, and Mona. When his painting completely stalled out, he took out the napkin with Mona's phone number on it, but couldn't get himself to dial the numbers. He didn't want to appear desperate. He'd intended to come up here and find peace and solitude, so that's what he was trying to do, except now that she'd been introduced into the mix, she continued to break his concentration. Again, they weren't purely sexual thoughts, though now he could admit that a few were definitely sprinkled in.

Mostly he thought about how lively and unpredictable she was, and how there was much more going on with her than met the eye. Normally, he didn't like unpredictable, but these days he was forced into dealing with things that made him uncomfortable. Mona seemed perfectly comfortable in her own independence, and that was something George clearly needed to work on himself.

He was just now realizing he and Melinda had maybe been a bit too codependent. That was made evident by the lack of people in attendance at the funeral. They had friends, but they weren't just Mel's friends or just his friends. They were couple friends. They would go to dinner with people occasionally, but they always went together. They traveled together, they relaxed together on the weekends, and they even shopped together a good majority of the time. And at the end of the day, they went to bed together every night. Sometimes they watched the news or a late night talk show. Melinda often read; George would do the crossword from the paper. He missed that, the feeling of having someone with him that just made everything feel normal. Maybe it hadn't been heated or passionate so much anymore, but it was comfortable.

Now, he wanted to put his head down and concentrate on himself and his relationship with his daughter for a bit, but he realized he was actually waiting for Mona to make another appearance. Her way was to just pop in, on her own time. He was fine letting her take the reins; he just hoped she wouldn't wait too long before her next appearance.

Dinner with Ella that next weekend was a successful one, in George's mind. The weather was cooperative so they met halfway at a little diner along Highway 61. George attempted to be relaxed and fun. He was still trying out this new normal. It was a different normal for him, and it was going to take some time, but he wanted to make things with his daughter work.

He decided not to bring up Jeff. If Ella wanted to talk about him, that was one thing, but he felt it was better to stay out of that specific zone if he could help it, unless she brought it up. Lucky for George, she did not.

"What's new?" Ella asked between their burgers and fries.

"Not much. Still just painting away."

"And it's not too quiet there?"

"I'm embracing nature," he said.

"Since when have you liked nature, Dad?"

"I mean, when I was a kid on the farm, I loved nature. But at some point I got my fill of it."

"Okay, so why now?"

"I don't know. I guess maybe it's soothing for the soul. Plus, I'd really only experienced Northern Minnesota in the warmer months previously. It's been very interesting seeing it in the dead of winter. I like it."

"I'm looking forward to spring."

"If you don't like winter, El, why do you live up here?"

"I didn't say I don't like winter. I just wish it wasn't nine months of the year. I'm over it. I want to be warm. By the way, what have you decided to do once your lease it up?"

"I'm not sure. Maybe I should take some of the money from Mom's life insurance and look at houses up here again? I like being this close to you."

"I've enjoyed it too," Ella said, giving George a warm look. "But I've also been thinking…"

"What about?"

"I know Mom was planning to do some traveling. What if you and I did that?"

"Travel? To where?"

"I don't know. Do you have any place you'd like to go? I mean, you're retired now. You can live it up."

"I'm not much of a live it up kind of guy, honey. You know that."

She sighed. "Come on, Dad. There's nowhere you want to see? I mean, you've barely left Minnesota."

"I'm content right here. I like Minnesota."

"Okay." Ella looked down and took a bite of her burger.

"Why? Is there somewhere you'd like to go?"

She looked back up at him. Her eyes twinkled a little with the possibilities. "Are you saying you'll do it?"

"I'll think about it."

"Some place warm," Ella said. "For sure. Maybe California, or Fiji. Someplace with palm trees and fruity drinks."

"Those are your two requirements? Palm trees and fruity drinks?"

"Yep."

"I see." He reminded himself about how he was going to work on pushing himself out of his comfort zone. And it would be another opportunity to keep working on things with Ella. It seemed like they'd been making some great strides here. He wanted to continue moving forward. "Well, I suppose it's not the worst idea," he said, finally.

"Great. I'll start doing some planning."

Chapter 17

After nearly two weeks passed with no word from Mona, the silence and the painting he couldn't seem to complete got the better of George. He began to feel claustrophobic in the small space and knew a trek out would help. He wished he could get the fourth painting done so he could use it as an excuse to visit The Grind, but it just wasn't happening. He told himself, so what? He didn't need a reason to go and see her. This was a new George. Sure, he was on the moving train, but he didn't have to be a passenger. He didn't have to let someone else drive. He could control his own destiny. So he got in his Prius and headed to town, throwing logic out the window on the way.

When he walked into The Grind, he saw a young man working behind the counter. Mona was nowhere in sight. Damn. He should have called her first. He decided to get some coffee anyway. He was already there, and he wasn't ready to go back into hiding just yet. His third painting was still on the wall as he passed by on the way to the front of the shop so he stopped to check it out briefly. Feeling the confidence come back to him, he stepped up to the counter.

"What can I get ya?" the pimple-faced barista asked.

"Large dark roast, please."

"Coming right up."

"Does Mona have the day off?"

"Uh…yeah, I guess."

"Okay, thanks."

He handed George his drink in a to-go cup. "Did you want to leave her a message? Are you her uncle or something?"

"No." George smiled as he handed him cash and fled to an open table near his artwork and sat down. He tried not to let the comment get to him. He should have expected it. To distract himself, he grabbed a loose newspaper from a nearby table and stared at it for a while. After he'd drunk about half his coffee, George took his phone from his pocket and dialed Mona's number. His hand was shaking a little and he felt ridiculous; like he was a prepubescent boy again, calling a girl for the first time. After four rings, he got her voicemail. "Hi. It's Mona. Leave a message."

He took a deep breath. "Hi. It's George calling. I just stopped in to the coffee shop and well, you aren't here. I guess you know that. I just wondered if maybe you were upstairs and cared to join me for some coffee. I'll be here for a bit longer if you get this and aren't busy."

After he hung up he replayed the message in his head and hoped he sounded casual enough. He set his phone on the table and looked around at the rest of the art hung on the walls. Some of the pieces were pretty good, but most looked like they'd been done by someone who conspired to the same artistic philosophy as Jeff. A little bit wilder and more like what George considered installation pieces, flash art. Looking back at his own piece, he wondered if maybe Jeff was right; maybe he was out of touch. His work did appear pretty straightforward, maybe even stuffy and conservative next to these others.

After a while, when he hadn't heard anything from Mona, he started to feel foolish. Maybe this really was all a huge mistake. She likely wasn't returning his call because he was an old geezer, and perhaps he was irrelevant after all. Still, he watched the door for a while longer as he finished his coffee, hoping maybe she'd get the message and just come blowing in, but she didn't. When nearly forty minutes passed and his phone hadn't rung, he gathered his things and headed out.

On his way back to the cottage, George made one last stop at the grocery store. He decided to get some Scotch since that's what Mona had requested the last time they had dinner, and he picked up another bottle of wine for his upcoming dinner with Ella.

"I'm sorry. Your card is declined," the cashier said.

"That shouldn't be. I just used it…" He realized he'd actually used cash at the last few stops. He hadn't used his card is several days actually. He pulled his other card out of his wallet and handed it to her. "Can you try this one instead?"

She swiped it through the machine and it beeped. "Sorry." She handed it back to him.

"Okay." He paid cash for half the items and left the rest on the belt. He felt like an idiot, but it didn't bother him that much because he knew it had to be a bank error. He had plenty of money in his account. In fact, after Melinda's life insurance payout, he had more than enough.

When he arrived at the cabin he pulled his cell phone out and dug through the little file folder he'd brought with him with important documents in it, and he pulled out his bank information.

"Hi, I was just told my card was declined, but that's not possible," he told the bank teller.

"What's your card number, name, and last four digits of your social? I can look it up."

After he gave the bank his information, the woman said, "I'm sorry, Mr. Altman. It looks like you currently have a negative balance in your checking account."

"I don't understand. According to my records, I should have a few thousand dollars in my checking right now."

"Let me see… It looks like there were several transactions yesterday. A few transfers from your checking account in large sums. You didn't have enough to cover the amount requested but you have your account set up to allow the bank to pull from your savings in case of overdraft. We only do that twice, which is what happened yesterday."

"What? No, I didn't…"

Something horrible began to dawn on George as he looked at the file folder, remembering the last time he'd touched it. Mona was standing in the cabin with him, watching him. He didn't want to believe it.

"Do you think this is fraud, Mr. Altman? We can put an immediate stop on your cards."

"Yes. I think it must be."

George hung up and dug back into the file folder. He pulled out the two checks Mona had given him for the paintings he'd sold. She hadn't taken them; still it was now all becoming clear. Mona stayed to shower on Saturday when he went to Ella's. He'd left the file folder sitting right out in the open, on the counter. It held his Social Security card as well as all of his bank information. Had she written down his personal information and somehow managed to use it to steal directly from his bank account?

Chapter 18

George continued to chastise himself over the next couple of days. He spoke to the bank a few more times. Once everything was said and done, the bank covered him for up to $10,000 but Mona had actually gotten away with nearly double that amount, withdrawing money roughly ten times over the course of the last three days. And now she was MIA.

The fact that the money was gone was less upsetting to George than the humiliation of being swindled. Financially he would be fine; he still had his 401k that he hadn't even begun to tap into because of the life insurance payout. He was just so fire-breathing mad, mostly at himself for letting his guard down and letting someone take advantage of him. He'd always prided himself on never falling for scams. Now it was clear he'd been such an idiot. This one he hadn't even seen coming. Looking back, he should have known. Why else would a girl like Mona feign interest in him? He couldn't even prove it though, nor did he care to do so. Even if he did, he didn't even know what her last name was, for Christ's sake.

And if he was being completely honest with himself—and he was after he'd drunk a good portion of the Scotch he got at the store—his heart was heavy. He didn't want it to be. George was painfully aware now that this girl hadn't actually felt a lick of emotion for him, but damn it, why did he still feel like she might have? Why would he even be concerned about whether she did or not? In the end, she screwed him over, in more than one way. He definitely now understood the meaning of feeling violated.

George spent the day coming in and out of clarity. There were some very defined moments of darkness, too. The liquor made sure of that. In the height of his rage and self-loathing, he decided he needed to get out. He contemplated going back to visit Harry at The Iron Ranger, but even in his state he knew that was a bad idea. He was feeling daring though so he took a bucket from the storage shed and hauled it out to the lake. It was now just past the middle of March and thus technically, by calendar standards, spring. Duluth had apparently not gotten the memo though, especially given the particularly long, cold winter.

So it wasn't unusual to find a handful of ice fishermen out still, probably also full of the same liquid courage as George, and one of them drilled him a hole. He didn't bother to even drop a line in. He just sat on his bucket, staring into the hole, searching the abyss for something deep down to reveal itself. The only thing he found was a runny nose and numb appendages. The man who drilled the hole returned an hour later and asked him if he was having any luck.

"No. I'm not," George said. He wasn't really referring to the fishing.

"Where's your lucky charm?"

"I'm sorry?"

"The girl who was with ya the other day?"

"She's gone."

"Oh. Where to?"

"Just gone."

"That's too bad," the fisherman said and started to walk away.

"Yeah. It is," George said.

***

Eventually, when he realized brooding wasn't going to get him anything more than frostbite, George returned the bucket to the storage shed and hauled several more bundles of wood into the cabin. Back inside, after he got a fire going and warmed his body, he plopped himself down onto the metal folding chair and stared through the canvas on the easel for a while. His logic was foggy, but in his state he thought maybe drinking was exactly what he needed to produce some amazing works of art. Hadn't all of the great painters been lushes? Something about fighting internal demons made for some fantastic outward struggles. George didn't know what that something was, but he was determined to see if he could find out. Maybe it was the exact formula he was looking for to make his work more relevant. He began fighting with the paint as he worked it around the canvas.

After a few more drinks, another thought arose. Had Mona really sold his paintings to legitimate customers? Probably not. She was likely using the sales as bait, so she had a reason to keep seeing him. Most of the lead-ins for her visits had been to deliver a check to him. He was stupid enough to fall for it: hook, line, and sinker. She was a good fisher woman; he'd give her that.

He felt like a complete idiot but he was stubborn. He didn't want to give Mona the satisfaction of destroying his passion for art. Besides, he hadn't come to Duluth intending to sell his work initially anyway. He was painting because he enjoyed it. He tried to remember that and he loaded a good dollop of paint onto the canvas and continued his struggle.

After pushing the paint around a bit longer, it was clear he was losing the battle. Frustrated, he gave up and moved the easel aside. He looked out at Lake Superior. He wondered again about what he was going to do. It had all been so clear before, but now his lack of confidence was perhaps more abundant than ever, no matter how much he wrestled with it. It was, he knew, a fairly ridiculous time to stop and take stock of one's life, yet here he was. Then again, maybe it was exactly the time to question everything. His wife was gone. Even though sixty-five wasn't that old, he felt his life was pretty much over now too. What had he accomplished? He'd always thought he'd have time to do more, to contribute something. He assumed art was the thing, the one talent he had to put forth to the world. Now he saw, even if art was enough, he wasn't an artist. The whole notion was suddenly so preposterous, especially seeing where it had actually gotten him. Nowhere. He was more lost now than ever before in his life.

Chapter 19
Present Time

Nancy quickly headed back to the station after she scribbled the name George Altman into her notepad. At her desk, she grabbed the final autopsy report from her box and read through it. Because of the cold temperature of Lake Superior and the way it preserved the corpse, the examiner couldn't put an exact amount of time the body had been in the water, stating it could have been two days to two months, but after having talked with Jenny, Nancy knew Mona was seen on Monday and turned up dead on Wednesday. The murder happened sometime between those two days.

The cause of death was strangulation without a weapon, not drowning. A homicide. Mona's hyoid bone was broken, and there was extensive bruising around the neck that differed from the bruising caused in the water, indicative of brute force done by hands. There was no water in her lungs. She'd died before she entered the water.

Nancy looked through the rest of the paperwork stacked up in her bin, then called the crime lab.

"Simmons here. Calling about Mona Clark. Have you had any luck with that cell phone?"

"We're trying to dry it out, but I wouldn't bank on it. It was submerged for too long."

"Right. Okay. Let me know if you get it working."

"Will do."

"Thanks. One more thing, was there any indication of sexual activity? Any additional DNA collected besides that of our victim?"

"None, but that doesn't mean much. The water could have eliminated that evidence. As far as visually, I didn't see any signs of rape, if that's what you're asking."

"It is. Okay. I appreciate it."

Nancy hung up and filed a report to get Mona's phone records. If she couldn't have the actual phone, she could at least find out where she'd placed calls and vice-versa. It wasn't as good as having contacts, texts, and voicemails, but it was something.

She checked her watch. It was almost lunchtime. Again, she'd forgotten to pack herself a lunch because she was eager to get going. She pushed on anyway because now that she knew for certain this was a murder, she had serious work to do.

She began searching the database for a George Altman. There were only three records listed in the state of Minnesota. One was a seven year old in Polk County near Crookston; the second was a ninety-one year old male in Rochester. The third was a sixty-five year old in St. Paul. She clicked the link for him. His records were cleaner than a newborn baby. He didn't even have a parking ticket on file. A little unusual, but not completely unheard of. It took her a little longer to find his whereabouts. She traced the address in St. Paul, which had a flag for mail forwarding, to a street just north of Duluth proper.

"This must be my man," Nancy mumbled to herself.

No signs of rape, and a strangulation—that could only mean one thing. This was not a random killing. The killer knew the victim. Generally, someone who used their bare hands to end a life meant they were allowed to get up close and personal.

This man, George Altman, had a connection to the victim, was living nearby, and may very well know something about what happened to her. She just needed to pull a motive out of him. What could cause an older man to kill a woman nearly forty years younger? Nancy looked back down at the photo of Mona in the case file opened up on her desk. Perhaps a better question to ask was why had a twenty-six year old become involved with a sixty-five year old? It seemed far-fetched, but according to Jenny at the coffee shop, there was something going on between them. Nancy had seen a lot of things as a detective and this wouldn't be even remotely the strangest. Sadly, it was all too common for love to be the primary motive for murder. She wasn't sure yet if that was the case here, but she had a definite lead now and she was anxious to get to the bottom of it.

She briefed the captain on her findings then she was off to pay George a visit. She knew she should take along a backup but the only one available was Balton, and she would rather get killed in the line of duty than spend any chunk of time with Balton. Besides that, she preferred to do her questioning alone. It always yielded better results. People seemed more eager to talk to a woman, she found. But the main reason Nancy chose to go alone was because she didn't need another person with her gumming up the works. She could handle things just fine by herself.

Chapter 20

George stood, drinking coffee and looking at the canvas from across the room. Now that he was sobered up he saw things for how they really were. The painting was awful, and he felt physically ill from the drink. He didn't care if he'd paid for the cabin for a full year, or how beautiful it might be up here in the spring or summer. It was time for him to go. If he stayed, he wasn't sure what would become of him and his mental state, or what it might do to his situation with Ella. She was the most important thing to him anyway.

He decided the best plan was to head back home. From there, he would either contact Michael Olson about looking for homes near Ella, or start working through those travel plans Melinda had saved on the home computer. Maybe the trip with El wasn't the worst idea right about now.

Whatever choice he made, he knew leaving Duluth and this cabin was the best thing for him. He started packing things up, almost as if the idea was so perfect, there was some haste to executing it. So that's what he was doing when he heard a knock on the cabin door.

He had a good majority of his stuff bagged and boxed up, piled on the counter and on the floor near the entrance of the cabin. He went to the door. His heart rate increased, though he wasn't sure why. He wasn't expecting anyone, and he'd made no plans with Ella. Before he pulled the door open, he peered through the peephole. In front of him stood a woman, maybe in her late forties dressed in a dark trench coat. She was adjusting her cashmere scarf.

"Can I help you?" George said as he pulled the door open, relieved and disappointed at the same time.

"Are you George Altman?"

"Yes."

She reached into her pocket and pulled out what looked like a wallet. Instead she revealed a shiny badge. "I'm detective Simmons of the Duluth PD. Wondering if I could ask you a few questions."

"What's this regarding? Is it Ella? Has something happened to her?"

"Do you mind if I come in, Mr. Altman?"

"Please." He stepped aside and let the detective in. He thought about offering her coffee but he was too nervous now. His thoughts immediately went to his daughter and that Jeff person. He just had a bad feeling about him. The detective walked to the counter and turned toward him. She pulled a small notepad and pen from her coat pocket.

"May I ask who Ella is?" she said, opening the pad of paper.

"My daughter."

"Well, to answer your question then, no. This isn't about your daughter." She looked around. "Are you going somewhere, Mr. Altman?"

"Yes. I'm packing to return to my home in St. Paul. What's this about?"

"It's about a woman named Mona Clark. Did you know her, Mr. Altman?"

"Yes. Did you find her?"

"We did."

"Do you need me to press charges?"

"Excuse me?"

"For the money she stole from me."

"She took money from you?"

"Yes. I thought that's why you were asking about her."

"No, Mr. Altman. She's dead."

"She's dead?" George heard himself ask the detective a second time. "How?" he managed to get to out. He wasn't sure it was even audible but she answered loud and clear.

"She was murdered."

He sat down hard as if it might somehow alter the situation, but when he looked up there was still a very tall, middle-aged woman wearing a black trench coat standing in front of him with a hard scowl and thin lips staring back at him, as if she were attempting to see straight into him. George's eyes went for the floor. He tried to stay calm.

The detective took out a recording device from her leather shoulder bag and hit a button. "I'd like to ask you a few questions. Is that all right?"

He nodded, head still tucked. He only half-heard the Miranda rights she recited to him, as if she were saying them from an entirely different room altogether instead of the enclosed space of a tiny one-room cabin. His thoughts clouded with all of the events that had taken place over the last few months. How had this happened to him? He'd assumed that once he retired, life would somehow be easier, quiet. It was touted as the golden years, after all. George had joked with his wife that it should be called the dead space—the time between living and waiting to die. It wasn't very funny anymore but he still didn't understand the reference to it being golden. For

George Altman, the only thing shimmering around him lately seemed to be the flames of the hell he was trapped in

Chapter 21

Nancy watched George's face closely as she delivered the fact that Mona was dead. He looked genuinely shocked, but Nancy didn't let it fool her. She'd seen some good actors in her day. And though the guy looked more like a teddy bear than a killer of young women, she continued to stand as she pushed on with her interview. She liked to use her height to intimidate possible perpetrators. The one disadvantage she'd been given, in terms of her physical appearance, was her blonde hair. It was shocking to Nancy how many people really did have preconceived notions and often had a hard time taking her for what she was, serious.

"It has come to my attention that you've been involved with Mona recently, is that correct?"

He shook his head. "Dead. How did she die?" He looked up at her now from the chair he'd practically fallen into after she delivered the news.

Nancy thought she smelled liquor on his breath. "That's what I'm here to try to find out," she said. "Now, what was the nature of your relationship with Miss Clark?"

"It's a long and embarrassing story." He sounded solemn. Was he experiencing remorse?

"I've got time," she said. That clock inside her brain was still ticking loudly though.

"Right. Well, I lost my wife in early January. I was two days shy of retirement. Our daughter is in Ely, so after my wife's passing I came here to get away and paint."

"How did your wife die?"

"She suffered a stroke as a result of chemotherapy from cancer."

"I'm sorry to hear that. How long were you married?"

"Forty-six years."

Nancy nodded.

"Anyway, I met Mona and I had no intention of anything happening, but she was a very persistent woman. After the identity theft, I figured out why she'd been pursuing me."

"Identity theft? Tell me more about that. Did you file a police report?"

"I felt too foolish to file anything."

"So you confronted her. Did you lose your temper?"

"No. I never saw her again, actually." He kept his eyes down, focusing on the table. "In fact, I can't believe I'm saying this, but even after she stole from me, I still cared for her. I don't know why."

"Did you kill her, Mr. Altman?"

"I…of course not."

"So you had nothing to do with and have no information regarding Mona Clark's death?"

"No. Nothing. I just said that I cared about her."

"Then you wouldn't mind if I get a swab of your DNA?"

"That would be fine," he said.

Nancy saw that George's hands were trembling slightly. She took out the kit from her leather bag and had George swab his inside cheek with the Q-tip. She continued with the interview as she sealed the sample back up and tucked it away.

"When exactly was the last time you saw Mona Clark?"

"Uh, I guess it would have been nearly three weeks ago Saturday."

"March 4th?"

"Yes."

"And had you been sexually involved with her on that occasion?"

George lowered his head. "Yes...but she left on good terms. I didn't figure out she took the money until several days after that and she was already long gone."

"Gone?"

"I mean, she stopped coming around and didn't answer her phone. I even went to the coffee shop but the kid behind the counter said he hadn't seen her. I assumed she'd left town with my money."

While Nancy formulated her next question, she glanced around the living room. There was an easel folded up and a painting on the floor next to it. "So, you're a painter?"

"It's just a hobby. Something to do to keep my mind off of things."

"But you'd been selling your work at The Grind?"

"Also something Mona got me to do. I never planned to sell the paintings."

"And you said you're heading back to St. Paul. Why is that?"

"After the incident, I haven't been able to focus on painting anymore, and I just wanted a change of scenery. I'm a city man. I thought I would enjoy this environment but it's beginning to feel confining."

"When you say the incident, what are you referring to exactly?"

"The theft, the relationship, the whole thing."

"Were you feeling guilty that you'd taken up with such a young woman, Mr. Altman?"

"Well, yes. I would never have done that normally. That's not me, but I was vulnerable after my wife died. I was lonely, and Mona was mature and smart and, as I mentioned, persuasive. Of course, I know now it was all an act."

George was still slumped over and he put his face in his hands. He looked less like a murderer and more like a victim in his demeanor, but things still mostly pointed in his direction, as far as Nancy was concerned.

"Okay, Mr. Altman. Here's the deal. I have no evidence to formally charge you at this time, but I may have some more questions for you. If this DNA yields anything, I'll need you to come to the station. I'd probably unpack your boxes and sit tight if I were you."

He nodded. "Should I get a lawyer?"

"That's your choice. Here's my card if you'd like to talk to me at any time." She set the card down on the table and moved toward the door.

George looked up at her. She could see his gears turning. She figured he was probably ready to confess, but instead he said, "Mona has a mother who needs looking after. She has dementia. She lives above the coffee shop. Can you make sure someone knows?"

"Already done, Mr. Altman."

He nodded from the table as Nancy walked out.

* * *

On her drive back up the hill to the station, she was conflicted. Killers didn't usually worry about the welfare of their victim's sick mother. That was not typical, for sure. But this guy had a pretty strong motive. He told Nancy he had feelings for this girl. There was some definite internal strife happening. He was clearly struggling with something. She needed something a little more concrete in order to get the judge to sign off on a search warrant. Even then, she could already tell this was not going to be as clear-cut as she'd hoped. A choking and a dumped body were not things that often yielded a ton of hard evidence. Her best chance now was for a confession. If he killed Mona, Nancy felt pretty confident he wasn't going to be able to keep it to himself for long.

Chapter 22

Nancy sat at her desk transcribing her recordings into her notes for the case file. She had four cups of coffee already today and not enough to eat. Her stomach was starting to roil in protest. She had too much to do to stop, so she went out into the main lobby area to grab something from the vending machines.

When she turned the corner, she saw Mr. Altman standing at the reception desk talking with Bonnie. She headed toward him.

"Hello," she said. "Have you come to talk with me?" She wished she'd made it to the vending machine before now. Confessions could sometimes take hours.

"Yes." He handed her some papers. "I thought you might want to have a look at the statements that came in the mail today from my bank, in regards to the illegal transfers."

"Oh." She took the paperwork from him. "Okay. Thank you."

He nodded and turned to leave. Nancy stood making small talk with Bonnie, the receptionist, for a few minutes until she was sure Mr. Altman was gone. She stepped outside the building and onto the sidewalk. She watched Mr. Altman get into a small silver Toyota and drive away.

With a bag of chips now in hand, she sat back down at her desk and went over the bank statements. It was clear that Mr. Altman hadn't been lying about the swindle. The bank had clearly marked the fraud charges in red. It didn't prove Mona Clark had been the one to take the money, but it would be easy enough for Nancy to verify if the money had entered into Mona Clark's bank account.

Again, it didn't clear Mr. Altman of any wrongdoing, though at this point Nancy wasn't ready to close the books on him either. She still had little evidence to go on, and it was important to keep the focus broad, though she had a hunch about George at this point. It was slightly more than a gut feeling. Too many things pointed in his direction. It was a bit of a strange move for him to bring the proof directly to her. Of course, people often acted odd and unusual under duress. Nancy had seen so many weird behaviors during her fifteen years at this. A possible suspect pretending to assist the police wasn't that uncommon. Psychopaths often thought they were smarter than cops, especially blonde ones. She'd even encountered guilty people who really believed they hadn't committed the crime, even when it turned out they had. People with schizophrenia and multiple personality disorders were prime examples. She had no idea what George Altman had going on. She felt certain it would reveal itself fairly soon, as it usually did.

Nancy filled out a few requests to obtain Mona's bank statements, and then she went over the phone records she'd received. She cross-matched George's phone number to those on the list. It appeared Mr. Altman had called Mona just one time, but she had not called him at all. This seemed to contradict his story that she had strongly pursued him.

Something else on the phone record stood out as peculiar. There were several calls made over and over to the same number. Nancy jotted it down and put it into her computer. It came back as an unknown cellular user, which usually meant it was what the kids called a "burner" or a cheap, disposable cell phone. They were often used in drug deals because they would swap them out, or burn them, often so as to not be easily traceable. She put in a request for a tracer on it anyway. Why was Ms. Clark making calls to a burner? One possibility was that she was a drug user. Could explain the need for the large sum of money she had allegedly stolen from Mr. Altman. She did have that prior on her record for marijuana possession, but it had occurred when she was a teenager, and Nancy would never make a bigger assumption on something like that. Most teenagers experimented with pot. Still, she would talk with the manager of The Grind tomorrow for some character references.

There wasn't much else to do until those records all came back. She went in to update the captain. He nodded as she prattled on about how she felt certain she could have the case solved soon. Of course, she was mostly just biding her time. She didn't have anything substantial yet, but she was confident in her abilities. All she needed him to do was somehow hold the media off for a little longer. He said he'd do what he could. It was the same as always. It was much easier to get her work done before the news stories started to come out. After, she'd be inundated with chasing a bunch of erroneous "tips" that came flooding in.

She grabbed the case file from her desk and headed out. She now felt very ill from all of the coffee and vending machine junk food, and she needed to get cleaned up and think in peace and quiet. Once she was able to eat a proper meal and relax, she knew her next move would come to her. She was thrilled that Roger was away and she could concentrate without any marital distractions.

The voicemail was flashing when she arrived home. It didn't surprise her. Roger had started a habit of leaving messages on the home phone when he was away on business. He said the same thing when he called. "Just checking in." It bugged Nancy that he did it on the phone he knew she wouldn't actually answer, but she didn't know why it bothered her. She didn't actually want to talk to him when he was away, which was pretty often lately, another reason she was irritated he'd moved her from her home state to this ice land. He was hardly ever bothered by the cold because he was hardly ever there.

Nancy opened a bottle of wine and poured herself a glass to go with the salad she'd picked up on the way home. She contemplated listening to the voice message but hit the delete button instead as she sat down to eat. When she was finished, she took her wine and headed to the bathroom to run a bath for herself. She'd never been a bather in California but in Minnesota, it had been routine. It was the only thing she found that warmed her up. It was a bonus that it also helped her relax and focus, which was essential when working a murder investigation. Need to solve a murder? Just let me soak for an hour and I can crack the case—that should be on her business card—she mused to herself as she slid further down into the sudsy water.

She closed her eyes. Her mind immediately began to go over the information she'd gathered about Mona Clark. So far it was possible she was a drug addict who found Mr. Altman an easy target, so she took advantage of him, swindled him out of some money, but didn't get out of the situation as easily as she'd hoped. She'd misread the older gentleman; he turned out to be less docile than he'd initially come across. He somehow lured her back to his place after he'd figured out her game, then he choked her to death and dumped her in the lake.

It presented itself as a cut and dry case but she would admit this George Altman guy was throwing a few barbs into her smooth theory. Say there was a slight possibility he didn't do it. Maybe he really was a vulnerable man who'd been taken by a money-hungry, nice-looking girl. That was a pretty big coincidence, but Nancy went with it for a minute. If there really was no connection between the heist and the murder, who else may have killed Mona and for what reason? She took George's money and went to buy drugs and was involved in a deal gone bad? Maybe she bragged to the dealer about the money she'd recently acquired? It was possible. Nancy wouldn't rule out any theory this early in the case.

She still needed more facts and until she collected them and put the case to rest, she couldn't relax any further, not even in the bath. She got out and wrapped herself in a towel, shivering. The worst part of a good soak in this climate was dealing with the aftermath. She shuffled toward her robe and slippers and regretted ever trying to warm up in the first place.

As she exited the bathroom, the home phone rang. She was dry and decent, but she didn't make a move to answer it. Instead, she casually walked to refill her wine glass and listened as the machine picked up. After the beep she heard Roger's voice.

"Hey, hon. Just checking in. Just got out of my meeting. Thought I'd let you know I made it okay."

Ever since the affair, these calls began. Nancy knew Roger was trying to show her he was being faithful, like a simple phone call could prove it. Even if it could, it was too little, too late, as far as Nancy was concerned. At this point, she was so far out of love with Roger that it didn't even matter to her if he did cheat. She almost wished he would resume the affair so it could just be over for good. Instead, he did everything he could to try to make it up to her, and she felt too guilty about leaving him. Besides, where would she go? As much as she hated Duluth, she hated the idea of starting over even more. She was too old. What was the point? She knew she was a huge chicken, but she'd rather just keep telling herself one day she'd love Roger again and things would be fine. It seemed easier that way. She'd rather avoid the conflict altogether.

Besides, it wasn't all his fault. She was just as much to blame. He might not have had the affair if she wasn't so closed off, at least that was what he argued. He was right, too. She'd kept her own secrets from Roger. She wished she could call it even and move on. Instead, she mostly felt like being alone. That was just how things had evolved. If you wanted to be a homicide detective, you had to be tough, impenetrable. Maybe Nancy had taken it too far, because most days she felt just as hardened as the people she dealt with in her line of work.

Chapter 23

Nancy got a few hours of sleep and was feeling refreshed and ready to tackle the case. She went back to the station and checked her inbox. The information on the burner phone was among the paperwork. It looked like whoever the owner was seemed to get around. They did a triangulation on the number and tracked the signal to several locations over the past month, including many places between Duluth and the Twin Cities. The signal was now stable and reading not far from there, so she sent a squad out to have a look. This often meant the phone had already been burned and was sitting at the bottom of a dumpster or more likely in this scenario, Lake Superior. She wouldn't waste her own time tracking it down but she still needed to cross it off the list.

Copies of Mona's bank statements were also among the things in her box. She had a total of $47.51 in her account. That seemed like another strike against George Altman. Had he concocted the whole identity theft just to throw them off? Nancy hadn't the faintest at the moment; though she was confident she'd figure it out, but not before coffee.

What better place to get it than the location she also needed to gather more information. The Grind. She bundled up and headed out. The wind was blowing up an unpleasant March storm, which was probably going to end up being more sleet and freezing rain than snow and often made for horrible driving conditions. Hopefully Nancy would have the case solved before that happened.

When she walked in, she looked around for someone who might be the manager, but just like the last time she'd been in, she didn't see anyone who looked older than seventeen working in the place. It was Saturday, so it was possible these were high school kids. Nancy approached the counter and waited behind a woman with a small child, weaving between his mother's legs. She was on her phone even though it was just barely seven in the morning.

The toddler tried to get Nancy's attention by sticking out his tongue and making guttural noises. Kids flocked to Nancy. They were like cats; they always seemed to know when someone was allergic to them. She was the one they wanted to snuggle up with and they went out of their way to get to her. Or maybe kids were more like dogs, they could sense her fear. This little boy was no exception. He wasn't going to stop until Nancy focused her attention on him. She smiled at him then pretended to look up at the menu board, hoping that would appease him. The kid had ideas of his own. He broke free from his mom's leg and stepped boldly toward Nancy.

"Why are you so tall?" he asked, looking up at her.

Nancy looked down at him. "Oh, because that's how I was made."

The kid's mother turned and looked at her, ear still covered with her phone. When she saw Nancy was a woman, she smiled and resumed her phone conversation. Nancy sighed.

"Why?" he persisted.

"I don't know. Why are you so short?" she said, looking down at him.

He wrinkled his nose up tight. "I'm NOT. I'm a big kid!" He stomped his foot.

Just when Nancy thought he was going to have a tantrum, all because she didn't know how to answer a simple question from a four year old, Mom got her coffee and juice box and pulled the toddler by his arm away from the counter and Nancy. He turned and gave her one more sour look for good measure.

When the counter was clear, she ordered another complicated sounding drink so she would have the barista's attention for the time it took her to create her frothy concoction. This girl wasn't quite as chipper as Jenny had been. She had jet-black hair, clothing to match, and a hoop through her nose. Her nametag said Jax.

"Jax," Nancy said, "I'm actually a detective, and I was wondering if you could help me with something. I'm hoping to speak with the manager."

"Why? Did I do something wrong?" Jax asked.

"No. It's regarding another employee. Mona Clark."

"Mona *was* the manager."

"Oh."

"Yeah. I think she got fired or something. Anyway, Jenny just got promoted to take over, which sucks for the rest of us."

"Who does the hiring?"

"The owner. I dunno. I've never seen him before."

"Do you have a card I could have so I can contact him?"

"Yeah. In the back. Just a second." Jax handed Nancy her coffee and went behind a curtain.

She returned with a card, which she exchanged with Nancy for cash to pay for the drink. Nancy thanked her. There was no one behind her in line so she said, "One last quick question. It sounds like you liked Mona as a manager. Why is that?"

Jax shrugged. "She was decent, as far as bosses go. I dunno, she was better than Jenny."

"She always showed up on time and was responsible?" Nancy asked.

"Yeah. She worked way more than the rest of us. Sorta weird she quit. She seemed to actually like this job. She had friends and junk here."

"Friends?"

"Like she actually liked the customers, talked to the regulars and knew their names."

"Regulars? Anybody in here now that I might be able to talk with?"

Jax looked around and shook her head. "It's usually weekday weirdos."

"Was there anyone who might have been doing more than getting coffee? Like a drug dealer maybe?"

Jax laughed. "Mona? No way. She was squeaky clean. But I guess she did have a stalker once."

"Do you know his name?"

"No. It was before I worked here."

A man approached the counter. Nancy said, "Thanks for your time, Jax. And the coffee."

"No problem."

Nancy walked toward the door. She almost missed seeing someone she recognized sitting at one of the tables along the wall because she was busy thinking she'd clearly been wrong about the drugs. An addict wouldn't have been able to hold down a manager job, even if it was just at an indie coffee house. Nancy stopped and turned back toward the person sitting at the table.

"Hello, Mr. Altman."

He had a cup of coffee and a spiral notebook in front of him. He looked up. "Detective."

"What brings you here so early this morning?"

"Probably the same as you. I'm trying to figure out who killed Mona."

"Is that right?"

"It is."

"Well, can I join you? Maybe we can compare notes so far?"

He nodded. Nancy slid into the seat facing George.

"Mona's bank records came up clean. She had less than fifty dollars in her account," Nancy said.

George looked directly at her. "I've been thinking, she must have had a partner."

"Who might that have been?"

"I don't know. A friend? Maybe even a boyfriend."

Nancy said, "The girl behind the counter mentioned to me that Mona had a stalker here at the shop. Did you often come here to watch Mona work, Mr. Altman?"

"No. Of course not. She was probably referring to the time… Oh my God. The ex!"

"Care to indulge me?" Nancy said curtly.

"Mona told me her ex-boyfriend had wanted to move in together a few years back. When she told him no, he came in here one night at closing time with a gun. Maybe he did this to her?"

Nancy took out her own notebook. "Did she tell you the boyfriend's name?"

"She did but it's not coming to me. He went to jail but she said he was probably out by now."

Nancy looked at her notes. She flipped back a few pages. She recalled Mona's mother giving her some names of boyfriends. "Was it Paul or Ben?"

"Ben, I think," George said. "No, Bobby! That was it."

"Okay. I'll have a look at the police reports." Nancy got up.

George said, "I suppose this still doesn't clear me?"

"Not quite yet, Mr. Altman."

He nodded. "One more thing. Would it be okay if I went upstairs and checked in on Mona's mother?"

"She's already been moved to a facility."

"Oh. That's good. Thank you."

"I'm sure I'll be in touch, Mr. Altman."

He furrowed his brow and stared past Nancy. She exited the coffee shop and climbed the stairs to the apartment. She'd cleared it with the captain yesterday to do another walk through now that Jan Clark had been moved to a nursing home. Officer Balton was already inside when she arrived. Usual protocol said that two or more officers should be present during a full sweep, especially if there would be evidence collection, but Nancy knew Balton didn't care about protocol. She could tell he'd done his sweep alone already, rather than collaborate with a woman, especially one who outranked him. It didn't bother her. She wanted to be alone with her thoughts while she checked things out.

"Find anything?" she asked him.

"Not much. No diary or journals, not many personal effects really at all besides a few books and an iPod."

"What about a computer or purse?"

"Didn't see either of those."

"Okay. I'm going to have a look."

"Here's the key. Leave it under the mat when you're done. I've got a meeting," Balton said.

"Under the mat?" Nancy raised her eyebrows at Balton. "Not a very safe practice for an officer…"

"Give me a break, Simmons. You're lucky we got the owner to agree to the search at all. He was antsy to get the place cleared out. I'm sure he needs to get it rented out again as soon as possible. Besides, he's not local. It was the best arrangement we could make, especially given the storm brewin' out there."

"Okay. Okay," Nancy said. Then she begrudgingly offered up a "Thanks," as much as it killed her to do so.

He nodded and showed himself out. Once she was alone in the apartment, she put on her gloves and wandered through the kitchen, picking up random things here and there. The apartment was small but clean. It was clear Mona had taken good care of her mother. The fridge was pretty well stocked and the dishes were done. The floor looked like it had been swept and mopped fairly recently and even the windows looked pretty good for March in Minnesota. Nancy couldn't say the same about her own windows. By this time of year they looked like they could use a good hosing off.

Nancy headed back through the living room and sorted through the papers on the desk. Some bills and other mail was piled up neatly. Nothing stood out as she examined a few pieces closer. It seemed a bit odd that there was no computer, but then again, most twenty-somethings were opting to go without these days. Mona probably couldn't afford one, not with less than fifty dollars to her name, and her mother certainly didn't need one. As a coffee shop employee, she really had no need for it, but it was unfortunate for Nancy. She'd likely done all of her electronic transactions on her phone, which was now defunct.

She opened a desk drawer and saw a few brochures for in-home care facilities. She picked one up and paged through it. These were no surprise. Mona was probably tossing around the idea of putting her mother into a home. She certainly couldn't blame her for that. If she hadn't had those strangulation marks on her neck, Nancy would probably go back to her initial suicide theory. She could see why Mona might be depressed. It couldn't be easy taking care of an ailing parent. Nancy hadn't had to do that herself. Her father had died when she was young, and her mother was still healthy and active, though Nancy hadn't seen her for a long time because she was still back in San Diego.

She put the brochure back into the desk and headed for Mona's bedroom. It was exactly how she'd seen it the last time she'd been there, only last time she couldn't touch any of it. Today she moved toward the books and looked at the titles. A few best sellers. Nancy had even read one of them herself. There was a flyer for an art exhibit sitting on her dresser. It had already happened, but Nancy took out her notepad and jotted down the information.

There was no sign of a handbag, not on the dresser, side table, or anywhere on the floor. Seemed likely Mona had it in her possession when she was killed, so it was probably at the bottom of old Gitchigumi right now.

She picked through the dirty clothes in the basket and opened the drawers of the dresser and dug her way through them. She found nothing terribly significant. She looked up and saw the two paintings on the dresser again. She turned one over. It had been painted by George Altman. She knew it looked familiar. The second painting had also been done by George. Why did Mona have two of his paintings? This might be something worth following up on. She made a note in her pad.

Nancy opened the closet and pushed several articles of clothing around on the hangers. Mona's closet was full of designer clothes that Nancy actually found herself coveting. If only she were a petite size. It was rather expensive taste for a girl who had no money in her checking account and likely couldn't even afford a computer. It wasn't really what Nancy generally saw on the racks in Duluth stores— California maybe, but not Duluth. She pulled a hanger off the bar and examined the soft pink silk blouse. A tag still dangled from the sleeve. It came from Saks. There certainly wasn't a Saks in Duluth. Closest one was probably the Twin Cities. This shirt was an Eileen Fisher. Nancy didn't know many twenty-six year olds. Bonnie from the office came to mind. She wore jeans and sweatshirts, not Eileen Fisher. Nancy grabbed the sleeve of the shirt and looked at the tag. $79.99.

"Please tell me she didn't scam money from a retired man so she could buy designer clothes," she said. She didn't put much past millennials though. They'd grown up in a very materialistic society. They thought they were entitled to everything. This situation felt slightly different though. From what she gathered so far about Mona, she apparently worked hard at the coffee shop, took good care of her sick mother, and besides the clothes, didn't appear to have much, including a computer. So, were the clothes a gift? Usually people didn't leave the price tags on gifts, unless maybe they wanted the receiver of said gift to see how much was being spent. And in this case, it was a lot. Who did Mona know who could afford eighty dollar shirts that maybe came from the cities? George Altman. Or maybe Mona had a bad shopping habit and was ordering things online and accrued credit card debt she was trying to get herself out of? That was another possibility. Nancy made a note to go back and check both Mona and George's bank statements for large department store purchases, as well as pull Mona's credit information.

She quickly went through Jan's bedroom, which had been mostly packed up by the state workers who helped her move to the nursing home. There wasn't anything odd in it so Nancy moved on. The last room to look through was the bathroom. She slid open the medicine cabinet. There was nothing in it to indicate Mona had been a drug user. In fact, there was little medicine in it at all besides some Ibuprofen. The rest was makeup and hair products, basic toiletries.

She knew from her years of experience people often kept their secrets hidden in plain sight, but she didn't see anything here. Still, she searched the linen and coat closets, and leaving the worst for last, she went through the trash. There was nothing but food wrappers and table scraps. The place was clean, so much so that Nancy hadn't even bagged anything to bring back to the lab. That was rare.

As she walked back to the station, tiny pellets of ice began to fall from the sky. This never happened in California, she grumbled to herself. Who would have thought there could be such a thing as a snowstorm in spring? It made no sense. Back at her computer, she did some searches for Mona's ex boyfriend, Bobby. It wasn't easy, given she had no specific dates of the event that had occurred and no last name for Bobby. She plugged in what little information she did have, an arrest that took place at The Grind within the last few years. After shuffling through a few hundred crime reports, she found the one she was looking for and pulled it up on her computer, full-screen.

Bobby Jacobs was charged on an ADW: Assault with a deadly weapon charge. He was convicted on July 17th, 2012 and sentenced to two years and four months because it was his first offense. But it was a felony charge and therefore he served time in the Stillwater State Penitentiary. He was released six months ago, two months early due to good behavior. His current residence was in Stillwater. Of course it was. Nancy knew she wouldn't get out of driving during a Minnesota snowstorm. She didn't know much about Stillwater, but she did know it was at least a two and a half hour drive due south on a good day. She also knew those signals on the burner phone could have easily been placed between there and Stillwater, possibly between Bobby and Mona since he'd been released.

She went in and told the captain of her travel plans to Stillwater to pay Bobby Jacobs a visit. He gave her the name and number of a good buddy of his, a Washington County law enforcement officer, to get in touch with so they knew she was coming and for what purpose. This was standard procedure when conducting an interview in a jurisdiction other than your own. She made the call before she left so she could be sure to focus all of her attention on the road while she drove through an ice storm

Chapter 24

George went back to the cabin after speaking with the detective in the coffee shop. He hadn't expected to see her, but now he was glad he had actually. Perhaps he'd managed to pull the focus off of himself by putting her on the track of the ex-boyfriend.

He was trying to hold it together, and on the outside he thought he was doing all right, but on the inside he was a mess, maybe even worse than when Melinda died. He stocked up on more alcohol while he was in town, and as much as it disgusted him, he opened one of the beers now and sat down on the little sofa in the living room. He mostly stared out at the lake. He kept the radio on, tuned to the local station in case there was any news about Mona. So far, he'd hardly heard anything reported. The paper had printed Mona's picture and a small blurb about her body having been pulled from the lake, but that was about it.

The hardest part of all of this was trying to keep himself busy. George was used to going to work everyday and being more or less occupied; at the end of the night he generally slept well, having spent his energy, physical and emotional on an average day. Now, he had nowhere to go with all of the panic and dread. The anxiety was building and starting to make him feel crazy. The little cabin's walls were closing in on him. He needed to keep focusing on a purpose, which at this point was drinking. The alcohol wasn't quelling the noises in his head like he hoped it would though.

George thought again about Detective Simmons. He wasn't sure what to make of her or how much he should be worried by her. She seemed like a phony. There wasn't much worse to him than a person who attempted to put up a strong front but it was clear they were just regular old people, with regular old problems, like the rest of them. George had gotten pretty good at discerning people who were acting. He tended to veer toward genuine souls, like Mona. She wasn't trying to fool anyone. He saw her cracks. They gave her character.

As he opened another beer, his head swirled. It didn't matter what he thought of the detective on a personal level. He just needed to figure out a way to get her off his back.

George's phone rang, causing him to flinch. He knew he was on edge, but he hadn't realized just how much. He walked to his cell phone, which was on the kitchen table, and answered.

"Hey, Dad. We still on for dinner?"

"Dinner?"

"You know, that thing we've been having together on Saturdays?"

"They've been saying on the radio freezing rain's on the way."

"I'm actually already in town for a meeting so I don't have far to come."

"Oh," he paused. "Okay then."

"You sure? I'm not keeping you from anything am I?"

"No. I just don't have much in the fridge, that's all." He looked around the cabin. His boxes still sat in piles around the entryway and beer bottles were strewn about the kitchen.

"You want to have dinner out? There's a place across the street from the hotel I'm staying at that looks pretty good," Ella said.

He could have things looking back to normal in an hour or so, he decided. He couldn't go anywhere right now. Not in his condition. "Out? No. I'd rather do it here."

"How about I bring some take out?"

"That sounds fine."

"Great. Six-ish?"

"Okay." When he hung up, he went to the things he had stacked near the door and pulled out the easel. He set it back up near the little front window, along with the metal folding chair. He knew there was no reason to even consider the possibility of painting again but he needed to make it appear like he had been. He sat down on the folding chair and looked out the window. He ran his hands through his hair and took a few deep breaths. He needed to pull himself together. He glanced at the half-finished painting he'd set on the easel. Maybe it was the beer, but at the moment it actually didn't look that bad. Maybe he should have another crack at it. It might be just what he needed to relieve the boredom and ease his conscious.

He got up to put some coffee on. He needed to sober up before El came. He could do this. He turned the radio volume up and dug his paint supplies and smock out of a box. Just as he sat at the folding chair again, something on the radio caught his attention.

"The vehicle of a woman who was pulled from the lake last Wednesday has been found by police. It was parked off of a Highway 61 wayside rest

area, about 17 miles north of town. Police are asking
if anyone may have been at the rest stop that day or
saw anything suspicious to call them. The woman was
twenty-six with shoulder-length brown hair and
brown eyes. She weighed approximately one hundred
fifteen pounds and was reportedly wearing a black
parka and knee-high leather boots."

George stood frozen. What could this mean
for the investigation? It caused his slightly settled
demeanor to go askew. He set his coffee aside and
cracked open another beer. His mind was buzzing.
What was he going to do? He got up and paced the
small cabin. Perhaps he should come clean to Ella? It
would feel good to get it off his chest, where it had
been sitting like a brick for the last week, causing him
to feel like he might have a heart attack at any
moment. Although, maybe having a heart attack right
now wouldn't be a bad thing.

Fog hung over the lake, shrouding George
and the little cabin as if it was trying to choke him.
The approaching storm was creating a hazy doom
that he felt was coming right for him. Something
about not being able to view the water out the
window made it feel like he couldn't see what was
coming. Was it a premonition or just the effects of
the alcohol? George sunk deeper into a state of
distress.

By the time there was a knock at the door,
George was out of his head. Perhaps it was the
culmination of all of the things simmering, or maybe
it was because he was deeply ashamed of himself.
Either way, he answered the door looking a haggard,
distraught old man.

"Dad? Is everything okay?" Ella asked, holding two plastic bags with Asian take-out in them.

"Come in," he said and turned back to the kitchen table. He sat back down to his awaiting beer and focused on it.

"Have you been drinking?" Ella said, setting the food down. Her expression said all George needed to know about her thoughts on the subject.

"Yes."

"What's going on?"

"Can't we just eat? I'm starved."

"I…" Ella stood looking at him, then with pity in her eyes, she warmed a smidge and went to the counter and grabbed some plates and forks.

They sat down and ate the food in silence for a short time. Then Ella said, "I know it's been rough since Mom died, but I don't want you to revert to bad habits."

"I can handle things," he said, a bit harsher than he intended. When he drank, an ugly monster crept into him that he disliked. The patient soul he was got buried, and he said things he could usually keep inside. "Are you still seeing that guy? What was his name again?"

"Jeff," she said. "Yes. I'm still seeing him. Why?"

"I don't like him."

"I knew it! Why not?"

"Honestly, he's an idiot. What do you see in him?"

"He's not an idiot! You don't even know him."

"I could tell. You have nothing in common with that guy."

"Why are you acting like this? Is it because of the drinking?" Ella stood up.

"No. I just don't think he's right for you," he said.

"What's going on with you? You're acting weird, and it's pretty clear you're drunk."

"What's going on is that my wife died." He pounded his fist on the oak tabletop.

Ella raised her voice in response. "You weren't acting like this the last few times I saw you. Does this have anything to do with that woman?"

"What woman?"

"Dad, I saw a picture of her in the Duluth paper today. The one who was here that night I came for dinner. She's dead."

"Mona," he said.

"How'd you know her? What was she doing here?"

"I don't know."

"God damn it, Dad. Could you just please talk to me for once!"

George's voice got low and quiet. He lowered his head. "I can't."

"You're freaking me out here."

He got up and started to pace the room again.

"Would you stop and just talk to me?" Ella pleaded.

He sat down on the metal folding chair at the easel and put his face in his hands. He wept. He hadn't meant to but he couldn't contain it. When he came back up, Ella was sitting on the loveseat looking at him. She had tears in her eyes now too, and she said softly, "Please, Dad."

"Okay," George began, "I've been keeping something from you. I did something unforgivable."

Ella nodded for him to continue.

"I slept with her. I didn't…it wasn't something I planned."

"You what?" Ella said. "Jesus, Dad. When I told you I gave you my blessing, I didn't mean for you to jump in bed with a teenager less than three months after Mom died."

"I know. That's why I didn't tell you."

"So, that makes it okay? That you lied to me?"

"I didn't lie to you. I just didn't tell you. I was sparing your feelings."

"That's what you always do. Were you off the wagon when this all happened?"

"That's not fair. I…"

"Dad, you know you can't drink. You know what happens. What else aren't you telling me? Why is that girl dead? Dad… You didn't have anything to do with it? Oh, God. Did you?"

"Ella, I… Is that what you think?"

She stood up. She was crying full bore now. "I don't know what to think. I need to go, Dad."

"Ella. Wait, please."

"No, I can't do this…"

George's daughter grabbed her purse and bolted from the cabin, slamming the door behind her. He was left alone to face the fact that he may have just lost her. His only family. He knew it was a possibility when he agreed to see her. He'd almost lost Melinda in the same way, all those years ago. Now it all came flooding back to him, things he'd avoided thinking about for years.

When he was twenty-one years old, he and Melinda married. Ella was around a year old by then. They bought a house and were struggling to pay the bills. He worried incessantly that Melinda wasn't happy with him, that it was his fault they didn't have enough money. Upon reflection, he should have realized she was more likely stressed from having a baby while getting her teaching degree, but he was sure at the time he wasn't living up to her expectations. On top of that, he wasn't fitting in at the factory. It was tough for a guy who never felt like he belonged, knowing he was meant to be an artist not a laborer. He started going out with some of the guys after work in an attempt to bond with them but when things felt overwhelming, he started to drink his problems away. He'd come home to Melinda and honestly had a hard time the next day remembering what had transpired beyond the fact that he knew they'd argued, which only made him want to drink all the more. He hated himself. He would never have eagerly opposed his wife had it not been for the dark place the alcohol had taken him.

One Saturday morning after a night out, he woke to an empty apartment. Melinda and the baby were gone. There was a note for him on the counter saying she wouldn't even consider returning unless he cleaned up. She never did come out and tell him specifically what he'd done, what had transpired while he was in that blackout stage, but he was too afraid to ask. He was embarrassed. He knew it wasn't the real him. He didn't want it to be. He didn't want to be like the rest of those roughnecks at the factory.

The thought of losing Melinda and Ella was enough to make him stop then. They were everything to him. He made the decision to put his wife and daughter first. He quit drinking cold turkey then and there, at twenty-two, without looking back and without regret.

Over the years, George wondered if Melinda and Ella had discussed what had happened when he'd been drinking back then. Of course they had; this conversation confirmed it. But what had Mel told their daughter? What had George done to Melinda? Melinda had only ever said he'd been a mean drunk. Was that really all or had more transpired? It was too much to bear thinking about, so he had pushed it so far down he never touched it again.

Was this why his daughter had always held him at arm's length? George wished he could talk openly with Ella about it; find out exactly what Melinda had told her, but that wasn't the kind of relationship they had. They never could communicate as freely as Melinda and Ella had done. Was Ella scared of him because of what Melinda had reported? Had his wife disclosed an ugly side of him to his only offspring, putting him at an unfair disadvantage from the very beginning? He didn't think his wife would do such a thing intentionally, but he wouldn't blame her if she had.

Melinda had been right about one thing though—he was a nasty drunk. He let all of the stuff he never brought to the surface when he was sober fester only to break out eventually in some kind of uncontrollable explosion. It was disgusting. George was disgusted with himself. It was no wonder his daughter didn't trust him. Even he wasn't sure what he was capable of doing.

Chapter 25

The next morning, the air hanging over the lake was cold, colder than the water temperature, and added to that ample amounts of moisture created a spectacular and stunning sunrise event known as sea smoke. A wall of billowing haze made it look like the clouds were on fire directly above the lake. It unnerved George, even if it was a beautiful sight.

He made several attempts to get a hold of Ella, but she refused to take his call. He left her messages but she didn't return them. He got in his car with the intention of driving up to Ely to see her, but not long into the drive he realized it would do no good. He couldn't prove anything to her that would change things. He wasn't even sure he could prove things to himself. He found himself instead going to the rest stop along Highway 61 where they'd reported on finding Mona's pickup. He didn't know why he wanted to go and see it and even knew it was probably a really bad idea. If Detective Simmons were to see him there, it would only add fuel to her fire. He wasn't a complete idiot; he'd seen enough cop shows to know that criminals often came back to the scene of the crime. Yet, he was still pulled to go, like a gawker at a crash scene. He needed to take a look, even if it would cause pain and possible trouble for him. It was just something he had to do.

When he pulled in, he parked his car far away from the area roped off with police tape and orange cones. There was a young uniformed cop there, keeping people away from the truck. He didn't see Detective Simmons anywhere. The rest area itself was fairly remote and overall quiet, just a few other cars around. There was a small restroom and a picnic table off a ways in the grass. He parked a good distance away from Mona's truck. After a bit, without thinking much, he got out of his Prius and wandered over to look at the water.

The Knife River was a fast flowing tributary that fed into Lake Superior just a few miles away. The air had warmed somewhat and the fog lifted. Birds were singing. Melting snow banks trickled water that dripped down onto the boulders built up along the sides of the fast flowing current of the river.

George closed his eyes and had a moment of serious contemplation. He wasn't sure what he was searching for. The spring scene should have created some solace, but instead the churning water only made him that much more uneasy. A strange thought occurred to him. He stepped over the thin wire barrier that was keeping people from slipping over the edge and looked down at the icy water again.

This could be a way out. Maybe he should take it? Why not? He was getting old. The love of his life was gone, his daughter wasn't speaking to him, and he was a suspect in a murder investigation. Another step and he could put an end to the mess he'd gotten himself into. He'd never have to think about the look on Ella's face again as she contemplated whether or not he'd killed someone. He felt dizzy. Instead of tossing himself, he vomited over the edge. He wiped his face and looked over toward the cop, hoping he hadn't brought attention to himself. The officer was still standing near the truck, looking straight ahead.

George gathered his thoughts, which were so circular he knew he would never find closure, and he hauled himself back over the wire and got in his car. He started it up and drove slowly past Mona's truck. With nothing else to do and nowhere else to go, he turned around and drove back to the cabin.

Chapter 26

Nancy pulled into Stillwater after a grueling, white-knuckled drive through the ice and hail. Two and a half hours turned into almost four, accompanied by a headache that was likely the result of the tense hours behind the wheel. Nothing sounded worse than checking into a crappy roadside chain hotel after what she'd gone through to make it there in one piece, but the only other option Nancy found was a fancy B&B. She wasn't a bed and breakfast gal by nature, given her need for privacy, but she'd take it to the possibility of bed bugs and a hard mattress. She deserved a little pampering for her suffering.

The place she chose was called The Sweetwater Inn. It was in a quaint historic part of downtown Stillwater, just a few blocks from Main Street. Stillwater reminded her of Duluth in that it was on a hill looking down over water, only in this case it was the St. Croix River instead of one of the great lakes. The Inn was fancier than she would have liked, but it was clean and not part of a strip mall. She was tired and hungry, but the dining room was closed for a wedding reception.

She put her bag in her room and asked the woman at the desk if she could recommend a little cafe nearby. The sleet hadn't reached this far south and it felt slightly warmer here than it was just a couple of hours north. Nancy couldn't conceive of getting back into her car at this point, so she bundled up and walked a few blocks down the hill toward the place recommended to her called Dockside Cafe. It was right on the water and just what Nancy had in mind. She needed to get rid of her headache before she went to talk with Bobby.

As she ate, she looked out at the St. Croix, which was tiny in size compared to the Superior, and at this point it was actually showing some signs of spring. She noted the old lift bridge to her north, another thing Stillwater had in common with Duluth. Nancy opened her leather bag and pulled out her notepad to jot down some questions she wanted to ask Bobby. In the middle of doing so, her cell rang. She looked at the screen, figuring it would be Roger. It was the station.

"Detective Simmons."

"It's Anderson. We've got Mona Clark's truck."

"Where?"

"MNDOT worker called it in. It was slated to be towed because it'd been sitting at the rest stop at Knife River for several days. He checked the plates and boom, they match our victim."

"Okay. I'm in Stillwater right now to question one of her ex-boyfriends. I can't be back until tomorrow afternoon at the earliest. Can you tape it off and keep it cleared until I can get back?"

"Sure thing."

"Thanks." She hung up. This was bad timing. That car might hold the clues she needed to put this thing to bed. Well, she rationalized, it had been sitting for several days already, what was one more going to hurt?

Reluctantly, Nancy got back in her car at the hotel and headed west up Myrtle Street until she got to Greeley. She took a right and found Bobby's home a few blocks to the north. She parked along the street and got out and examined the old Victorian home. It was tricolored with faded paint and lacked any charm at this point. It had clearly been made into duplexes, with three doors lining the front porch. The neighborhood was nice except this yard had some old tires piled next to a beat up car, old lawn furniture, rusty bikes, and some other random junk lowering the value of the beautiful historic homes surrounding it.

A dog barked from inside as Nancy approached the porch. The light of the day was almost gone and she had a slight moment of hesitation before knocking. She'd holstered her weapon before she left the B&B, just in case. The dog continued to bark from somewhere behind the lower level apartment, which was Bobby's, but after a second knock, there was still no answer, and besides the barking, all seemed quiet within. There were no lights on, as far as Nancy could tell from a quick peek in the front window. After everything, she wouldn't get to speak with Bobby today. Damn.

***

The next morning, Nancy woke early and checked out of the B&B. She wasn't taking any chances on stopping for breakfast even. She wanted to get to Bobby before he left the house for work. She approached the duplex again and knocked, feeling a little less apprehensive the second time around, in daylight hours. A moment later, she heard footsteps approaching and the familiar barking of a dog, which increased in volume two fold as the door swung open. A Doberman greeted her with snarls and bared teeth. He was being held back by a shirtless man in greasy jeans.

"Can I help you?" he said.

She flashed her badge. "Bobby Jacobs?"

He nodded.

"I'm Detective Simmons. I was wondering if you would mind answering a few questions for me."

"Uh... Okay." He opened the door wider and pulled the dog out of the way. "In your crate, girl." The dog retreated to a kennel and laid down. "Come in. Sorry about the mess," he said, though Nancy didn't see one as she followed him through the home to a kitchen. The place was surprisingly tidy when she considered what the lawn looked like. She wasn't expecting it. When they got to the kitchen, she noticed a high chair near the table but she didn't see or hear anybody else now that the dog had quieted.

Bobby offered her a chair at the kitchen table.

"I'd like to record our conversation for my notes, if you don't mind..."

"That's fine."

She clicked the recorder on. "Before we begin, I'd like to remind you of your rights." She recited Bobby the Miranda laws then she said, "Do you have children, Mr. Jacobs?"

"You can call me Bobby. Stepchildren. Two of them."

"Where are they now?"

"They go to daycare in the morning. My wife just left with them for work. I was just getting ready to leave for work myself."

"I won't keep you. You may have heard that Mona Clark is dead. Her body was pulled from Lake Superior last week."

"Mona? Holy shit! I hadn't heard that. Excuse my language."

"That's fine. So, I just have to ask you if you've been with Mona or anywhere near Duluth within the last few weeks?"

"No."

"And where, specifically, were you on Tuesday, March 21st?"

"Tuesday? I was at work."

"And where's that?"

"I'm a mechanic at the Chevy dealer in White Bear Lake. They have my timesheets, and any of the employees can verify I haven't missed any work."

"Okay. And that evening? Where were you after work?"

"Uh. Oh, I actually took my wife out to dinner that night. It was our one year wedding anniversary. We got a sitter and we ate at a fancy place downtown."

"All right. So, you haven't been in contact with Ms. Clark at all since your release from prison? You haven't been calling her?"

"No. Absolutely not." Bobby looked at his watch. "Sorry, I don't want to be late. I'm doing everything I can to keep things together, ya know? This isn't going to cause me any problems with my parole, is it? I haven't seen Mona since…you know, that night."

"Tell me about that night."

"I was young and stupid and thought I loved her. I would never have actually hurt her. I was crazed when she said she didn't want to see me anymore. I thought if I could just talk to her, convince her…"

"By waving a loaded gun around?"

"I did have some anger issues, but I loved Mona. Truly. I just really wanted us to make something. I just always wanted a family and...well, what I have now. I'm doing good here. I want to keep it that way, ya know?"

"Okay, Mr. Jacobs. I'm going to follow up on the information you've given me, and if everything comes out clean you have nothing to worry about."

"It'll check out. I promise."

Nancy clicked her recorder off and got up.

Bobby walked her back to the front door. "So, you think it was a murder though? She didn't, I mean, I know she got down about her parents and stuff. She had a hard life. Could it have been suicide, at all?" he asked.

"It was a homicide. Do you have any idea who might have wanted Mona dead?"

"No. Mona took care of people. She was good."

"That's what I'm finding," Nancy said. "Well, thank you for answering my questions, Mr. Jacobs. Good luck to you."

"Hope you figure it out."

"I will. Here's my card in case anything comes to you." She handed Bobby her card and walked away, no closer to knowing who killed Mona Clark.

Chapter 27

Nancy would have normally gone to talk with the employees at the car dealership and the parole officer next to verify Bobby's story, but she had arranged for the Bureau of Criminal Apprehension mobile unit from the cities to meet her up at the rest area in Knife River. She wanted to make sure they didn't miss anything when they went through the truck. The best way to ensure that was to use the high-tech gear of the BCA's unit.

When she arrived at the rest stop several hours later, there was a younger beat cop on the scene, standing near the taped off area. She'd seen him at the station now and again but she knew little about him. She approached, wishing she had some warm coffee to offer him. "Afternoon, Officer Lansing. You must be freezing." It was hovering around 36 degrees but it was overcast and the moisture present in the air was the kind that chilled you right to your bones.

"Nah. Not too bad out today," he said.

Nancy gave him a sideways sneer.

"Guess I'm used to it." He chuckled. "I bet it don't feel like this in California in March."

"It definitely does not."

"Someday I'll go there. Always wanted to see palm trees. Did you know they aren't native to America?"

"Is that right?" Nancy said. She looked around the rest area. "Has it been quiet here?"

"Yeah, except I thought I mighta had a jumper a while ago."

"Really? Tell me more."

He nodded. "A guy in a flannel shirt walked to the edge over there and stood looking down for a long time. Then he vomited and got in his car and left."

"Do you recall if he had a grayish beard?"

Lansing nodded. "Ya know, I think he did."

"Was he driving a silver Toyota?"

"Yep. One of them environmental cars, I think."

"I see. Okay. What do we know about the cameras here?"

"There's one set up at the entrance of the restrooms, but I don't think it captures footage this far out into the parking lot, just people going in and out of the bathrooms."

"Okay." Nancy made a mental note to have someone check the footage to see if Mona was on it, or perhaps George. Just as their conversation was wrapping up, the boxy yellow BCA truck turned into the parking lot.

Nancy thanked Lansing and sent him on his way. "Go get yourself warmed up."

"Good luck, Detective," he said, getting in the squad parked next to the police tape.

She stood jotting down some notes as the two people with the mobile unit parked and got out of the vehicle to greet her. She was pleasantly surprised to see a black man and a female approaching. You were hard pressed to find any diversity in Duluth, and she hadn't seen a single woman colleague since she'd been here. Since this unit was from St. Paul, it shouldn't have been a shock, but it was nonetheless.

"Thank you for coming. I'm Simmons," she said, shaking hands.

"Becker," the woman said, "and this is Thomas."

"What have we got?" Thomas asked.

"Homicide. Twenty-six year old, Caucasian female, turned up in the lake with a COD of strangulation. This was the victim's vehicle."

Nancy saw Thomas look at his partner and give her a little smirk.

"Is something funny?" she asked him.

"No, it's just...well, you don't have the accent. We were expecting the accent."

"Ah. Right. I'm not from here," Nancy said. He nodded. "Sorry."

"Anyway, I want the handles swabbed for prints, any possible DNA samples collected and all loose items inside the car bagged."

Becker said, "No offense, Simmons, but we've done this a few times before."

"Of course you have. Now I apologize."

"We're even," Thomas said, smiling.

Nancy said, "All right. Let's get going then before we freeze to death out here."

The crime lab experts gloved up, and Becker began snapping photos of the car, inside and out. Thomas got out a swab kit and started to work the outside door handles for possible prints. Nancy stepped back to give them room and to inspect the area around the car. She pulled her scarf and wrapped it around her neck an extra time. She looked on the ground near the car. There were plenty of dirty tread marks worn into the snow but tire tracks would do her no good at this point since who knew how many other cars had been in and out of the lot since the day of the crime. She walked to the edge of the river and peered down at the water below. There were some jagged rocks jutting out, and water from the strong current bashing against them splashed up close to Nancy's feet.

She walked back to the vehicle, pondering a whole new series of questions she had floating around her head regarding how Mona's vehicle had gotten here. Becker was inside the car now. Thomas was standing, working the passenger door handle with the swab kit.

"Question for you," Nancy said to him. "If someone tossed a body into this water, how long would it take to make it to the lake?"

He turned toward her. "Not too long. That fast moving current, I'd say maybe a half hour."

"What about once it reached the lake? Would it submerge then?"

"Yes, if it didn't get snagged on a rock or debris—branches, logs, that kind of thing."

"And how long before it would surface?"

"In this temperature, usually a pretty long time. Lake Superior averages about 41 degrees. It could take several months to float, if at all. You're new here right? So you might not have heard the expression, Lake Superior doesn't give up her dead easily."

"Thanks," Nancy said. So much about this new information didn't add up. George Altman said he'd last seen Mona on March 4th. Jenny at the coffee shop saw her on March 20th. Her body was discovered on the morning of the 22nd. That meant her body had been in the water for only two days, maybe less. Still, Nancy didn't think the body was dumped here. Even if it had been, and it surfaced faster than normal for whatever reason, it would likely never make its way all the way to Canal Park from here. Once it hit the lake, there would be no more current to allow for it to flow down to where they'd found it and certainly not in that short amount of time. This was miles from the location it was found.

So, maybe Mona met someone here and they left together. For whatever reason, between that time she was strangled and then dumped in the lake at Canal Park. The body never actually sunk but instead stayed afloat, maybe it was the puffy parka acting almost as a life preserver, or the fact that Mona was very tiny in stature, or during the dump the body or an article of clothing got snagged on something, maybe the rock itself, maybe some debris just under the surface of the water causing it to stay at the surface.

Why was Mona here in the first place then? Nancy looked around again. This was a wayside rest between Duluth and Two Harbors. It was in a desolate area and had nothing to offer. She was clearly meeting someone for a specific reason. She left with someone. That someone was likely her killer. The fact that George Altman had been here earlier was where Nancy's confusion lay. The puzzle pieces didn't add up. She knew sometimes killers returned to the scene of the crime, though just why they did never made much sense to her. Did they want to be caught? Did they want to see other people reacting to what they'd done? Initially, she suspected George was here for one of those reasons, but now? If he had done it, he obviously hadn't thrown the body in here.

Why not? Because this wasn't where it happened. If it had been, Mona's body would still be at the bottom of the lake right now. That meant this wasn't the scene of the crime. So why come here today and risk being caught? And since Nancy now knew this wasn't where Mona's death occurred, why was her truck parked here, nearly twenty miles north of her body?

**

When they finished up, Nancy offered to take Thomas and Becker to a legendary mom and pop cafe right off the highway called Bertha's Pies so they could thaw out. It was also sort of selfish because she was hoping to spend a little time with some like-minded individuals, maybe even run her notes from the case by them and get their feedback, but they declined the offer, saying they had a long drive and wanted to get back to the cities before dark.

Disappointed, she went home with more questions than answers. She was losing heart. She made some notes in her case file while she ran her bath water. Just as she sank into the tub to try to find some clarity, she heard the garage door opening. She'd completely forgotten that Roger was returning tonight. After several more minutes, he knocked on the bathroom door.

"Come in," Nancy said.

"Hi. I'm back."

"Hi."

"Couldn't be bothered to return any of my messages?"

"Sorry. I've been really busy on this case."

"Nanc, I..."

"Can we not do this right now, Roger? I've had a long day, and I'm tired."

"Fine." Roger turned and left the bathroom.

Nancy pushed her knees up and plunged her head under the water and just stayed that way until she had to come up for air. She listened as the garage door opened again, followed by sounds of Roger's car driving away. They often fought, but Roger had never actually left before. Usually they just avoided each other for a day or so and then finally one of them would apologize and they'd go back to their normal way of handling things. She couldn't let it distract her right now. She had to keep her mind focused on the case.

**

The next morning, Roger had still not returned, but Nancy couldn't worry about him. He was an adult and could take care of himself. She looked in the bathroom mirror, did a double take at the size of the bags around her eyes, then splashed some water on her face. If she hadn't been anxious to get going, she might have put some concealer on, but she was and so she didn't. She pulled a brush through her hair quickly and headed for the station.

On her way, she drove through a coffee shop so she wouldn't have to get out of her car. It was one of those Marches that held on tightly to winter and wouldn't let it go and made Nancy feel like staying under her covers all day. She might have if this case wasn't pressing on her.

When she got to her desk, she went through the papers in her box. Toxicology had finally come back, and just as she had suspected, Mona was clean. Her system had no drugs or alcohol in them at the time of her death. There was nothing back from the BCA yet, but she assumed as much. It would probably take another day or two for that report. She'd gotten Anderson to go through the surveillance footage from the rest area, and his email indicated there were no signs of Mona or George on the film.

Nancy was at a bit of a dead end. She updated the case file then flipped through her notes, combing over the tiniest of details. Her head throbbed. She pulled her chair away from her desk and concentrated. She tried to put herself in Mona's shoes. Who else might have wanted a coffee shop manager dead? Maybe the next in line for the job. Jax had said that Jenny had been promoted. Jenny had come across as a bit odd when Nancy first spoke with her. This was something Nancy would follow up on.

She hated to keep her focus on one person, in case her gut instinct was wrong—and sometimes it was—but she still kept coming back to the same name when she reviewed her notes. George Altman. All the arrows still seemed to be pointed right in his direction. She decided it was time to pay him another visit. If nothing else, she might spot something in the cabin to give her enough probable cause to get a full search warrant. And there was always that chance that he might be ready to talk.

Chapter 28

She arrived at George's cabin just before lunch. She had to knock twice, which caused her a bit of concern. Had he done something drastic? The last time he was seen, he was standing at the edge of a cliff. Worse yet for Nancy, had he flown the coop? He was allowed to legally at this juncture, but for her sake, she hoped he hadn't. It would only make things harder for her. She was about to go around to peer into a window when he threw open the door.

"Mr. Altman."

"Detective."

"Everything oaky?"

George looked less put together than the previous few times she'd seen him. His flannel shirt had paint on it, and if she didn't know better, she'd say that his beard had a significantly larger amount of gray running through it than before.

"Just great."

"Do you mind if I come in?"

"Why not?" He opened the door wider to let her in.

When she was in, he closed it and offered her a chair. She stayed standing. He sat down in the same chair he'd done the previous time she was there, the one at the little round table jammed between the kitchenette and living area.

"I wanted to let you know your DNA didn't turn up on Mona, but we're still running a cross check with the BCA on the car. You haven't sought counsel yet?"

"I haven't done anything to warrant needing it."

Nancy looked around the cabin. It looked mostly the same, maybe a little bit more disheveled. And there was a painting on the easel that looked half-done. "Back at painting?" she inquired.

He shrugged. "Not really."

She walked over to the canvas. "I saw some of your work at the coffee shop. You have talent."

"Next I suppose you'll want to sleep with me and steal my money," he said flatly.

She turned back to him. "Mr. Altman…"

"Call me George."

"Okay. Why did you go to the rest stop yesterday?"

"I went because I wanted to see if it might give me any insight into why she might have been there. Same as you."

"Did you come up with anything?"

"No. You?"

"I'm not going to compare my notes with you, Mr. Altman."

"I understand."

She looked over things in the little cabin a bit more from her new vantage point at the window. George's eyes followed her.

"You can look around if you'd like. You don't have to get a warrant. I'm not hiding anything."

She nodded.

"Can I ask you something?" he said. "It's not about the case."

"All right. If you do me a favor."

"What?"

"Come in to the station and give me your fingerprints."

George nodded. "That's fine. I already said I'm not hiding anything."

"Okay. What's your question?"

"Do you have children, Detective Simmons?"

"No."

"How come?"

Nancy adjusted her stance. "It's complicated."

"It's just as complicated when you do have them, I can assure you."

"Is this about your daughter. What was her name again?"

"Ella. She's about your age, actually, if I had to guess."

"Does she live in Duluth?"

"Ely. I came up here to be closer to her but now it doesn't matter."

"Why not?"

"Relationships are complicated, just like you said, Detective."

"You're fighting with her?" Nancy prodded.

"She and I have never been close, to tell you the truth. I just don't know how to relate to her for some reason. But still…there are some solid principles in life that you assume and it's hard when those things don't stand up when everything else goes to pot."

"Such as?"

"I don't know…"

"Indulge me. Like I said, I don't have children."

"That your kid believes in you. I don't think she's ever respected me. How could she? I was just a lowly factory worker. She's a smarty-pants scientist. She doesn't get that I did what I needed to do to take care of her. I sacrificed for her to be a scientist. I gave up things to give her a better life. That's what parents do. In return, it's expected that they will stand behind you."

Nancy nodded in hopes he would continue. When he didn't, she said, "Is there a reason she wouldn't believe in you?"

"I didn't tell her about my relationship with Mona. I rationalized that it was to spare her but I know it was really because I was ashamed. Just another failure on my part as a father."

Nancy raised her eyebrows. "Another?"

"I started drinking again. I'd done it when she was little, and it wasn't good. I went to treatment and got clean." He ran his hands through his hair and took a long, deep breath.

"Were you drinking when you were with Mona?"

"No. I hadn't touched a drop, not even after my wife died. I assumed that part of me was so long over with, it hadn't even occurred to me to start back up, until well, all of this began. I couldn't cope. I thought it would help, but just like last time, it only made things worse. I'm done now. You can check the trash. I threw it all out yesterday." He paused. His voice was quivering, and Nancy worried he might begin to cry. "It hurts, you know? My own daughter. Melinda would have stayed by my side. I miss my wife." Another long pause. George cleared his throat and looked up. "Are you married?"

"Yes, but that's...not what I'm here to talk about, Mr. Altman."

"George. Right. Sorry. Anyway, I've been thinking, maybe it was another artist."

"What?"

"Mona. She arranged all of the art consignment at the gallery. That's how she lured me in. Maybe she was doing the same with other artists. She was pretty involved with the art community. Hung out at the Artist's Loft a lot, I believe. I was thinking about it because my daughter is involved with this sleazy artist up in Ely. I don't like him. That's one of the things we argued about before she stormed out."

Nancy got out her notebook and jotted down some notes. "Okay, Mr..."

"George."

"I'll check out the Artist's Loft."

"Thanks," he said.

"I'm not doing it for you. I'm doing it for Mona."

"Not for that. Just for listening."

She nodded.

***

Nancy returned to the office and met with the captain to update him on the case. Now, far more than forty-eight hours had come and gone, but Nancy was still feeling good about the leads she'd gotten thus far. She asked for a few more days to focus solely on the case before the captain started giving her other assignments. He agreed.

She sat down at her desk to make some calls. The first thing on her list was to check Bobby Jacobs' alibis. She dialed the number for the Chevrolet Dealership in White Bear Lake.

"White Bear Chevy. This is Brian. How can I help you today?"

"Hello, Brian. I'm looking to speak with the manager."

"I'm him."

"Great. I'm Detective Simmons, calling from Duluth. Could you please provide me with documentation that Bobby Jacobs was at work on Tuesday, March 21st?"

"Okay. Let me have a look at the computer records here."

"I appreciate it."

"I've got it here. Uh..."

"Yes?"

"March 21st, you say? Looks like Bobby took a sick day that day."

She sighed. "Okay. I'm gonna need a copy of that. Let me give you the fax number."

"Is he in trouble?"

"I'm not sure yet."

"I hope not. He's the best mechanic I've got."

"There's nothing certain at this point. No reason to worry unless I tell you differently, okay? I've still got more checking to do."

"All right."

She gave him the fax number then said, "Thanks for your time."

Nancy hung the phone up. So much for crossing Bobby Jacobs off her list. This case seemed to be going backwards. She looked at her watch. It was now past lunchtime. She decided to pick something up on her way to the Artist's Loft. After looking up the address, she grabbed her coat, scarf, and bag, and headed out.

On her way to the Loft, she was eating fast food in the parking lot of the restaurant when she got a text from Roger. Roger wasn't a texter. He worked in corporate sales. He always grumbled that texting was impersonal and cold. He liked to talk to people, the way communication was meant to be, in his opinion. This was how she knew he was serious about storming out last night. The text was asking her to meet him for dinner tonight, to talk. She replied that she would, even though she really shouldn't be taking time away from the case, but she'd been avoiding Roger for days now. They agreed on a time and location. She finished her lunch and drove the rest of the way to the Artist's Loft.

The Loft was a big old warehouse on the edge of town that housed artists' work studios. When Nancy entered, she stood in an atrium, a large open area that doubled as a lobby and a gallery space. There was everything from paintings to sculptures, pottery, and glass cases filled with jewelry. There were big pieces of material hanging from exposed beams near the top of the high ceilings, which Nancy surmised was some type of fiber art, but actually looked like a jumbled mess of weaved blankets that needed mending, in her opinion.

There were two floors of doors that circled around the outer portion of the building and must have been the individual artist spaces. Nancy wasn't sure where exactly to start with her inquiries. She had no specific artists' names, and there didn't appear to be any type of reception desk or directory anywhere. There were a few spaces with open doors. That looked like her only option. She walked to the first open studio and knocked lightly on the side of the door. She peered in and saw a young man working on a screen-printing machine.

"Hello," he called, looking up at her.

"Hi. I'm Detective Simmons. I don't want to interrupt your work, but I was wondering if I could ask you a few questions."

"Sure, if you don't mind coming in. I'm right at a point where I can't walk away from the machine."

"Thank you." She entered the space. "Do you happen to know anyone here who knew a woman named Mona Clark?"

"Mona? Sure. A lot of us knew her. It sucks to hear she died."

"How well did you know her?"

"I didn't know her that well. I'm not a painter. The painters know her better. She was always looking for artwork to consign at The Grind."

"Can you direct me to someone who may have known her well?"

"Yeah…maybe talk to Pete. He's two doors down."

"Okay. Thanks."

"No problem."

Nancy left the screen printer's space and went the two doors and glanced in. Here was another young man painting a giant canvas that took up the entire back wall of the studio. His back was to Nancy. All she saw of him was long, dark dreadlocked hair that hung almost to the middle of his back.

She knocked. He turned, and his long, matted hair swung with him. "Yo," he said. He was dressed in jeans and a t-shirt, both of which were covered in splotches of dried paint in every hue imaginable. He had a scruffy beard and yellowing teeth.

"Good afternoon. Wondering if I could ask you some questions about Mona Clark." She showed him her badge.

"Mona? Okay. Yeah."

"May I come in or would you like to come out?"

"I need some coffee, so I'll come out."

They walked through the big open area in the middle of the building toward a small hallway near the back where there were bathrooms and a small room with a few vending machines and some tables and chairs. Nancy bought Pete a cup of coffee and they sat at one of the tables, which was covered in a mural.

"Can I get your full name, first off?" she asked after she began recording.

"Pete McGuire."

"How well did you know Miss Clark?"

"Pretty well. She came to gallery shows here a lot and hung out, had tons of friends. I was bummed when I heard."

"Have there been any rumors circulating around here about it?"

"Just the usual, people wondering what happened."

"When was the last time you saw her?"

"Maybe a month or so ago."

"Did you two ever date?"

"No." He laughed. "Not to offend the dead or anything, but she was a little too...normal for me."

"How so?"

"You know, just...nice clothes, a little too, sort of, professional, I guess. She was mostly just interested in the artists so she could get them to consign stuff at the coffee shop. I think she got some sort of commission on it."

"Did you ever do that—consign your work?"

"Not really my scene. I do larger scale stuff mostly."

"But others here did?"

"Sure. Lots of people."

"Can you give me a few names?"

"Uh, Jesse Thurman and Tanya Miller I think both have stuff hanging up there right now."

"So, you go there a lot, The Grind?"

He held up his cup. "I'm a coffee fanatic, so yeah. I go there sometimes."

"Do you know an employee named Jenny who works there?"

"Sure."

"What can you tell me about her?"

"She's pretty normal, like Mona. They were friends, or used to be."

"Used to be?"

"They got into some kind of epic fight a while back. It was here actually, during an art opening. That's the only reason I know about it."

"Do you know what it was in regards to?"

"I dunno. Chick stuff."

"Can you be more specific?"

"I think Jen was dating one of the artists, and she wanted Mona to put his stuff up at The Grind, but Mona didn't think it was good enough. Jen was pissed, and they fought about it. Standard petty girl crap."

"Who was that—the artist they fought about?"

"His name is Doug something or other. I don't really know him well. He's a pompous douchebag, if you ask me. One of those people who give artists a bad reputation."

"Does he have a space here?"

"Yeah, it's across the gallery on the west end."

"Okay. Thanks for your time, Pete. I appreciate it."

"No problem."

"If you hear anything else, any rumors or something that might be linked to Miss Clark's death, could you let me know?" She handed him her card.

He studied it for a second then said, "I'm not a snitch or anything but killing someone is pretty cold. Make art not war, that's my motto." He flashed her a peace sign with his fingers.

She smiled at him. "Have a good day," she said and stuck her recorder back in her coat pocket. She headed to the opposite end of the building to see if Doug was in his studio.

Most of the studio doors on that side of the building seemed to be closed and dark, but as Nancy's luck would have it, she spotted a little plaque on the wall outside one of the spaces with an open door that said, "Douglas Samuelson. Artist with a vision." This must be the right place, she thought.

She knocked, and a short man with a clean-shaven face and a button-down shirt appeared before her. He was clean, as in he had not a drop of paint on him. He didn't look like the typical artist, but Nancy didn't usually stereotype. In her line of work, nobody was what they seemed.

"Are you Douglas Samuelson?"

"Depends on who's asking," he said stiffly, then he laughed dryly.

"I'm Nancy Simmons with the Duluth PD. Wondered if I could ask you some questions regarding Mona Clark."

"Mona? What kind of questions?" He propped himself up against the doorframe of the studio.

"I've been told you knew her. Can you tell me what your relationship with her was?"

"Uh, we dated casually for about three months like a year ago. That's about it."

"You dated? What happened?"

"It just didn't work out."

"And am I correct that you currently date her friend Jenny?"

"Yeah. Jennifer and I are engaged. Why? What does this have to do with Mona?"

"Can you tell me about the fight they had?"

"It was just stupid. Mona was jealous that I'd moved on to someone else."

"So Mona ended her friendship with Jenny because of your past relationship?"

"Yeah. She hated seeing that we were happy together."

"And it had nothing to do with her not consigning your artwork at the coffee shop?"

"Absolutely not! Did she tell you that?"

"No. She's deceased, Mr. Samuelson."

"Right. Anyway…no, I think she still liked me. She was bitter about the engagement. It was her way of getting back at me, not taking my stuff at the shop, but it really didn't bother me. I have my sights set higher than on some pathetic coffee shop."

"So, you and Mona ended things mutually, but you think Mona still wanted to be involved? Why do you think that?"

He shrugged his shoulders. "It's just something guys know."

"But she never told you that specifically? She didn't text you or leave voicemails to indicate that to be the case?"

"Well, no…"

"I see. So, she and Jenny fought, but then they went on working together."

"Yeah."

"And they were okay? Nothing else went on between them after the fight?"

"No."

"Okay, and when's the last time you had any contact with Mona yourself?"

"Uh, I guess I saw her at a show. I had a few pieces in the gallery at the U. That was late February. You know, now that I think of it, she was with some geezer. Said it was her date. He looked like a creep to me. You should check him out."

"By chance do you recall his name?"

"No. Beard, brown hair. Sort of a belly."

"Does the name George sound familiar?"

He snapped and pointed at Nancy. "Totally. That's it."

"Thanks for your time. That's all the questions I have."

"Jenny's not in trouble is she?"

"No."

"Good. We're getting married this summer."

"Congratulations."

Chapter 29

In the parking lot, before leaving the Artist's Loft, Nancy made some notes. She didn't really believe that Mona was jealous of Douglas and Jenny's engagement announcement. Bobby Jacobs had told her that the reason he'd flipped was because Mona had no desires to get married. And Nancy knew Mona had been sleeping with George Altman; not really something one did when they were pining for another individual. Still, she wasn't ready to cross Jenny off her list just yet, and while she was at it, she added Douglas Samuelson to it. Her list seemed to be growing instead of shrinking, and she now had a headache.

Nancy wanted to track down Jenny while all of these thoughts were still floating around in her head, but she didn't have enough time to devote to it right now because she needed to meet with Roger for dinner soon. She had just enough time to go back to the station, file her daily report, and head out. She really didn't want to be doing this tonight, but she knew she couldn't put it off any longer. The timing couldn't have been worse.

When she got to the restaurant, she parked and checked her phone before turning it off. She took a few deep breaths trying to get herself ready for what she figured was about to happen, then she went inside. The restaurant they'd agreed upon was a small steak place, which had amazing food but wasn't pretentious. When you walked in, it felt like you were stepping back in time, like Neil Diamond or Tony Bennett would be singing on stage while you ate steak and baked potatoes as big as your head. Nancy loved it because it reminded her of a place her dad used to take her to on Friday nights. The place even smelled similar, and when she walked in, memories of her father flooded her every time. It felt comforting and sort of painful all at once, but she embraced both of the emotions, even tonight.

She saw Roger already seated in a booth toward the back of the place, and she walked toward him, still breathing in the nostalgia.

"Hi," she said, slipping into the booth across from her husband, trying to pretend he didn't feel like a stranger.

He gave her a smile that she knew. It was one he gave when he was looking for pity. She hated it. It reminded her of the affair. Those thin lips were a constant for weeks after Nancy figured out what was going on with him and his co-worker. Like she wouldn't have figured it out. He married a detective—a damn good one at that. Nancy wondered if they were back to sleeping together. Maybe that's what all of this was about.

"So," Roger said. "Thanks for meeting me."

She nodded.

"Do you want to order before we talk?"

"I suppose." Nancy picked up her menu and pretended to look at it while she wondered why he'd bring her to a public place to discuss something like this. She started to get annoyed. Roger was a persuasive man, so she figured he was probably trying to make sure she couldn't get up and walk away. He wanted to make sure she heard him out, but there was no way she was planning to take him back this time. She was ready for it all to be done.

The waiter came and took their orders and menus. Nancy didn't have anything to hide behind anymore. She took a deep breath. "Okay. Let's get this over with."

"Here's the thing then. I'm just going to say it. I know you're going to be upset, but I want you to know that I love you very much, and this wasn't intended to hurt you in any way."

She started to feel warm and wondered if she could really do it suddenly.

"I'm taking a new job. It's back in California."

Nancy sat staring at Roger, trying to process what he'd just said. For some reason, her first inclination was to think he was actually leaving her. "What?" she heard herself say.

"I should have asked you first, but I know how much you hate it here, and I didn't want to miss the opportunity…"

She let that sink in.

Roger went on, "I know things haven't been great here, and I know you never wanted to come in the first place."

She nodded.

"I'm hoping we can go back and start over."

When she still didn't respond, he said, "Nancy? Are you listening?" He started to explain the whole thing to her again.

She finally snapped with it and said, "No, I got that part. I just…I was expecting something else."

"What were you expecting?"

"I don't know."

"Okay. So, you're not mad?"

"Mad? I…no. I'm not mad. I thought you were mad. Why'd you leave last night?"

"Because I hate when you're all wrapped up in a case and you don't talk to me. I needed to get some stuff done back at the office, and then it got late and I just slept on the couch there. I didn't realize how tired I was from the traveling, and I had an early meeting. I knew calling wouldn't matter because you were in case mode and hadn't answered my calls in four days."

"Oh."

"So, what about going back to Cali then?" Roger had a look on his face that indicated he really had no idea what Nancy was going to say. And the truth was, Nancy wasn't sure what she was going to say. She definitely hated living here, but for some reason, right at that moment, she didn't want to say yes to moving. It wasn't the move, necessarily, she was rejecting. She'd expected to come in here and finally call it quits with Roger. She was so sure it was finally going to be done. Now? He'd taken a new job without even broaching the subject with her, and she was just supposed to wag her tail and follow him again.

"When is all of this happening?" she asked.

"Fast. I actually already gave notice. I've got a project beginning next week in Sacramento, so…"

"Sacramento?"

"Yeah. I know it's not San Diego, but it's not Minnesota either." He smiled at her, still trying to win her over.

Why was he still interested in what she wanted, she wondered. "I don't know, Roger. I've got this case, which is proving to not be as open and shut as I thought it might be and…"

"You can stay and finish it up then, sell the house, and meet me there when everything is tied up here."

"What if I can't get a job in Sacramento?"

"Sure you will. You're the best homicide detective in Duluth."

"That's not funny."

"You're killing me right now, Nanc. Can you just agree to come?"

"Why do you even care if I go? You didn't bother asking me before you took the job."

"For Christ's sake…because you're my wife."

"That doesn't feel like a good enough reason."

He launched himself toward her from the other side of the booth, so their faces were inches apart. His voice became intense as he said, "Because I love you. Can you say the same?"

She looked at his eyes then looked away. Why was it so easy for him to say that? She didn't think he actually believed it. You didn't cheat if you truly loved someone, but she wasn't going to bring all of that back up. Not here. But he was right. She couldn't answer him back, not as easily as he could. She couldn't make those words just pour from her mouth. Not when she wasn't sure she meant them. She didn't just say things for fun. She had to mean them. She stayed silent.

Roger pulled back, shook his head from side to side, and looked down at the table. Their food came. Nancy stared at her plate; Roger started cutting up his steak like a man who hadn't eaten in a week. She knew his anger was building because his cheeks were puffed out. They did that when he was mad.

After his meat was all carefully and methodically segmented out, which was totally Roger and completely annoyed Nancy for no real reason, he turned his attention back toward her. "What the hell do you want from me?" he asked, finally showing his full frustration. "What can I do to make you say, 'Yes, Roger...I'd love to go with you'?"

"I don't know."

He shook his head again slowly, displaying yet more emotion. "That makes two of us."

"Can I just have a little time to think? My head is wrapped up in this case right now."

"That's always your excuse for everything."

"It's not an excuse! It's the truth. I have a job too, you know? You aren't the only one who gets to be a big, important person. I'm trying to figure out who murdered a twenty-six year old girl. What are you trying to do? Sell some goddamn steel?"

"Okay, calm down. Can we just finish eating? I still have to go back to work tonight. I have piles of stuff to get done before I leave." Roger started to eat his steak in silence. Nancy picked at her potato. She wondered what would happen if she just came right out and said she was done. Right here. It could all be over. She wanted to, she really did. But she couldn't make the words form. She was a coward, but she was a confused one. Why was she suddenly fighting to stay in this city? She couldn't wrap her head around it. She snuck a few looks at Roger and tried to see him for the rugged, handsome man she used to love, when they were younger, when things were simple. She searched, but she couldn't see that man because he was hidden behind all the years of arguments and differences; the wall that Nancy had built up after he cheated. He wasn't the same man, but she knew she wasn't the same woman either.

She was spiteful. She should never have left San Diego. She was happy there, for the most part. She had friends and great colleagues who respected her and the work she did. Now, she was too old for anyone to respect her, or to love her. She resented Roger for keeping those things from her. She was angry with herself for not having the guts to stay in San Diego when he decided to relocate here. It was too late. For her and Roger, and for Nancy alone.

Roger paid the bill and looked up at her briefly before he slid out of the booth. "You'll think about it? Let me know your decision?"

She nodded and waited until he left the restaurant before she could move. She slowly got up and went to her car. In the darkness of the parking lot of Howard's Steak Palace, Nancy sunk down in the driver's seat and did something unexpected. She cried. It was the first time she remembered doing it in years. She was not a crier. Even when she found her father with blood pooling around him on the kitchen floor she hadn't cried, or when she confronted Roger with the affair last year. And now, as the tears spilled onto her lap, it felt alien to her. She hated the out of control sensation in her body, the raw emotions forcibly surfacing up from the depths of the place she'd locked them. Now that they were unleashed, they poured out of her like she was a cat trying to release a hairball, in undignified gurgling fits and starts. Glad for the darkness, she gave in and just let it all come out, hoping that if she expelled it all— everything she'd pushed down, suppressed for such a long time—that this would be the end of it.

Chapter 30

The next morning, Nancy went to the station and looked for the crime lab report in her inbox but it wasn't there yet. She went to the fax machine on her way out of the office and grabbed the timesheet for Bobby Jacobs. She knew she was probably going to have to make another drive down to Stillwater but she had a few more things to do before she did. One of them involved coffee.

She walked into The Grind and saw immediately that Jenny wasn't behind the counter as she'd hoped. Instead, it was a pimple-faced boy whose nametag said Tony.

"Good morning. Could I have a large coffee and a blueberry muffin?"

"Sure thing," Tony said.

As Nancy waited, she contemplated her next move. She had the coffee shop owner's card in her case file back at the office. She'd have to go back there and call him or her to get some more info on Jenny. This wasn't the morning she was hoping to have. She really wanted to be able to cross at least one person off of her list by the end of the day.

Just as Tony handed her the coffee and bag with the muffin, Jenny appeared from behind the curtain. She had a clipboard in her hand. Nancy paid Tony then said, "Jenny? I don't know if you remember me but I spoke with you about Mona Clark…"

Jenny looked up at her. "Oh, right."

"I was wondering if you had a few minutes to talk again."

"Okay."

They went to a small table toward the back of the shop. Jenny still looked like the perky blonde Nancy remembered from the first time she saw her. Once again her hair was pulled back in a ponytail. She was wearing a baggy sweatshirt and jeans and chewing gum in an exaggerated way, which reminded Nancy of the cheerleaders from high school.

"First of all," Nancy said, pulling out her recorder and notepad and discussing rights. "For the record, can I get your full name?"

"Jennifer Stevens. Am I in trouble?"

"No. I just have a few questions. I imagine your fiancé mentioned that I spoke with him yesterday."

She nodded.

"Well, I just wanted to hear your side. I've been told that you and Mona had an argument. Can you tell me what it was about?"

"It wasn't an argument. More like a disagreement. I just got annoyed with her attitude, that's all. You know how sometimes your boss can be a jerk? I got sick of it."

"I thought you two were friends?"

"I told you last time. We were work friends, not friend-friends. I was nice to her because she was my boss. I didn't really like her."

"Why not?"

"There wasn't a specific reason. We just weren't compatible. Not everyone is."

"But you know nothing about what happened to her?"

"Nothing."

"And March 21st. Where were you?"

"I was here that entire day actually. I remember because I had to pull a double to cover for her. She called in sick, which I remember being odd. She never called in sick. You can ask Tony too because he was working the night shift with me. Or ask that guy sitting in the corner. He's a regular…a writer, I think. He's here like every day."

"Okay. Thanks for the information, Jenny. I appreciate it."

"We're done?"

"Yes."

"K. Am I…good then?"

"For now. I'll need to follow up on the things you told me, but if it all checks out, then yes. Unless any new evidence is brought to light. There's nothing else you want to tell me?"

"Nope."

"Then we're done."

"Cool," Jenny said and got up.

Nancy picked up her coffee and muffin and went back to the station. An additional look at her email for the crime lab report came up empty. The case file was sitting on top of her desk. She opened it and found the card for the owner of The Grind. She dialed the number.

"Mike here."

"Hello, Mr. Olson. I'm Detective Simmons calling from the Duluth PD."

"Uh huh."

"I'm calling because, as you know, one of your employees at The Grind, Mona Clark, has died."

"Yes. I was sorry to hear about that. Mona was a great employee. I was sad to lose her."

"How long did she work for you?"

"Uh, I'd have to go back to the timesheets to be completely sure, but I think it must have been close to four years."

"Well, I'm sorry for your loss," Nancy said.

"Yeah. It's a shame."

"I'm curious about another of your employees, Jenny Stevens. Wondering if you could verify her work schedule the week of March 20th."

"Jenny? I can check my records. Can I ask why?"

"I'm investigating Mona's death. Just dotting my i's and crossing my t's. You know, standard protocol."

"You think Jenny had something to do with it? Should I…I mean…would it be appropriate to let her go?"

"No. Jenny's innocent until proven otherwise, and that's what I'm trying to do, so I'd really appreciate the timesheets for verification of her whereabouts that week." She gave him the fax number.

"Okay. Sure. Right. That's good. I'd hate to lose another employee. I mean, not lose in the same way we lost Mona, but, well, you know what I mean."

"Yes. Okay, well, if you could fax that paperwork to me that would be very helpful."

"Sure. No problem."

"Have a good day, Mr. Olson."

"You too."

Nancy sighed. She'd been putting off going through the anonymous "tips" that had come in through the hotline since they released the information regarding

Mona's vehicle, yet it had to be done. Looking on the bright side, not that Nancy usually did that, if Mike faxed the timesheets over soon, maybe she'd be able to at least set Jenny aside for the time being and focus her efforts somewhere else.

After sifting through three dozen calls, there was only one that could not be completely eliminated. It was from a witness who said they saw a couple arguing at the wayside rest area that night. Of course, the tip was anonymous so it couldn't be followed up on. What could Nancy glean from it? It was apparent Mona was not alone at the rest stop because she'd left there somehow, not in her own vehicle. So, what was the reason for being there and who did she meet? Perhaps the person who she'd been calling on the burner phone. The fact that someone had referred to them as a couple made Nancy question her original thought that it had been George Altman. If Nancy saw George and Mona together, she wasn't sure if she'd automatically assume they were a couple; perhaps father and daughter, or even granddaughter, but not lovers. The word "couple" usually insinuated two people who were roughly the same age. Who would Mona have been with who was around her same age? Or maybe it was too dark for the anonymous tipster to see them very well? Maybe they assumed it was a couple because they heard a man and a woman having a disagreement?

Nancy got up and went to Balton's desk. He was writing out some paperwork.

"Hey, did one of your officers follow up on locating those pings from the radio towers I requested?"

He looked up at her. "Yeah. They did. The closest triangulation points indicated Canal Park. They didn't find anything in the dumpsters or alleyways after a thorough search. Phone is probably in the bottom of the lake along with the rest of the secrets of this town."

She was afraid of that. "Okay. Thanks."

She checked the fax machine on her way back to her desk. Still nothing from The Grind owner. Back at her desk, she typed Jenny Stevens into the records database to get her home address and waited for the results. Surprisingly, Jenny wasn't so squeaky clean. She had a misdemeanor assault charge for fighting at a local dive bar. That wasn't something Nancy was expecting, though it shouldn't have surprised her since she'd fought with Mona at the Artist's Loft, but it was nearly three years ago and didn't appear to have any connection to this case. The next item might though. She was questioned on suspicion of check fraud just last month, though the charges were dropped. Could it have anything to do with George Altman's stolen money? Were Mona and Jenny working together to siphon people's bank accounts? Perhaps that was the real reason for the public brawl at the Loft?

Nancy got up and checked the fax machine again. Nothing. She was exasperated. As she turned the corner to talk with Bonnie, she saw George Altman sitting in a chair in the waiting area.

"Hello, Mr. Altman."

He stood. "I'm here."

"Fingerprints. That's right. Thank you for keeping your promise. Follow me."

She'd asked him for the prints because, though she had his DNA, prints were a quicker read and she was hoping she could match them as soon as she got the report back from the BCA, rather than wait for DNA analysis, which could take up-words of a month to come back from the lab, even with high clearance.

She went back to her desk after George left and was about to head out to pay Jenny another visit when her computer pinged to let her know she'd received a new email message. She looked up at it. It was the crime lab report she'd been waiting for from the BCA.

Chapter 31

Now that George had once again—for the second time in his life—given up drinking, he had nothing to do with himself. But he felt slightly better because he thought he'd made a little headway in convincing the detective that he was innocent, and he hoped by now she was starting to believe him. She had seemed somewhat more pleasant at the station while he got his fingerprints taken and had even shared a few pieces of information with him regarding her current leads. She said she was hopeful things would be wrapped up soon. George took this to mean she was concerning herself with someone else, but he still wasn't planning to leave until he was certain that was the case.

Besides that, Ella was still not answering his calls, and he didn't want to leave without trying to repair things. He wanted to give her some time before he tried again. So while he waited, he stayed holed up in the yellow cabin on Lake Superior. He'd been given a little boost of renewed confidence from the detective in another area, whether she knew it, or not. She'd commented the last time she was there that she thought he had talent. It had drawn him back to the canvas and he was working up a new piece when there was a knock at the door.

He answered, still in his paint smock. "Good afternoon, Detective."

"May I come in?"

"Please."

George couldn't help but notice that Detective Simmons looked like she'd had a rough couple of days since he'd last seen her. She didn't appear to be wearing any makeup, and her hair looked like it had gone through a windstorm, even though it was a pretty mild day. She had bags under her eyes and her clothes weren't as crisp and pristine as they'd been on previous visits. She held a large cup of coffee in her hand as she came through the door.

"Not sleeping?" George inquired.

She gave him a rather terse look, but didn't answer. He offered her a seat at the table but she remained standing per usual.

"Your fingerprints were found all over Mona's car, Mr. Altman." Her tone was one of almost disappointment. George thought it reminded him of Ella's tone the last time she was here.

"I rode with her to an art exhibit at the college. It was snowing that night and she insisted she drive because she didn't think my little Prius could handle the conditions making the climb to the University."

"Do you have anyone to corroborate your story?" she asked him.

"Uh, no."

"I see. Why didn't you tell me this sooner?"

"I didn't think of it. Wait…Mona did speak with someone there. She even introduced me to him. A young man that she had dated at one time. I don't recall his name. He was another artist, clean cut, rather smug."

"That sounds like Douglas Samuelson," Detective Simmons said.

"Yes, Doug. That was his name. You know him?"

"I've spoken with him, yes."

"In connection to the murder?"

"That's none of your business."

"Wait, was it when you went to the Artist's Loft?"

"Again, I'm asking the questions here, Mr. Altman."

"Right. Anyway, he spoke with Mona. I don't think she told him my name, but I'm sure he'd remember me."

"And that's the only time you were in Mona's car?"

"Yes."

"Was Mona ever in your car?"

"Uh, no. I don't believe so."

"I'm going to need to verify that by having the crime lab come out and take a look. Would that be a problem?"

"Not at all."

"Good." Nancy slurped her coffee.

"You're welcome to sit," George said.

"I think I'm done here."

"Anything else come out of your visit to the Loft?"

"Mr. Altman…" She eyed George in another scolding manner.

"Fine. Listen, could I just get you to have another look at my painting? I need a good critical eye like yours to tell me if I'm on the right track." He walked her to the front window. "Do you think it needs a little more white here?"

"I don't…I'm no artist, Mr. Altman."

"I thought you were calling me George. Please, if you could just look at it and see what you think."

Chapter 32

She walked to the painting. She hadn't expected to have an opinion, though she didn't know why that would be the case. She was a very opinionated lady. She figured this work would appear similar to the ones she'd seen previously, abstract with bold colors, but it wasn't at all like those other paintings. This wasn't even an abstract piece. It was the view from out the window.

Nancy, exhausted and emotionally spent, wanted to just mumble her approval and be on her way. She still had to drive to Stillwater, though the thought of it made her want to curl up in the fetal position. But when she looked at the painting, something overcame her, something unexpected and raw. She wanted to blame the stress and lack of sleep, but it was more than that. The colors were muted and subtle, and the light hit the lake in a very serene way. The water was the exact right shade of blue. Nancy hadn't ever really stopped to notice just how lovely the big lake really was. Something about all of it made her get a little emotional. It probably had less to do with the painting and more to do with the stuff she was dealing with, but she stayed looking at it longer than was necessary in an attempt to conceal her fragile state from George Altman, who she knew was watching for her reaction.

George said, "Is it so terrible that you don't know what to say about it?"

"No. It's really...I didn't know you could paint realistic stuff."

"Neither did I, but I've had some time on my hands, and the lake was singing her siren song to me."

She turned to him finally. "I need to be going. I've got a long drive ahead of me."

"Where to?"

"Stillwater."

"Today still?"

"Unfortunately."

"You look like you should take the night off and go in the morning."

"I can't. I wish I could."

"Why not?"

"Because. The longer I wait, the harder it is to get answers."

"Can I ask you a question?" George said.

"Okay."

"What motivates you to do this work?"

"Solve crimes? That's easy. I do it for the victim."

"What about you? Doesn't it take a toll on you?"

"For me, it's temporary. Think of Mona. She'll never have the opportunity to recover from it."

"But you will?" he asked.

Nancy didn't know how to answer that question at the moment. She turned to him, his face was sincere. He had concern in his eyes.

"I'll be fine, Mr. Altman."

"George."

"Goodbye."

"Drive safely," he said.

Nancy couldn't help think he sounded like a father talking to his daughter. She let a small smile escape, then she turned and left.

Chapter 33

The drive to Stillwater was more pleasant than the last one. The road conditions were good, and Nancy actually took George's concern to heart. She realized she did need some time, and on the road she had just that. So, as she drove down I-35 headed south, she thought not about the case but about Roger. There was a lot she needed to work out.

By the time she reached the interchange to take her to Highway 61, to the Chevrolet Dealer, she still hadn't come up with a definitive plan regarding her standing with her husband. It was so complex and circular that she'd resolved nothing in two and a half hours of driving and thinking.

The clock on her car dash said it was 5:11 when she reached the car dealership. She hoped Bobby Jacobs would still be there. If she could talk to him now, she could turn around and make it back home by 8 p.m. and get a little rest. She parked in the lot and went in through the service door. Inside, behind the counter, was an older man wearing a set of blue coveralls.

"Can I help ya?" he said. He was typing something into a computer. His fingers were caked in grease.

"I'm looking for Bobby Jacobs."

He looked up at her. "Did he service your car?"

"No. I need to speak with him about a private matter. Is he still in today?"

"Uh, yeah. Let me call him. Can I tell him who would like to see him?"

"Yes. I'm Nancy Simmons."

Nancy had a seat in one of the plastic chairs lining the lobby. A few minutes later, Bobby came through the backset of doors with a greasy rag in his hand. Nancy stood up. "I'm sorry to inconvenience you, Mr. Jacobs. I just have a few follow up questions and I'll be on my way."

"Oh. All right. Uh…let's go out back."

She followed him out through the garage with cars hoisted up on jacks. The noise of drills and other tools echoed through the dingy room. They went around a corner and out another set of doors, which put them outside, behind the building. Bobby closed the door, muffling the noise of the shop. There were several used cars in the back lot, but nobody else was around.

"Do you mind if I smoke?" he asked.

"Good ahead. Mr. Jacobs, I checked your alibi. Your manager said you called in sick on March 21st."

"Oh, shit!" He almost dropped the cigarette dangling from his lips. "I forgot I had a meeting that day."

"A meeting with whom?"

"As part of my probation, I have to attend anger management classes once every three months. I call in sick so my boss and wife don't know about it."

"Your wife doesn't know?"

"Do you think she would've married me if she knew what I was really in the slammer for? She thinks I went to jail for vehicular manslaughter. That I accidently killed someone on an icy road but they charged me because I was a little tipsy at the time."

Nancy grimaced. "How long was the class?"

"Five hours. From ten to three."

"Can you provide me some documentation on that?"

"Sure. I gotta sign in each time so my probation officer has proof I attended."

"Okay. I'll speak with him then." Nancy paused to think for a second. "That only accounts for half the day. What about after three? Technically, you could still have driven to Duluth and back after three."

"After three, what the hell did I do? Oh! That's right, I picked the kids up at daycare that day because I was off so early, and then like I said last time we spoke, we had dinner reservations, so I dropped the kids at Kim's mom's house after I got them fed. You can check with the daycare center because you have to sign them out at the front desk when you take them. I can give you my mother-in-law's phone number. She babysat while we went out."

"Okay. I'm gonna need your wife's cell number, the name of the restaurant, as well."

He nodded. "I suppose you'll need to tell her why?"

Nancy turned and looked at his face. "Not necessarily," she said. "I just need the facts to check out."

He smiled. "Thanks."

"Well, that's all I need for now then."

"Sorry about that. I really just forgot about the damn meeting. Seriously, what are the odds that it would be on the same damn day that Mona…" He shook his head. "Really, I've done my time. I'll do whatever it takes to not go back to jail."

"Hopefully this will be the last time we need to speak, Mr. Jacobs."

"I hope so, too. I better get back to work." He threw his cigarette down and stepped on it.

Chapter 34

Now that the weather was getting better, George decided to head to the art store to buy a new canvas and some other supplies he was running low on. He really wasn't sure if the detective had liked his painting of the lake, but he felt like he was breaking through some of that hard outer shell she'd initially presented to him. She was warming to him, it seemed, if just a little. Either way, whether she liked the painting or not, he was finished with it and was anxious to start another one. It was the only thing keeping him preoccupied and sane.

Just as he was putting his jacket and boots on, his phone rang.

"Hi," Ella said softly. "I'm just calling to make sure you're okay."

"I am. Are you?"

"I'm not sure. I'm still angry."

"I've stopped drinking," he said. "And I'm sorry about what I said about Jeff."

"Can you just tell me you didn't do it?"

"I don't feel like I should have to…it should be something you just know about me."

"Well, I don't."

"That's upsetting to hear," George said. "What have I done to warrant you to think that way about me?"

"You haven't said you're innocent, Dad."

There was silence on the line.

Ella said, "I guess until you can tell me that, I'm not sure…" She sniffled into the phone then the line went dead.

George put his phone into his jacket pocket and went out the door. On his way to the art store, he went through a cycle of emotions. The problem with him and his daughter, he rationalized, was that they were too much alike. George wondered if all father/daughter relationships were this difficult. What had caused Ella to build up such a protective wall around herself? It actually reminded him of Detective Simmons.

As George walked into the store, he felt very lonely suddenly. He missed his wife. George wished he could talk to her about all of this right now. She would have been the one to straighten things out with Ella. Wouldn't she? What would she think of him right now? He supposed if she looked at all of the facts, Melinda probably wouldn't forgive him for what he'd done either.

With purchases in hand, George made his way back to the cabin, which was feeling more like a prison each day. Maybe he should get used to it. It might be where he ended up when this was all said and done. It was a very real possibility; one George hadn't really let himself think of much until now. What would an old man like himself do in jail? Did it really even matter at this point? He was alone, without a plan. Maybe prison was for the best.

George considered ending it all before that happened. He didn't want to put Ella through any more pain because of his stupid mistakes. There was no reason to go on. He could be with Melinda again. He missed her so much; he really hoped that was true. He'd never been a religious man, but he wanted to believe that he could be with his wife again. He never got a chance to tell her things, at the end. It was all so abrupt and final. He never got to say goodbye.

He pulled into the drugstore parking lot. He cut the engine and sat there for a few minutes trying to figure out what he could purchase inside the store that would help him end his life. Now that he was thinking about it, realistically, he wasn't sure how to even go about something like this.

He walked through the aisles trying to find something to make it swift and relatively painless. He didn't think he could actually go through with anything as deliberate as a hanging or shooting. When he got to the end of the last aisle, he'd found nothing suitable to for the task at hand. He wanted to be certain he didn't screw it up. It needed something strong and final. Cough syrup wasn't going to do the trick.

He went back to the Prius frustrated he couldn't even accomplish something as simple and straightforward as killing himself. He'd failed again. He rested his head on the steering wheel and was hit with a feeling of overwhelming exhaustion. His daughter's words played through his head. Tears welled up, and instead of tamping them back down, he just let it all out right there in the middle of the drugstore parking lot in broad daylight. He cried, and he cried hard. He felt like a blubbering idiot, especially knowing anyone might see him, but he couldn't stop.

After he cried away all of the tough emotions plaguing him of late, he came up for air. He felt better too because as he sobbed some clarity had found its way to the surface. He would go back to the cabin, call his doctor and request some strong sleeping pills, paint this one last painting while he waited, and then he'd say goodnight. He was happy to finally have a plan.

Chapter 35

Nancy was home by 8:02. She was exhausted but hopeful that her trip out to Stillwater wasn't for naught. She'd double-check Bobby's alibi with the parole officer in the morning, but for now, she was mentally crossing Bobby off of her list. Today's mission had been completed, and with little time to spare. Nancy was starving. She was so focused on narrowing her leads; she hadn't even stopped to eat.

When she walked in the house from the garage, Roger was in the kitchen behind the stove. It smelled like garlic bread, which meant he was making the one thing he knew how to cook.

"Pasta Florentine at eight o'clock?" she said.

"Yeah. Busy day. Have you eaten yet?"

"No, actually."

"Good. It's done."

"Perfect."

Roger dished them each up a plate of noodles and put a piece of garlic toast on the side. "You want to eat in here or the living room?" he asked, handing her the plates.

"Living room."

"I'll bring you a glass of wine."

"Thanks."

Maybe it was because she felt like she'd made some progress on the case today, or because this was exactly what she needed tonight; either way, she was in a good mood. This felt normal, sitting in her living room with her husband, eating dinner while watching television. Did she really want to give this up?

They didn't talk much. It was clear they were both worn out. Nancy was too tired to do anything but focus on the screen. When she finished eating, she collected their plates and took them to the kitchen. She rinsed them then decided she'd tackle the rest tomorrow, after she slept. Just as she was setting the plates in the sink, Roger came up behind her and slipped his arms around her waist. He began kissing her neck. It had been a while since they'd been intimate, but Nancy knew if it was going to happen, tonight was probably the best time. She was tired, too tired to fight, and she did love to have her neck kissed. It was dark in the kitchen with just the TV from the living room casting a tranquil amount of light in. Nancy closed her eyes and let Roger go for a little longer before they moved into the bedroom.

***

The next morning, Roger was gone from the bed when Nancy finally stirred. It was nearly nine a.m. She'd slept way longer than she'd meant to and she felt the familiar weight of everything on her shoulders, the ticking in her head, when she jumped up and headed for the bathroom. In the shower, she turned the water up to the hottest setting it would go. It felt like an evil contrast to the cold of the room, but she wanted it to sting. She wanted it to wash away the guilt she was feeling after her night with Roger. She knew she'd misled him last night by letting him whisk her into bed. It was selfish of her, she knew. She wanted that one last feeling of strong desire for closure.

Now, as she washed her body, she no longer felt needy; she felt like a coward. It was over and she knew it. She'd have to confront Roger within the next few days and tell him so. She wasn't going to go with him. What exactly it was she was going to do, she still wasn't sure.

Nancy stepped out of the shower and pushed any thoughts she was having about her and Roger to the back of her head. She needed to keep all of the available space in her brain working on figuring out who killed Mona Clark. The days were quickly slipping away, and the captain wasn't letting her forget it. As she dried and dressed, she made a mental list of all of the things she needed to get done today.

When she made it to the station, she went through the stack of papers in her box. There were still no timesheets from The Grind for Jenny Stevens. She called and arranged to have the Duluth Crime Scene Investigation Unit (CSIU) process George Altman's car. Time was becoming a factor and she hoped to gain some ground soon.

Between these two things, she had to find what she was looking for. If George had been with Mona at the rest stop, perhaps he'd taken her to another location in his car; in which case, the evidence would be there, in the silver Prius. And then there was Jenny. It was possible she could have been involved somehow, but Nancy still had more digging to do to find out for sure.

In the meantime, she called Bobby's parole officer, who verified he'd attended the anger management class. She then followed up with the daycare and restaurant. They also checked out like he said they would. Finally, maybe she was making some headway.

Next, she pulled out the copies of the bank statements George had given her. She looked for purchases from big department stores for expensive clothing, but found none. Then she thought more about Mona stealing from George and wondering again if Jenny Stevens had been involved somehow. Identity theft was tricky to crack. If it were easy, people wouldn't be doing it as rampantly and successfully as they were nowadays.

Nancy went to the vending machine for some lunch. She still had too much to do to stop. On her way back to her desk, she paid Officer Anderson a quick visit. He was the station resident expert on all things fraud. He'd recently taken a class on ID theft. Nancy knocked on the side of his door, which was partially open. He called her in.

"What can I do for you, Detective?"

"Working a case that involves some money fraud. Wondering if you can point me in the right direction. Any good tips from that class you took?"

"The main idea was to follow the money trail. There's a new intranet site in the system you can use, it's just for law enforcement and investigators, called E-information. It can track the flow of money."

"Great. That's exactly what I need. Thanks."

"Anytime."

Nancy went back to her desk and plugged in the information she had on George's bank account. Follow the money trail. That was the phrase she repeated to herself as she dug into it. Where did that $20K go that Mona had managed to siphon from George's account?

"Follow the money" was a common saying in the world of crime fighting. It could more often than not lead you to a perpetrator. But Nancy had learned over her years working cases that just following the

215

dollar signs could also blind you from other possible motives. People killed for many other reasons too: love, revenge, jealousy, hate. Sometimes it was a combination of some or all of them. It was a complex thing, killing.

Eventually, Nancy stumbled upon a secondary bank account, set up in George's name at a small independent bank in Lake Elmo, Minnesota. Nancy quickly checked the map and saw that Lake Elmo was a neighboring town to Stillwater. The money had all been withdrawn and the account was now sitting inactive. She called and spoke with the manager. She requested camera footage from the day the account was created. If Nancy could ID this person, this might be her killer—if, in fact, the money had something to do with Mona's death. It was still possible the two crimes were not connected, though it seemed highly unlikely.

The money had been withdrawn on March 24th. That was two days after Mona's death. Had she simply obtained the information and passed it along to a fraud ring for a cut? Or had she been working with someone she knew? Jenny Stevens had previous experience with check fraud.

"I guess it's time I follow up with our cheerleader," Nancy said, putting her trench coat on and grabbing her leather bag.

***

She parked her car half a block in front of Jenny's home, which was a pretty standard middle-income house in the Hunter's Park neighborhood. Still lived with Mom and Dad, Nancy figured. There was a beat up old Oldsmobile in the driveway, which probably belonged to Jenny. Nancy cut her engine and waited.

If she knew twenty-somethings, Jenny would be going out for the evening before too long. She wanted to see what kinds of things this girl got up to when she wasn't selling coffee or getting in fights.

Sure enough, around six-thirty Jenny got in the Olds and headed out. Nancy followed at a distance. After about eight minutes, they arrived at a nightclub called the Pink Flamingo on the outskirts of town. Nancy parked toward the back of the lot and watched. Jenny got out of the Olds, grabbed a tote bag and threw it over her shoulder. Her long blonde hair wasn't pulled into a ponytail tonight. She walked in wearing some deadly high heels.

"Oh, Jenny," Nancy murmured. "Turns out you aren't a cheerleader after all."

Nancy looked at herself in her rearview mirror. She was gonna stick out inside the so-called gentlemen's club, but there wasn't much she could do about it unless she could transform herself into a man. Sometimes she wished she did have that ability; tonight wasn't really one of those times though. She felt dirty just walking into the place. The lights were practically off, it was so dark inside. There was a stage toward the back of the room, which created most of the ambience the place offered. Nancy took a seat at a table as far away from the stage as she could but kept her gaze there, assuming Jenny would be making an appearance upon it at some point.

A short time later, a cocktail waitress approached. Nancy looked up and was surprised to see Jenny Stevens standing in front of her. She was wearing a tight glittery shirt and a short black skirt. At least she wasn't a dancer, Nancy thought.

"What can I get…" Jenny said before she fully looked at Nancy. Once she did, she said, "Detective? What the hell? Are you following me?"

"Hi, Jenny. So, you're moonlighting, huh?"

"Moonlighting?" She had a confused look on her face.

"Never mind," Nancy said.

"You can't tell Doug about this."

"You haven't told your fiancé about working here?"

"No. He'd kill me."

"So, why do it then?"

Jenny shifted the tray in her hand and blew her stringy hair out of her face. "You think I can afford to pay for a wedding on the money I make at the coffee shop? I took the crappy promotion to manager hoping I could quit here soon, but I dunno. I still have to pay for the dress and caterers. I had to give a down payment to the venue a few months ago and the damn check bounced. They wanted to press charges."

"So that explains the check fraud on your record."

"Yeah. I told them, 'It's not fraud, I'm really broke.'" Jenny did a half-snort, half-laugh then blew a bubble with her gum.

"What about Doug? Isn't he helping pay for anything?"

"Are you kidding me? He's an artist." She made air quotes with her fingers when she said the word in a snarky tone. "He keeps telling me if he can sell just one piece to some New York gallery we'll have it made, but until then…We'll probably stay living with my parents for the rest of our lives." A patron walked by and smiled at Jenny. She batted her lashes a little for him then turned back to Nancy. "So, you wanna order something? I gotta get back to work."

"No. I think I'm done here."

"You sure? Everybody loves our chicken wings."

"Thanks. I'll take a rain check."

Jenny shrugged and headed to another table. Nancy hightailed it from the Pink Flamingo.

Chapter 36

That evening at home, Nancy felt sick. She wanted to blame it on the case. She was exhausted and still didn't have a clear picture of what transpired in order for a young girl to be pulled up dead from the icy waters of Lake Superior. But in truth, she was actually worried about seeing Roger when he got home. She was hoping to avoid it altogether until the case was over, but the way it was going, she wasn't sure that was ever going to happen, and now Roger was planning to leave for California soon, and she knew he was expecting an answer from her.

She wished she did still love him. It would make everything so much easier. She wished they had both wanted the same things out of life, that she could have given him what he needed, that he wouldn't have cheated. So much had come between them and happiness; it seemed obvious in many ways why it was over, but what made it hard was the fact that he was a good man and he still loved her. She hated that she couldn't say the same, especially since she really didn't know what she wanted or needed, only that it wasn't Roger. It seemed an impossible task to tell someone that. There was a reason she'd put it off for so long.

Nancy brought take out home and paced the kitchen floor. She grabbed plates out of the cabinet and considered dishing the food out onto them, only she wasn't very hungry anymore. Instead, she took out a glass and poured herself some wine. She sat down at the kitchen counter and waited.

Halfway through the glass of wine, she relaxed a little and was feeling slightly better about talking with Roger, when the home phone rang, nearly causing her to pitch from the bar stool she was perched on. She got up and took the call.

"Hi, hon," Roger said. "I'm not gonna make it for dinner. Still trying to tie up all the loose ends here."

"Okay."

"Sorry."

"It's fine."

"You didn't make something special for me, did you?"

"Just my usual. Take out."

He laughed. "Don't wait up. I'll probably be pretty late."

"Okay."

Once she hung up, Nancy opened the Styrofoam box and filled her plate. Miraculously, she'd regained her appetite.

***

The next morning, she got to work and checked the fax machine and her box, still waiting for Jenny's timesheets to come from The Grind. Still nothing. She sat down at her desk and turned on her computer. Hopefully, she'd have that bank footage to look through.

Once her computer was fully up and running, her calendar popped up to remind her she had an appointment with her therapist in half an hour. She'd almost forgotten, which was odd considering she'd held the same monthly appointment since she'd come to Duluth. She usually looked forward to the meeting. She liked the doctor and found the sessions to be incredibly helpful. Still, now wasn't the best time. Nancy had so much work to do on this case. She picked up the phone to cancel the appointment, but a few clicks through her email showed she didn't have the footage from the bank yet, and without it or Jenny's timesheets, she was in limbo. Plus, now seemed like a really good time to sit down across from the psychologist and talk everything out with regards to Roger.

***

On the way out of the clinic after her session, Nancy was on a different planet. She was still turning things over based on her conversation with the therapist. The therapist advised her to come clean with Roger. If she got everything out in the open, she would be more likely to move past it all and start fresh. She was trying to figure out how she would do that when she nearly careened into someone in the lobby. She looked up and was nose to nose with George Altman. Their eyes met in a very knowing way. He looked almost as crazed on the outside as she felt on the inside. He had a small white prescription bag in his hand, which he quickly tucked into his jacket pocket.

"What are you doing here?" she asked, regaining her senses.

"Oh, I...I've been having some trouble sleeping, as you can imagine, so I had my doctor phone over a prescription for something to help. What about you?"

"I... You know, it's a good thing I ran into you actually. I was planning to call you today. I got a warrant. I'll be bringing the lab techs over tomorrow morning."

"All right."

"So, I guess I'll see you tomorrow then."

"I guess so."

***

On her return trek to the station, Nancy was shocked to find the sun actually warming her skin. Her trench coat felt like the right amount of protection from the elements for the first time in a long time. She wished she could be happier that spring was actually making an attempt to work some magic on this frozen land, but she had too many other things to worry about at the moment.

She checked her email again and finally received the footage from the bank. She began reviewing it, frame by frame, second by second. This was a very slow process, as she needed to examine every face at three different bank teller counters within an eight hour period. Luckily, this was a small bank and they had no drive through options. The faces were clear enough, so she scrutinized them all, waiting and hoping to see one she recognized.

After several hours of fast forwarding, rewinding, and pausing, Nancy had looked at the entire reel and hadn't seen Jenny, George, Bobby, or Mona in a single frame.

"Damn it," she muttered under her breath. With little else to go on, Nancy knew she was stuck again. She went in to update the captain, though she framed it in a way that made it sound like she was on the brink of cracking the whole thing wide open. If she didn't, he would assign her a new case and though she had a few other cases still open from before this one, they weren't murders and held less weight. She felt sure if she had just a little more time with this one, she'd come up with something. The captain seemed less sure, but gave her another week to keep the file classified as a top priority.

On her way out that night, she lingered, trying to find a way to put off going home for as long as possible. She really wished she had a lead she was following, but even without one, she considered calling Roger and telling him she was going to have to pull an all-nighter. It obviously wasn't implausible since she was knee-deep in a homicide investigation, so Roger wouldn't suspect anything out of the ordinary. The bigger question was what exactly would she do? All she really wanted to do was go home and soak in her bathtub and try to figure out her next moves on the case, but as soon as Roger got home, she knew that wouldn't be possible.

She stopped to make small talk with Bonnie the receptionist on her way out. Bonnie was a twenty-nine year old single woman. Nancy didn't know much about her personal life except that from the outside she appeared a bit mousey, but that couldn't really be the case because she regularly went out with others from the station after work.

"Hey, Bonnie…you don't have a fax for me up here do you? I've been waiting for some timesheets to come from The Grind Coffeehouse."

Bonnie looked through some loose pieces of paper scattered around her desk. "No. I haven't seen anything."

"Okay, thanks." She started to walk away then paused and turned, "Hey, is anybody going out after work tonight?"

Bonnie looked up at Nancy with a curious expression. "You're asking to go out with us?" she said.

"Is that weird?" Nancy played dumb.

"Not weird. Just not normal. You've never gone out with us before."

"I know but this case has me all tense, and," she lied, "my husband's out of town, so…"

Bonnie said, "Actually, a bunch of us are going over to Superior Brew for some pizza and beer if you want to come."

"Yeah? Okay. I'd like that."

"Great."

Chapter 37

The next morning, Nancy had a headache. She wasn't hung over, necessarily, but she'd definitely had more than she usually did. She was a one glass of wine type of girl. She hardly ever drank beer, and never more than one. She'd had a few. It was more than enough. But it had been an unexpectedly decent time. Nancy actually enjoyed getting to know some of her colleagues a little better, even if she'd only done it to avoid her husband. She'd been successful in managing to do so; Roger was fast asleep when she crawled into bed next to him when she returned at bar close.

Now though, headache or not, she pulled herself together because she had to get over to George Altman's cabin. She popped a few Ibuprofen and said goodbye to Roger, who was packing some bags.

"Hey, I might be a bit late again tonight because it's my last day and they want to take me out for a little going away thing." He looked up at her from his luggage. "Actually, do you wanna come along?"

"No. I won't know anybody."

"Are you sure? It'll be fun. Come on!"

"Nah. I have a lot to do on this case still."

"Another all-nighter? You making any headway?"

"Yeah. I'm so close."

"Okay. Let's have dinner tomorrow night. We can talk then."

"Sure. Sounds good," Nancy said.

***

She got to George's cabin at 8:04. The CSI Unit had already started prepping his car for processing. They decided to tent it to use the blue-light. If there was any ammonia or bodily fluid dried into the car upholstery, they'd find it this way. After Nancy checked in with them, she walked back to her car. She was planning to go over the case file while she waited. She hadn't seen George at all yet. She eyed the cabin once she sat down with the file propped up against her steering wheel. It appeared quiet within. Nancy tried to concentrate on the file but she kept getting an irritating nudge to go and check on George. Something about seeing him yesterday wasn't sitting well with her. As much as she tried to push it out of her head and read through her notes, she couldn't let it go.

She set the file back in her bag and got out of the car. Two steps from the front door, George came flying out of the cabin toward her. Nancy took a quick step back, slipped on the wet ground, and fell down. "Jesus!"

"Detective, I'm sorry." George crouched down to help her back to her feet. "Are you okay?"

"Yes. And I see that you are also."

"I…just got a call from the Ely sheriff. Ella's been in a car accident." He looked at his car covered in a canvas tent. "She's in the hospital. It's serious. Can you drive me?"

Nancy didn't know what to say. This wasn't standard protocol, but his car was clearly out of commission at the moment, and technically she didn't need to be at the site any longer. She turned and looked at him. It was very apparent in his expression that before her was a man who loved his daughter.

Nancy knew that face. She was a seventeen year old girl again looking into her own scared father's eyes just before he died. "Okay," she said.

Without hesitation, he jumped into the passenger seat of her sedan. She explained to the CSIU agent that they could leave when they were finished processing the Prius and to send the results to her as soon as they were ready. She contemplated telling one of them, or calling the captain, or even Roger, to let someone know she was getting in a car with one of her prime murder suspects, but it sounded so stupid, even she was too ashamed to say it.

George gave her directions to the hospital in Ely. After a half hour of dead silence, she noticed George's right knee bouncing up and down rapidly. She said, "I'm sure she's going to be okay, Mr. Altman."

He didn't reply.

"Can I ask you a question? Not on the record."

He nodded.

"What are you really planning to do with the sleeping pills?"

Again he stayed silent.

"I'm planning to tell my husband tomorrow that I'm leaving him," she said calmly.

George turned his head toward her a little.

"I don't know what I'm going to say yet," she went on. "I think it will probably have something to do with the fact that I feel guilty I was never able to give him children. See, he thought we were trying for years and it just wasn't happening. The truth is, I was making sure it never actually happened."

"Why?" George asked softly.

"I was seventeen years old, in the 11th grade, when I came home from school one day and found my father lying in a pool of blood on our kitchen floor. He'd been shot. He died in my arms. That's why I became a detective.

"When they couldn't solve the case and they called to tell us it had gone cold, I think I did too. I just knew I didn't want that to happen to other people. It was a horrible feeling. Helplessness. Someone out there took something from me, and there would be no consequences for it. They could just go on…being. And I would never be able to do the same. The injustice of it was something I could not fathom.

"I also knew that when I decided to become a detective, there was a greater possibility that I could be killed in the line of duty. I didn't want my child to have to go through what I went through. So, no kids for me. I ended up falling in love with one of the only men on the planet who actually wanted to have kids. I failed him. Then he failed me. Now it's over."

"I'm sorry," George said.

"My point is, killing myself because it didn't work out isn't the answer. I'm in a tough spot, just like you, but I need to push through it. Somehow it will work out. At least, that's what my therapist told me yesterday."

George laughed a little. "Thank you," he said.

Nancy nodded.

***

When they got to the hospital, Nancy stayed back while George hurried in to find out some information about his daughter. Eventually, Nancy took a seat in the main lobby of the little hospital, which was about the size of the clinic she went to in Duluth, and pulled the case file from her bag to resume going over her notes to figure out what she was missing.

After about an hour, George sat down next to her. "She's in a coma. She was heading to a water collection site early this morning on a very rural road. It was hazy, and the roads were wet and slick from all of the melting, so she didn't stop in time. She hit a moose." He sniffed.

"I'm so sorry," Nancy said.

"Am I allowed to stay here? I don't want to leave her in case she wakes up."

"Sure."

"Thank you for driving me."

"No problem. I'll bill the station for my mileage." Nancy smiled and closed the folder in her lap. She stood to go then stopped. "Can I ask you something?"

"Yes."

"Did you love Mona Clark?"

George's gaze went to the floor as if it made him invisible to Nancy that way. "I think I might have," he said. "She was exactly what I needed at the time I needed it. Besides, love doesn't always follow rules. Sometimes it's just there…or it isn't."

She nodded and left the hospital.

Chapter 38

The next day crawled by. Nancy was so full of nerves, she actually reached the point where she just wanted to get it over with—the dreaded "talk" with Roger she'd put off for so many months. She assumed it would never happen. But today was it. Roger was leaving for California tomorrow so whether she wanted to discuss it now or not, she was going to. She knew George Altman was right. Love didn't make any sense. She was tired of trying to make it.

Nancy assumed the report from the crime lab wouldn't be back for a few days, but it was there in her box when she arrived in the morning. She looked it over with a trifle of dread. She wanted to catch her man, but at this point, she wasn't sure she wanted it to be George. Except he still had the strongest motive, the worst alibi, and the most unusual story. He had the makings of a killer on paper, yet there was something about him that struck Nancy.

It didn't matter. She followed the evidence, not her emotional reaction to a suspect, and looking at the report in front of her, the evidence was not in the Toyota Prius. It was clean, and by clean, she didn't mean it had been cleaned with ammonia in an attempt to hide blood. The only fingerprints on the car at all were those belonging to George. There were no hairs or skin flakes that pointed to anybody else having even been in the car, not even George's deceased wife.

If George had dumped Mona's body in the Superior near where she was found, she would have needed to have been transported from her car at

Knife River to somewhere near Canal Park, alive or dead. She hadn't gone in George's car, and she hadn't gone in the pickup truck. How did Mona leave that rest area? Why was she there in the first place?

Again, Nancy went back to the drawing board and started to re-read the case file, exploring it from multiple angles. She was now completely out of new leads and ideas. She left work early because she was upset with herself. She couldn't believe she'd failed Mona Clark and her marriage all in one day.

***

At home, Roger was already waiting for her with dinner. He had placed a dozen long-stemmed roses in a vase on the center of the dining room table. She'd never hated herself more than she did at that moment. If she could take one of those thorny stems and jam it straight into her heart right then and there, she would have.

She tried to swallow down the giant lump sitting in her throat as she sat down and faced Roger sitting across from her. She wished he had more sense to know what was about to happen, but it seemed clear he did not. He was oblivious as always, which was probably another part of their problem.

This was the time she needed to find some strength and pull it up from the murky depth of her soul. She took a deep breath. "Roger," she said, her voice so shaky she barely recognized it as her own. "I wish I could go with you to California, but…"

"I knew you weren't going to come," he said calmly, stabbing at his salad with his fork.

"What? You did?" Relief flooded her. Maybe this was going to be easier than she thought.

"Sure. Don't you think I know you well enough by now? How long have we been married? Twelve years, right?"

"And they were good years…"

"You make it sound like it's over," Roger said, laughing a little.

That's when Nancy realized he wasn't understanding. "Uh…"

His salesman voice came out now. "We'll be apart for a while but it's not the end of the world. You can just come after you wrap up the case. I know you. You can't leave until you've marked the case closed."

"Oh. Roger, I…"

"The reason we work so well is because we want the same things," he went on. "I've been thinking about how perfect it is that we are both so independent. We can let each other be our own person. I know how dedicated to your work you are…and it's okay because I am too."

"Right." She took a gulp of her wine. She wasn't sure why Roger had changed his tune from their last conversation. Maybe it was his sales tactic. He just wasn't going to let her say no. Or maybe it was because of the other night. She knew she shouldn't have slept with him; it had obviously sent the wrong message. The familiar guilt wrapped around her like a blanket. It was overwhelming. All she wanted to do was get away from the table.

"So, do you think you can handle the sale of the house yourself while you're in the middle of the case?" he asked.

"I…think so."

"Great. I'm so excited to get the hell out of this cold. Have you looked at the openings in the Sacramento Police Department yet?"

"No."

"Well, I'm sure you'll find something. You might want to consider doing a desk job, or even training. I think this case is really wearing on you. You look...tired."

Nancy just nodded. Maybe now wasn't the best time to do this anyway. She'd sell the house and then tell him after he got all settled in California. She'd formulate a plan for what she was going to do next herself and then tell him. Yes. It was better this way. Roger would go to California, and she could focus on the case and deal with her marriage after.

She finished her glass of wine and got up from the table. "I'm going to take a hot bath," she said.

"Sounds good, hon."

Chapter 39

George sat helpless, hunched over his daughter's unresponsive body as she lay in the hospital bed, the beeping of the machines the only sign she was still of this world. He got up to stretch then sat back down in the chair he'd been glued to for the last few days and took Ella's hand. The doctor advised him to talk to her. It could help pull her out. Now seemed like the right time. He obviously hadn't been able to do it while she was conscious.

"Sweetie," he said softly, "I know I've made mistakes, but they aren't the ones you think. Your mom and I, we were so young when we met. I came to the University from a small town in rural Minnesota, not so unlike Ely. I was so naive. I had hardly experienced life yet. My parents were farmers. They didn't get me. They didn't understand art or my desire to paint. As a result, I was very isolated growing up. I was shy and awkward. I didn't know how to express myself like other people, not through words anyway.

"I don't blame my parents entirely, but farmers are busy people, and really, they aren't the most expressive people either. So, I just never learned how to interact with other people the way I probably should have. But the land, that's what I cherished the most about my childhood. It was my savior. It was beautiful to me. It was the only thing that understood me, and in turn, I it. As a young boy, it was my only friend. It was pristine and open, a gorgeous sprawling prairie with a creek running along the edge of our property, with groves of trees creating a visible force field between me and the rest of the world.

"There was a huge old oak tree that shot up in the middle of the flat pasture. The cows often mingled around it like it was their god. I would sit outside the barn and paint the tree during sunsets, never able to capture it the way it really appeared. The way the light hit the haystacks and reflected like gold across the fields. The dull color of the red wooden slats on the barn. Those were the things I thought about most; how to turn them into 2D images with paint. My parents never supported my passion, never tried to connect with me or make me feel that this was normal. That's how parents are, I guess, because I'm just now realizing how much you and I are alike. You love the land too and protect it with your work. You and I express it differently in our actions, yet neither of us seems to be able to use words very well.

"Anyway, when I left the farm, my parents were angry with me. They took it personally. I think I might have taken it personally when you moved away from Mom and me, too. I felt like you'd kind of abandoned us, which is so stupid. I mean, I'd done the same thing, hadn't I? Anyway, I don't know why. I guess you just hope your children love you so much they'll always want to be around you. I guess maybe to prove you did right by them? I don't know.

"My parents wanted me to stay and take over the farm someday. Why would I want to get a college degree, one for art no less? they asked. They never understood that I wasn't a good farmer. I loved the feel of the country, but I had no desire to plant things or feed cattle. I wanted to express myself, to be understood, through the visuals I put on the canvas.

It was the only thing I'd ever wanted in life until that point.

"I came to the city at eighteen as a boy, one who'd never had a true relationship with anything or anyone except the landscape…until I met your mother. She was as beautiful as the sunset to me. She knew how to interpret my nervous energy and form words for me that I couldn't form myself. Needless to say, I quickly fell in love. It took over. I was no longer concerned with painting, or eating, or even breathing, unless your mother was with me. She could light up a room with her energy. She was from the city. She was a confident, assertive, bubbly young lady. She was everything I was not.

"Being so blindly in love, did we make some mistakes? Absolutely. I can admit it. We should have been more careful, but I felt so happy to find someone like your mother, someone who got me, I wasn't thinking about the consequences. When your mother got pregnant, everything changed. At first, I thought we'd made a horrible mistake. I was mad, but it was only at myself. I was sure I'd ruined your mother's life. She had dreams to become a teacher, and I knew she'd make a great one. I felt helpless, until you were born. Then I held you and looked at your tiny face, and I realized that we hadn't made a mistake.

"You, my flesh and blood, my child…you were the thing. You made it okay that I wasn't pursuing an art degree, that I was going to a monotonous job every day, that your mom was cranky because she wasn't sleeping, that we were in debt and struggling. These things no longer mattered. You were all that mattered. You mattered so much we didn't even feel the need to have more children because we didn't have any more love to give…we gave it all to you because you deserved every last bit of it.

"And all I wanted was to protect you, to make sure you were happy. I wanted to be the best father to you. And I know I failed you. I'm so sorry, Ella. I'm sorry I couldn't be the dad you deserved."

***

After George wiped his tears, he was drained. He needed to clear his head, and maybe getting out of the hospital for a short time was the solution. He also desperately needed a shower. He found Ella's house keys in the bag with her belongings that the sheriff had collected from the accident site. He called a taxi and went to her house.

When he walked in, he heard noises coming from the bedroom. There was a faint glow of light coming from the hall. He looked around for some kind of weapon. When he didn't see anything in his immediate reach, he made his way quietly to the kitchen and pulled a knife from the drawer. He tiptoed down the hall, following the sounds, and peered into the bedroom.

Jeff was lying in Ella's bed, his arms folded behind his head. A small TV on the dresser was playing at a low volume.

"What the hell are you doing here?" George yelled, coming into full view in the doorway.

Jeff's eyes went wide as he honed in on the shine of the kitchen blade, but when he looked up at George's face, he yawned and stretched. "Oh, hey, George. I'm just hanging out. What are you doing here?"

George set the knife on the top of the dresser. "Checking on my daughter's house while she fights for her life in the hospital. Why haven't you been there? I left you several messages."

"I was there...yesterday. I must have missed you," he said, getting out of the bed. He stood in a pair of red boxer shorts.

George's hands became tight balls. "That's a lie. I've been at Ella's bedside the entire time."

"Oh, I..."

George didn't know what came over him, but he took a step closer and faced Jeff down. "You are a pathetic excuse," he said. Jeff didn't budge, which only enraged George more. Before George knew what he was doing, his clenched fist rose up and launched at Jeff's face.

Jeff wobbled for a minute then grabbed at his cheek. "Ouch! What gives, old man?"

"Get out of this house," George spat, rubbing his knuckles. He turned and headed for the shower.

A few minutes later, George stood in the bathroom outside the shower stall listening through the stream of hot water until he heard the front door slam shut. He relaxed a little, knowing Jeff was gone. He finally got into the water, still shaking a little from his own actions. He didn't really hate Jeff that much, he'd just been pushed too far past his breaking point. He was angry with himself, knowing there would be consequences to pay for losing his temper. He hadn't realized they would be with the police and not his daughter.

By the time he stepped out of the shower, a police car was pulling up to the front of the house. George threw his worn jeans and flannel shirt back on and opened the door, getting to the officer before he got to him.

Chapter 40

Nancy had come to a decision in the bathtub. She hated the idea of bothering Mona's mother, especially knowing her fragile mental state, but she was desperate to collect more information. She really needed something, anything to help guide her toward the right path. So the next morning she drove straight to the state-run senior living home, in order to speak with Jan Clark again. If nothing else, she felt it was her duty to check in with her and make sure they were treating her well.

"I don't know if you remember me, Mrs. Clark. My name is Nancy Simmons. I know you've been informed about your daughter. I'm a detective working on her case."

Jan nodded. "Mona's dead," she said.

"I know. I'm very sorry for your loss."

"They said someone killed her. Who would do that?"

"I don't know yet, but I'm working on it. That's why I'm here, actually. I was wondering if you could answer a few more questions for me."

"I can try. My memory isn't what it used to be."

"Anything might help." Nancy cleared her throat and hit record on her little device. "When I talked to you the last time, you mentioned a few names to me. Ben and Paul. You said one of these was the name of Mona's boyfriend. Do you remember that?"

"I think so."

"What else can you tell me about her boyfriend? Does one of those names still seem right?"

"I don't…I'm not sure."

"Okay. Maybe you can help me with another question. Why do you think Mona might have needed a large sum of money?"

Jan's eyes lit up. "Oh. That's an easy one. Mona had a dream. She wanted to move to the cities and open up a fancy art gallery. She even had a friend who was helping her with it."

"A friend. Who was that?"

"I don't know his name."

"It was a him though?"

"Yes."

"And when you say 'cities,' you are referring to the Twin Cities?"

"Yes."

"So, she had a friend helping her with this art gallery. How so?"

"He was helping her look for a place. I told her she should stay and do it here in Duluth. She didn't need to be in that dangerous city. So much crime there, but she insisted Paul was safe."

"Paul? You mean St. Paul. That's the Paul you're talking about? The gallery she was hoping to open was in St. Paul?"

Jan nodded. "I never met him. He was a secret, you know? I wasn't supposed to tell people about him."

"Why is that, Mrs. Clark?"

"Because he was married. I think he even had children."

"The man who was helping Mona in St. Paul was married with children?"

"Yes. Do you know when John's coming back?"

"John? Your husband?"

"Yes. He's on the road. He's a trucker."

Nancy knew that Jan's husband was deceased and this was just the disease talking again, but she'd put Jan through enough for the moment, she didn't want to cause any more pain for her. "I bet he'll be back soon," she said.

"That's what Mona always says," Jan said.

"You've been very helpful, Mrs. Clark. Thank you. Are they treating you well here? The accommodations adequate?"

"Oh, yes. Mona never wanted me to come to a place like this. She said I deserved better, but it's nice here. They take care of me. Not like Mona did, of course, but they're nice too."

"Good. That's good," Nancy said. She got up to leave, but Jan pulled her hand back down.

Nancy assumed she was just lonely and wanted to talk some more, but her voice got serious and she said, "You'll find them, right? The person who did that awful thing to her."

"I don't plan to stop until I do."

"You would have liked her. I could tell the first time I met you, you're like her."

"How so?"

"You're determined."

"I guess that's true."

"I may be slipping, but sometimes I'm glad about it."

"Why's that?"

"It makes these things easier."

Nancy nodded and this time managed to get all the way out of her chair. "You take care, Mrs. Clark."

"You too. I mean it. You're going to find this person. Promise me you don't kill yourself in the process."

"I won't."

"You come talk to me again, okay, Mona?"

"I will." Nancy let the name slip go. She knew how dementia worked. Jan Clark was working between two realities during their conversation, which made it hard to decipher what was fact and what wasn't, but she had a little more to work with than before she had talked to Mona's mother, so that was something.

When she got into her car, she jotted down notes onto her pad. Had George and Mona known each other before George's wife passed? Was this the man Jan was referring to as Paul? George was a man from St. Paul with a wife and child. Had they begun the affair while George's wife was still alive? Perhaps that's why he promptly moved to Duluth after her passing. He was an artist and she had aspirations of opening an art gallery. They could have crossed paths earlier. This was something Nancy hadn't speculated previously. And continuing with that train of thought, often times when couples had affairs, they had them in hotel rooms.

So that might explain why Mona's body was found in the lake just outside of Canal Park where all of the major hotel chains in Duluth were located. She and George met at a hotel, things went bad, he killed her and dumped the body just steps from the hotel, into the lake. It would explain why she wasn't dumped just north of there, at the yellow cabin.

Nancy put the car in drive and headed for Canal Park. She turned east onto Canal Park Drive and made note of the various inns, motels, and hotels that lined the waterfront side of the street. On the southern side of the park, this touristy area of town boasted quaint aquatic-themed stores and adorable candy shops, which made traffic unbearable, even in the spring. Nancy inched her way along, becoming mildly irritated by the lack of available parking.

She had one of those plastic city parking permits to stick on her rearview mirror since she drove an unmarked car, but even if she hadn't left it sitting on her desk, it didn't matter. There weren't any spots available, metered or not. She almost just gave up in frustration. She was suddenly so exhausted. But she knew she couldn't, especially not after her talk with Mona's mom. She needed to push through this. She couldn't let a parking spot deter her. She might be onto something here. She had to get her patience level in check—for Mona, the innocent victim in all of this.

Finally, she found a space at a metered spot with a one-hour limit. With the number of hotels she might need to visit, she knew this could make for a much longer visit than an hour, but she was anxious to get going, so she put her quarters in the meter and reminded herself to come back and move the car if necessary. Maybe she wouldn't need to though—she was due for a break in the case. Hopefully, she'd find what she was looking for before the hour was up. God, she hoped so.

Before she stepped out of the car, she tugged at the photo of Mona, detaching it from the paper clip that held it to the inside of the case file and slipped it into the pocket of her trench coat. She then purposefully crossed the street and entered Lake Superior Lodge, which looked nothing like what came to Nancy's mind when she conjured up a lodge. This place looked like a large chain hotel. The lobby was busy. It was shocking to Nancy that people in this state would pick this particular city to visit as a spring break destination. It was sunny, sure. But warm? That was relative to people in Minnesota, Nancy had come to learn after only two years here. For some reason, Minnesotans loved Duluth. She still didn't get it.

It physically pained her to have to wait in the check-in line at the lobby desk. There were two people working the registration desk, but they were moving slow. Everyone around her was staring at their smartphone seemingly oblivious to the world around them. This lack of observation is what made Nancy's job harder by the day. Technology was giving people an excuse to mind their own business. By the time Nancy reached the desk, her parking meter had already practically expired, and the hope she'd built up was dashed.

She held the photo of Mona up to the tall, slender man behind the counter wearing a cheap and poorly tailored suit. "I'm Detective Simmons. Wondering if you recall seeing this woman checking in here on occasion, or perhaps meeting a friend, coming and going through the lobby?"

"Sure. I've seen her."

Nancy's heart began racing. "Really?"

"Yeah…her and a million other women who look just like her. In fact, I've checked in at least five of her within the last two hours."

"Please, this is important. Really look at her."

He looked at the photo again and shrugged his shoulders. "It's like asking if I've checked in anybody with the last name Johnson recently," he said smugly. "Or someone who draws the long o sound out when they say Minnesota. After a while, they all blend together. Sorry."

"Thanks," Nancy said.

"Next," he shouted in her face.

Nancy glanced at the photo of Mona as she walked to the next hotel. He was probably right. Mona was not an unattractive woman, but there wasn't anything striking about her facial features necessarily that made her stand out. She looked like a Midwesterner: shoulder-length, wavy brown hair, dark eyes, a light complexion, a round face. Was there anything Nancy knew about her that might help identify her better, or was this a losing battle? She glanced at her watch. She had ten minutes left on the meter. In defeat, she decided to head back to the station. This wasn't going to get her anywhere. So much for thinking she could solve a homicide in an hour.

She lugged herself back to the station and wondered if Roger's flight had departed from the MSP Airport yet. What did she feel about it? She still felt like a coward mostly, but there was nothing to do about it now. No reason to dwell on it. He was gone, and she was still in Duluth. What a strange turn of events. She'd always figured she would be the one to fly off and leave Roger stuck on this iceberg. Had she only gotten the guts to do it sooner, maybe that would've been the case. She sighed.

Sitting down hard at her desk, she tried to clear her head. She had to think. She was determined, damn it. She wasn't going to let this hotel angle get the better of her. She turned her computer on and realized she just needed to pull the hotel registries for the last few months to see if either George or Mona had booked rooms under their names.

After she filled out a massive pile of paperwork arranging for the hotel reports, she was about ready to call it quits for the night when Officer Lansing approached her desk.

"Hey, California."

She looked up at him. "Did you just call me California?"

"Sure. Everybody calls you California."

"Not to my face."

"That's just because they're intimidated by you. You're smart and confident and good at what you do. Frankly, everyone here admires you."

"Oh, well...thanks. I..." Her face went hot, and she knew she was blushing.

Lansing politely pretended not to notice. "Besides, California has palm trees and beaches. Who doesn't love palm trees and beaches? It's a compliment."

She smiled. "I'd never thought about it like that before..."

"Anyway, Bonnie said to tell ya we're all going to grab a beer here shortly if you want to join us."

"Oh, yeah? Where to?" She was thinking maybe this was a better idea than going home to sulk in the bathtub.

Before Lansing could answer, her cell phone rang.

"Sorry. Excuse me," she said to him. She hit talk. "Detective Simmons."

"Yah, this here's Officer Rinken. Callin' from over here in Ely." Nancy cringed at the bite in Officer Rinken's accent. "I got a guy here says to give ya a ring. He got himself in a bit of a pickle. Name's George Altman. Ya know him?"

"A pickle? What kind of trouble could he have gotten himself into? He was supposed to be at the hospital."

"Yah, we brought him in on assault."

"Who did he assault?"

"Guy by the name of Jeff Young. Anyhoo, George says it'd be a good idea if you could come."

"Christ. Okay. I'm on my way." She hung up and looked up at Lansing. "I'm going to have to take a rain check. I appreciate the offer. Tell Bonnie I said thanks."

"No problem."

Chapter 41

How the hell had George Altman managed to get himself thrown in jail when she'd left him in the hospital at his daughter's bedside? That was all Nancy could ask herself for the duration of the drive up to Ely. She'd never been so conflicted by someone's personality as she was by George's. On one hand, he seemed like a gentle soul—introverted and thoughtful; on the other, he was continuously getting himself into unusually ugly situations. Either this guy was having some of the worst luck Nancy had ever seen, or George was not the person he seemed to be.

It frustrated her that she wasn't able to tell which it was. A homicide detective should have a keen sense about this stuff. Maybe she was losing it? Maybe Roger was right. Perhaps it was time for her to pack in her career. And now seemed like an excellent time to do that, except for one problem: Mona Clark's mother. Nancy couldn't get those eyes and that fragile voice out of her head. Jan was expecting her to bring justice to her daughter, and Nancy knew she couldn't stop until she did. Jan was right; Nancy was nothing if not determined. She just wished the case wasn't so damn elusive.

When she got to the Ely police station, she went in and talked with Officer Rinken. It seemed that Jeff Young was the daughter's boyfriend. Jeff was threatening to press charges, arguing that George had not only hit him but he had a knife, bumping the charges from a simple assault to assault with a deadly weapon. Nancy asked if she could speak with Jeff before the paperwork was filed.

Officer Rinken said, "I don't usually allow that kinda thing, but since yer a detective, and you seem to be involved in this somehow, I s'pose it's okay this time."

Nancy smiled at him and went out to where Jeff Young was seated in the waiting area. He was a younger man than she was expecting, maybe late twenties, knowing Ella Altman was in her mid-forties. He had a thermal shirt on with a ratty t-shirt layered over top of it. His jeans had a rip in the right knee, and he looked like he was stoned, or at least had been recently. He reminded her of a sulking teenager, the way he was slouched in the chair with one hand on a large bruise formed under his eye.

Nancy sat down. "I'm Nancy Simmons of the Duluth PD," she said.

"Jeff," he mumbled.

"Care to tell me what happened today with Mr. Altman?"

"The dude's a straight-up psycho. I was asleep at El's, and he just busted in and whaled on me. Not cool."

"Did you exchange any words beforehand?"

"I dunno. He was pissed 'cause I hadn't gone to see Ella at the hospital, but I hate the smell of those places. They're all mediciney and sterile, ya know? I'm a nature guy."

"Uh huh. So, your girlfriend was in a very serious accident, is in intensive care, and you were lounging? I guess I can see why her father might be a bit touchy."

He shrugged. "There's nothin' I can do."

"Right. Well...Mr. Young, given that George is distressed by his daughter's condition, I would advise you to drop the charges."

"I dunno. It hurts pretty bad." He rubbed his cheek.

Nancy was losing patience. "What if, say, you and Ella get married someday? It might be in your best interest, speaking long-term, if you found it in your heart to forgive her father for this, and maybe he'd do the same for you for not coming to the hospital."

"Whoa. Whoa. Back up." Jeff sat up straighter in his chair. "I have no intentions of marriage."

Nancy sighed. It was clear she needed to take a less mature approach with this guy, something he could understand. "Okay, listen. If you forget about the charges, I'll overlook the fact that you reek of marijuana. What do ya say...do we have a deal?"

"Oh, man. Fine. Deal." He got up from the chair.

"And," Nancy said, "I'd advise you to stay away from Miss Altman's home until all of this is resolved."

"Whatever," he said as he walked away from Nancy without looking back.

***

George was sitting in a little holding cell. His head was resting against the concrete wall, and his eyes were closed when Nancy walked in and sat down next to him on the long bench.

"I'm sorry," he said softly.

"For what?"

"Making you drive out here. Getting you involved with all of this. Just so you know, the knife wasn't intended for Jeff. I thought there was an intruder."

Nancy nodded in understanding. "For what it's worth, I might have decked that Jeff kid too."

George chuckled.

"How's Ella doing?" Nancy asked.

"Still unconscious." Then, from out of nowhere, George started to cry. It echoed in the little cell, amplifying it. Nancy shifted uncomfortably on the bench. She'd never heard a man release such emotion before, and a part of her felt like she was intruding on a private moment. She considered leaving George alone to his grief, but she also wondered if she was about to finally get her confession. It often happened after someone had been pushed beyond their limits. She waited until he was silent again, which took a pretty long time. She was about to attempt to coax it out of him when he turned his head to her slightly and said, "I didn't do it. I did not kill her."

"I want to believe you," she said. "I just need the proof."

"You know the worst part of all of this? It's that I never told Ella that. I should have just told her. I won't live with myself knowing she died thinking her father was a murderer. I just wanted her to already know that I wasn't capable of something so heinous. It made me sick to think she could possibly even consider that about me."

"You can still tell her."

"I'm not so sure."

"Well, not sitting in here you can't. Come on. I'll drive you back over."

"What? They're letting me go? How?"

"Let's just say Jeff and I understood each other. You're off the hook."

"You're a better person than I," he said.

"Maybe, maybe not. Let's go."

Chapter 42

Nancy sat with George in the waiting area of the hospital drinking coffee. It was now late in the day, and she was too exhausted to drive back tonight. She'd probably get a hotel room, but for now, she just needed coffee.

"My husband left today for California," she told George out of the blue. She'd been thinking about it so much, it felt good to get it off her chest.

"So it's over?" George asked.

"I'm still not sure."

"Why not?"

"I'm thinking this might be my last case. Maybe when I'm done, I'll go and see if I can figure things out with Roger. Maybe I won't. I just don't know."

"If by some miracle you manage to find Mona's killer, and I'm free to go, I don't know what I'll do either, if it makes you feel any better."

"There will be no miracle involved. I'm going to find the perpetrator. Anyway, what about your art? I don't think you should stop pursuing it."

"Eh. I appreciate that, but I don't see it amounting to anything. Not at my age."

"Mona thought it was good, too."

"How do you know that?"

"She had two of your paintings in her bedroom."

"Really? I thought she just bought them so she had a reason to keep up the scam. She brought me a check and then seduced me, stole my personal information. I was so upset when I figured that out.

She was clever, too. She must have paid the coffee shop owner for the painting then wrote out a new check from the business because she told me a stranger had purchased my work."

"She bought the paintings from you? I thought maybe she worked out an agreement with the artists. Her walls were lined with them. How much did she pay?"

"Two hundred and fifty a piece."

"She only had forty seven dollars in her bank account. How could she afford to do that?"

"I don't know. Maybe she was scamming The Grind somehow, too. I never thought about that. Once a scammer, always a scammer. Right?"

"Do you still have the checks she gave you?"

"Actually, I have them in my wallet. I had no way to deposit them up here, and after she'd clearly been through my file, I put them in my wallet for safekeeping." He took one out and handed it to Nancy. "Why? Do you think she was working with someone at the coffee shop?"

Nancy looked at the name on the check. "ORC? What's that?"

"Let me see." George looked at the check. "It's a corporation name. Olson Realty. I guess Michael Olson owns the coffee shop, too."

"You know Mike Olson?"

"He owns the cabin I'm renting."

"You rent that cabin?"

"Yes."

"Did you know that Mona was planning to open an art gallery? She must have been collecting those paintings for that purpose."

"What? No. She needed the money because she wanted to put her mom in a good nursing home. That's what she told me anyway."

"And she never lied to you about anything else, right?"

"You got me there," George said.

"I think I have a new lead. Hopefully this one gets me somewhere."

"Hopefully on your way to California to work out your issues with your husband."

Nancy gave him a sideways sneer.

"I mean, if that's what you want."

"Did you ever consider divorce in all your years of marriage?" she asked him.

"Not once. I loved Melinda every day. Even when things were hard. I guess I was just lucky that way."

"I guess we all have different luck," Nancy said, finishing the dredges in the bottom of her Styrofoam coffee cup. She stood up. "I'll check back with you tomorrow before I leave."
Just as she was about to walk away, a doctor came trotting toward them. "Mr. Altman! Your daughter's waking up!"

Nancy watched as George ran with the doctor, rounded the long hallway and disappeared. She was smiling as she walked out of the hospital for two reasons. She was happy for George—that he'd be able to tell his daughter all the things he'd put off. That resonated with her. Maybe, just maybe, there was a lesson for her in all of it. If she could just tell Roger all of the stuff she'd been putting off, maybe there was a chance the two of them could work things out. She'd think about that later though because the second reason she was smiling was that she had another lead that might put her one step closer to finding Mona Clark's killer—and she had a pretty good feeling about this one.

***

Nancy left the hotel early in the morning. The week the captain had given her was just about up. This was perhaps her last chance to figure it out, and she felt like she was closing in, for real this time. There was something very instinctive to her, when the conclusion was drawing near. It was like the sun had been hiding behind a dense fog, and suddenly the sky cleared and everything was crisp. She felt like that today. Everything seemed so much brighter, and her senses were fired up.

When she pulled into Duluth, she didn't stop at home. Instead, she headed straight for the station. She had a hunch she still wasn't going to find those timesheets she'd requested from Michael Olson for Jenny Stevens, and she was right. They were nowhere to be found. It wasn't because Michael Olson was trying to protect Jenny Stevens either. It was because he was trying to steer her in the wrong direction. Why would he want to do that? There could be a good reason for it.

Nancy traced the checks back to Olson and Sons Realty, just as George had suspected she would. It made a lot of sense. Mike was Mona's boss and her landlord. He lived in St. Paul. He was a real estate agent. He might be just the person to help Mona look for a space in the cities in order to open her art gallery.

Nancy pulled her phone from her bag and dialed George Altman's number.

"Hello," George croaked.

"How's she doing?"

"Well. She's come around. She's said a few words. The doctors are hopeful."

"I'm so glad."

"Thank you."

"I hate to ask you this now, but it's important."

"Go ahead," he said.

"How did you meet Mona?"

"She brought me the key to the cabin."

"She was the person you mentioned was helping Michael Olson care take?"

"Yes."

"Did she ever mention him to you?"

"No. Did he have something to do with this?"

"I'm thinking yes. I'll know more soon."

"Please keep me posted."

"I will."

Nancy hung up and went to her email. The reports she'd requested from the hotels were in. She clicked on the one from Lake Superior Lodge. The registry was long. She scrolled through the check-ins for the week of March 20th until the name she was looking for appeared. Michael Olson.

Chapter 43
February 2nd

Michael yanked the glove box open and grabbed the cheap flip phone out. He dialed Mona's number as he drove, heading to meet a client for a showing in Lowertown.

"Hello," she said.

"Did you get that key to George Altman?"

"I did."

"You're the best."

"Uh huh."

"I was thinking maybe I'd come up for a visit this weekend. I miss you." There was silence on the other end of the line, but Michael knew Mona well. She played it cool—always. "Hey," he said, "did you know that Altman guy is a painter?"

"Really? I thought he was cute," Mona said.

"Cute? You're a nut."

"Why? Besides, you know I have a thing for painters."

"I guess I'm in the wrong profession then."

"There's a lot of things wrong with you, Michael."

"Uh huh. Anyway, how about I get us a room at Superior Lodge on Friday night."

"The hotel? Seriously?"

"I just rented out the cabin, remember?"

"I know."

"Okay, babe. I gotta run in to this appointment now. I'll see ya Friday night."

"Ciao."

Mike flipped the phone closed and threw it back in the glove box with a grin on his face. Friday couldn't come soon enough. He just needed to find a good excuse for why he might need to be out of town for the weekend. Luckily, he had the rest of the week to figure it out.

He got out of the car and headed toward his brother Paul, who was already there, as usual, waiting for him outside the property. Paul was a pain in his ass. He was the more responsible one of the sons who made up Olson and Sons—always early for things, always selling more properties, always more likeable, even better looking, which really got Michael's goat. And though he had no reason to do so—he was already the clear family favorite—Paul still sucked up to their father like the little weasel he was. Mike truly hated his brother. Most guys bonded with their siblings. Mike and Paul were too competitive for bonding, had been since day one. And the prize was their father's love and respect.

Why did he always have to do these deals with his brother? This property could net some serious cash if Mike had the opportunity to work it alone. But no. They were "a team," as his father constantly reminded him, and that meant they had to do things together, which meant doing it by the books, on the straight and narrow. This property had been a thorn in their sides for a while now. They bought it with the intent to rent it out to small businesses, but they hadn't bargained for the high insurance premiums because the building was actually still zoned as industrial. They thought the space would sell as hip, trendy office spaces with its modern, light-industrial vibe in an up and coming area of St. Paul. After they worked the numbers and set the rent it was too high for any small businesses to bite, and the space now sat empty.

They had learned the hard way since they hadn't done an inspection until after the purchase. It was another shortcut Mike had taken behind his brother's back. His father wasn't pleased, but he could still fix it, hopefully today. He had an interested buyer. If he could flip it, he could potentially still earn a profit and walk away as the hero. He didn't think it was necessary to inform the potential buyer about this little downside with the zoning. He also wanted to spike up the cost to recoup their losses. His goody- -goody brother would have different ideas, Mike was certain.

"Hey," Paul said when he approached.

"Before he gets here, let's agree on something," Michael said. "I want to try to haggle a little. If we start throwing numbers around, we might be able to get this guy to bite on something a little higher than what we paid."

"Dad said we should just try to get rid of it. Not every deal is gonna be a win, Mike. Sometimes you just have to cut your losses."

"I don't admit defeat as easily as you, Paul."

"You aren't the owner of the company, thank God."

Mike breathed. "When are you gonna grow a set of balls?"

"When are you going to stop acting like a self-centered, juvenile delinquent?"

Mike didn't have time to form a rebuttal because he saw a man in a gray suit, carrying a briefcase, walking toward them on the sidewalk.

"Mr. Enders," Mike said, pushing his brother out of the way to shake the potential buyer's hand. "I'm Michael Olson. This is my brother, Paul."

"Nice to meet you," Mr. Enders said.

"Why don't we head in and take a look at the space."

"Great."

Paul unlocked the front doors, and they moved into the building. As they walked around, Mr. Enders said, "Can I ask why you're selling after just fifteen months? And why you didn't rent the space out?"

Paul said, "We had planned..."

Mike interrupted him. "We had planned to start a business here but our investors backed out, and we never found the capital to get it off the ground ourselves."

"I see," Mr. Enders said.

Mike's brother shot him a look. Mike ignored it. "I should be honest with you, Mr. Enders. We actually have another party interested in this property." He didn't even look at his brother as he went on, "It's going to go fast, I think."

"Is that right? Well, I do like what I see here. I don't think it would take much to get this place cleaned up. I think I'm willing to throw my hat in the ring."

"Perfect," Mike said.

"I'd like to do an inspection first."

"It could be too late by then," Mike countered.

"How much are we talking about?" Mr. Enders said.

"Five hundred and sixty-five," Mike said firmly.

"Uh..." Paul began. Mike shot daggers at him.

Mr. Enders said, "That's fifty more than the initial asking price."

"I'd be willing to let you have it today for five-fifty," Mike said, "but we'd like to forgo the inspection. I can have our last report sent over to you but I guarantee you'll find everything up to code."

"You drive a hard bargain, Mr. Olson, but I'm going to need to think about it."

"I wouldn't think too long," Mike said.

After Mr. Enders left and Mike stood on the sidewalk while Paul locked the place up again, he prepared himself for the scolding his older, wiser brother was about to dish out. Instead, Paul didn't say a word; he just turned and walked away.

Mike followed behind at his brother's heels. "Jesus. I suppose you're gonna run to tell Dad just like you used to do when we were kids." Paul didn't stop. "That's the business we're in. You need to be able to play the game right."

Paul froze abruptly, causing Michael to slam into the back of him, like he did when they were young boys and Mike tagged behind, in full big brother worship. Paul sighed and turned to him. "You don't get it, do you? We aren't used car salesmen, Mike. We need to operate under the laws. We need to be able to make decisions as a team. You don't get to do things flippantly, on your whim. You are not a team player, never have been. I'm sick of you risking my future, my family's future."

"So what are you gonna do about it? Squeal?"

"Yeah, I am. Let Dad be the judge. I think we both know who he's going to say is right."

"Yep. His hard-working, honest son, who will never amount to anything more than being a sad little pawn in his father's chess game."

"At least it's an honest game. You've never played by the rules in your life. I remember once you cheated at tag. I don't even understand how someone can cheat at tag, but you did. You figured out a way. Why would a twelve year old even think about cheating at something as stupid as tag?"

"I'll tell you why...because I took a boring game of tag and turned it into something interesting."

Paul shook his head and started walking again. "You're playing with the devil, Mike. I don't want anything to do with it."

"Trying to make a little money...that's playing with the devil?"

"Maybe not yet, but small things always have a way of getting bigger as they roll along."

"Okay."

"Wait and see," Paul said as he got to his car parked along the side of Broadway Avenue and got in.

"Wait and see," Mike repeated back like a toddler. He turned and headed toward his own car, kicking a small pebble along the sidewalk.

Chapter 44

The next day, on schedule, Mike's dad called him to his office. Mike was thirty-four years old, and he was still getting in trouble with his father. He couldn't take it. It made him feel like he was sixteen all over again and crashed the car less than a week after he got his driver's license. It hadn't been his fault, but his dad didn't see it that way, nor did he listen to reason. He came down like a hot iron, like he always did. The burn lasted for six months, after which he got his car keys back. Mike thought it was harsh and extreme, his father's specialties, and no amount of apologizing changed the outcome.

He walked in to Olson and Sons Realty, gave Paul the dirtiest look he could muster, then he knocked on his father's office door filled with anxiety and fear, as much as he hated to admit it. Even as an adult, his father had powers over him. But he wanted to get his scolding over with so he could get on with his day. He had six appointments lined up for showings.

"Come in, Mikey." His father was sitting behind his desk like a king on his throne. He was a big man, red in the face, thinning hair. Michael thought he could stroke out at any time if he didn't start cutting back on his salt intake. His blood pressure had been a problem since Mike was a little boy.

"Hey, about yesterday..."

"Mr. Enders' office called to say he was out," his father said, looking up from his paperwork and at

Michael for the first time. He was calm, for the moment.

Mike looked away. "I took a chance," he said. "I was trying to help. I'm sorry."

His father's fist came down on the desk. "Damn it, Mikey! I specifically said to just move the property."

"I know. I misread Enders. I thought..."

His father shook his head from side to side exactly like he used to do when Mike got in trouble at school. "I told you last time, you had one more chance. I meant it."

"Come on, Dad."

Mike's father looked back down and casually went back to work on the papers in front of him.

"You're being dramatic. I...just...I was going to fix everything."

His dad made him wait for a lengthy period of time while he signed half dozen checks in front of him. Finally, he looked up at Michael. There was no sadness in his eyes, no pity, no nurturing qualities Michael could discern in the expression.

"I thought you were better than this."

"Dad, please..."

"Pack up your desk. You're fired."

It was not unlike the car accident at sixteen. He knew once his dad made a decision that was it. It was done. It was firm, like everything his father did. Michael turned to go. His father twisted the knife by adding, "Give your brother your appointments before you go."

Mike kept walking, past his brother, ignoring his father's last request. He even slammed the front door of Olson and Sons on his way out. He marched to his car and sat in the driver's seat for a long time, just staring ahead of him. His father might as well have just punched him in the face. It stung like he actually had. *I thought you were better than this.* All his life, he'd been fighting his older brother for his father's approval, and now it was official. Paul won. He had a sudden surge of hatred toward the both of them.

I thought you were better than this. He was; he knew it. He was better than Paul, at least. Probably his dad, too. Though his father had built up a little realty empire from scratch, he wasn't a great guy. He acted more like an Italian mobster, not the Scandinavian he really was. He was short-tempered and demanding and drove Mike's mom away when he and Paul were very young. She literally walked out on them and never came back. Mike was ten and Paul was twelve. Since then, they'd looked to their father for the affection they no longer received elsewhere. It was almost comical to Mike how ridiculous a feat it was now that he thought about it, how long he'd tried to squeeze love from a stone.

His father had always hung the jobs over their heads, as a rationale for why they were constantly seeking his approval. "I made you two soft by giving you these cushy jobs. You never had to earn real respect," he said to Mike and Paul whenever they were too transparent in their needs.

Mike didn't need his father's acceptance anymore. Maybe, now that he contemplated it, his dad had been right. He should have left Olson Realty a long time ago. Striking out on his own was exactly what his ego needed. He was smarter and more willing to take the risks needed in this business. His father had been holding him hostage for too long, keeping him from doing the things he knew would give him his own measure of success.

He breathed and harnessed his anger into an energy. He had confidence in himself. He wasn't going to let this stop him. He had too much going for himself. He had a lifestyle to maintain. He had a big house, a family to support, three cars, a boat, and a girlfriend. At the thought of Mona, he calmed down even further. He was going to see her Friday. It was exactly what he needed right now. The weekend couldn't come soon enough. He put the car in drive and backed out of his parking spot at Olson and Sons for the last time.

***

Bright and early the next morning, Michael sat down at his computer in his office at home and dug in, making calls to old clients in an attempt to drum up some business. His wife kept butting in with food and drinks and then once just to chat. Then she sent the kids in so she could get some of her own stuff done for a little while.

Mike decided to take a drive after all of that, especially after none of his cold calls panned out. At least in his car it was quiet. He pulled the flip phone out and dialed Mona, but she didn't answer. He left her another message reminding her about the weekend.

The next day, Mike had a meeting with a firm looking for a consultant. He was sure he'd nailed the interview and was shocked when they contacted him on Thursday morning to say he hadn't gotten the job. He wasn't worried. He was doing fine for the moment. He still had the revenue from The Grind and the apartments above it, and he'd tucked away the money he'd been paid for renting the cabin out for the year. If he was being realistic though, he knew that all only amounted to a very tiny fraction of the money he needed to pay his bills.

He really just needed to get away and put the stress behind him for a few days, and then he'd come home and hit it hard. So, first thing Friday morning, he packed an overnight bag and got an early start. He stopped off at the mall on his way out of town, then he was on his way. No sense in waiting around. He was anxious to get there.

Mike reached Lake Superior Lodge by about noon. Check-in wasn't for another hour, so he decided to get some lunch at Granny's Restaurant, which was within walking distance from the hotel. Parking in this area was atrocious, so Mike parked at the hotel and walked to lunch. Granny's was practically an institution in Duluth. He tried to eat there whenever he was in town. He did enjoy their food. It was straight-up, good classic American, no gimmicks or weird themes, plus the cost was right. He had a burger and fries and pondered how he might wine and dine Mona later. He'd learned from the master, his father. After his mom left, his dad brought many a lady around the house. Not a single one of them showered Mike or Paul with much attention, but they certainly loved his dad, for a while—until they learned how nasty he could be, and how short his fuse was, and how after the gifts and sex, he wanted them to leave. He was done with serious commitment after Mike's mom left.

Mike considered his situation to be much different. He wasn't a bad guy, he was in a committed relationship, and he just needed to blow off some steam now and again. Besides, it wasn't like he was going to prostitutes or something. He only had one person he showered with gifts, and that was only because she was special to him. It was just a little perk of the job. She deserved the things he bought for her, even if she didn't always act like she wanted them. He knew differently. Mona was prideful, and he understood. So was he. They were a lot alike in his mind.

After lunch, he headed back to the hotel and checked in. He always got a lakeside room. He liked the ones on the main level with the patio door that let you go right out onto The Lakewalk. Obviously, in February that was irrelevant to Mike, but he still got the room just because he could. Looking out at the lake was the reason Mike had fallen in love with Duluth in the first place. It was his love of the water that drew him to this area of the state. He would have preferred an ocean view, but this was the closest thing he was going to get being landlocked in Minnesota. Still, he could use his imagination. When he looked out, there was no snow or cold, just water and blue skies. It was bigger than him. It wasn't something he could explain; Lake Superior was his refuge, had been since he could remember. That's why when he got his first real paycheck when he started working for his father at eighteen, he purchased the little yellow cabin.

He took a shower, crawled into the hotel bed, flipped the TV on, and waited for Mona. By the time she arrived, he'd already had several drinks from the minibar and was feeling slightly sleepy, but he perked up when she came in.

"Hey, beautiful."

She didn't say anything; just plopped herself down on the couch, removed her giant faux-fur-lined hood, and threw her purse on the floor. Mike patted the space next to him on the bed, but she remained on the couch.

"I got you something. It's in that box on the floor," he said.

Mona reached down and picked up the box with Saks Fifth Avenue written on it. She slipped the top off and held the cashmere sweater up to her chest. "Another sweater. Thank you, Michael."

"Don't you like it?"

"I like it, but I've already told you, you don't have to bring me gifts every time we see each other."

"I'm just happy to see you. I'm trying to show you what a good boyfriend I can be."

"You're not my boyfriend, Michael. You're married."

"I could change that."

"You have three children. Can you change that too?" Mona rolled her eyes at him. "Can we please talk about something else?"

"Okay, yeah." Mike sat up in bed. "Actually, I wanted to tell you that I found a cute little corner shop for rent in Lowertown. It's the perfect place for your gallery."

"That's great, but you know I don't have the money."

"Maybe I can help you out with that."

"I'm not taking your money."

"Well, think about it. I mean it, honey."

"Please don't call me that."

"You're impossible sometimes, Mona."

"Are you taking me to dinner or what?"

"We could stay in…"

"I'd rather go out."

"Okay. Whatever you want." He pulled the covers off and got dressed.

***

A week later, things were still not panning out for Mike. He'd resorted to begging and pleading with some of his old contacts, but things were feeling a little bleak. Not the end of the world yet, but too close to it for Mike's comfort level. He knew what he had to do. He needed to get a little scratch together so he could expand his own business. He'd already started with the coffee shop, but he needed more. He wanted to buy a few more cheap properties and rent them out, and maybe then he'd do some house flipping. The real estate world offered so many opportunities for big money if you knew what you were doing, and Mike was sure he did. This was good, he thought. Without my idiot brother and bullheaded father in the mix slowing me down, this will be a piece of cake. All he needed to do was get the initial money.

He met with the bank regarding a small loan.

"I'm sorry, Mr. Olson. After going over your numbers, we feel you are too much of a risk at the moment. Your debt nearly outweighs your income. When you have more coming in, we'd be happy to talk about it again."

"When I have more coming in, I won't need a loan!"

"Yes, well. That is sometimes the case."

"Doesn't my good credit account for anything?"

"Your credit is just average, actually."

"So, there's nothing you can do for me?"
"No. I'm sorry, not at this time."

Mike stormed out of the bank seeing red. He got in his car and found himself driving toward Duluth. He hadn't planned on heading up again so soon, but he did not want to go home, and driving always helped clear his head. He did his best thinking on the road.

He thought about calling Mona when he was about halfway there, but then he decided to surprise her. He had a few things he needed to take care of at The Grind anyway. The only downside to this spontaneous retreat was that his cabin was rented. It was where he'd often gone for solace at a time like this. At least he was still cashing in on his decision to rent it out. The idea struck him that maybe he should check on his renter. What a curious guy that was, George Altman. A retired factory worker who had somehow been able to plunk down several thousand dollars on a rental cabin. How had he accumulated that amount of wealth, and why spend it on a rundown cabin? If Mike had that kind of money, he'd get himself a real vacation home on a Caribbean Island. That was his measure for making it. That was his dream. Mike fantasized about heading to the Bahamas and plunking down a wad of cash. If a socially awkward old dude could do it, a successful and savvy investor like himself surely could.

All he needed was the initial capital. Where had the old man gotten his? Better yet, did he have more? Maybe Mike would pop in on Old Man Altman and ask if he wanted to be his investor. He thought back to his meeting with George Altman. No matter how hard he'd worked him, that guy gave

Mike nothing back in return. He was an odd duck. Mike wasn't sure if he wanted to try sucking up to Altman again. It made his stomach churn just thinking about it. Then he remembered Mona commenting that George Altman was cute. And all the dots connected.

***

"So, I've been thinking about stuff," he said to Mona in the back room of the coffee shop after hours. "You need some money to open your gallery, right?" He hopped up on the square safe and sat down.

"Sure," Mona said.

"I happen to know this guy who has enough money laying around, he can afford to pay cash for a year's lease on a cabin on Lake Superior. You don't do that unless you have a lot more where it came from…"

"George? He didn't seem rich to me."

Mike cocked his head at her. "George? You're on a first name basis with him now? That's perfect."

"Perfect for what?"

"So, here's my plan. All you're gonna do is dip your spoon into George Altman's soup. Just take a little taste of the good life. You deserve it."

"What are you talking about? I'm not doing that. He's a sweet old man."

"You want to get this gallery up and running so you can make enough dough to move your mom into a nice home, right?"

"Sure."

"Then all you need is a little chunk to get you started."

"And what about you? What's in it for you?"

"I'd take a small cut too, but I'm telling you this guy won't even know it's gone."

"Why's that?"

"Because he'll be so head over heels in love with you by then."

"I'm not doing that."

"Yes, you are."

"No. I'm not."

"Then you're going to stay working at a coffee shop, caring for your mom for the rest of your life. This is your chance. It's a way out."

"No," Mona said, but it took her a while this last time. Michael could see he'd taken a slight chink out of her armor.

He went for the kill. He kicked the safe he was sitting on with the back of his boot. "Besides, I know you've been buying paintings with my checkbook. I almost missed it. You've got some skills with your bookkeeping. You can put those skills to work on someone else now."

Mona picked up the gift he'd brought her, another sweater, rolled it in a ball and chucked it at him. "You're an asshole, Michael."

"Maybe, but I'm doing it for you, baby."

"Don't call me baby. And don't do me any favors."

"No? So I should stop employing you? Should I also stop giving you cheap rent? I should stop bringing you expensive gifts?" When she didn't say anything, he picked up the sweater and threw it back at her. "That's what I thought."

Chapter 45

A few weeks later, Mona had the day off. She sat with her mom on the couch, looking through brochures for care facilities. Right away this morning, Mona knew it was going to be a bad day. Her mom had asked when John was coming home from work. Mona's father had been dead for several years.

"He'll be home soon, I'm sure," Mona said. She often tried to play along until her mother got on a different track. It probably wasn't the right thing to do, clinically speaking, but it was just easier sometimes. She'd tried logic; it rarely worked on a day like today.

"Oh good. I hate when he goes on these long trips, don't you?"

"Yeah." Mona's father had been a truck driver. It was true, he would often be gone for weeks at a time, so she could see where there might be some confusion. Still, she hated her father for leaving her to take care of her mother by herself. As far as she was concerned, he was selfish and she'd never forgiven him, especially on bad days. "This one is particularly long," Mona said dryly.

"I miss him, don't you?" Jan said.

Mona didn't answer. She used to miss him, when she was little and he was on the road. Not anymore.

Then Mona's mother started to tear up. "Why hasn't he called?"

Mona put her arm around her mom. "He can't call from the truck, Mom."

"Maybe I'll call him," Jan said, getting up, moving toward the desk near the window.

"Mom…" Mona followed her to the phone.

She picked up the receiver and stared down at the keypad for what felt like an eternity to Mona. Mona had to let it play itself out. This was often the point where she just set the phone back down and went on to something else. Not today. Jan said, "I can't remember his number. Do you know it, darling?"

"No, Mom. I don't know it either."

"Well, for heaven's sake. That's the strangest thing. Why isn't it written on this paper with all of the other numbers?" She set the phone down and began to shuffle papers around on the desk frantically. "It must be here somewhere."

"It's not here, Mom."

"Do you think something happened to him on the road? It's snowing pretty bad out there." Jan and Mona stared out the window for a minute, looking at the storm outside. "Maybe we should call the police?"

"No, Mom. We don't need to call the police." She took her mom by the shoulders and led her back to the couch. "Look, The Price is Right is on. You love that show."

"Oh. I do. Can I have some tea while I watch, dear?"

Mona breathed a sigh of relief. "Sure. I'll get you some."

"And those good cookies I bought from the bakery yesterday?"

"Uh…sure, Mom. I'll find you some cookies to go with your tea."

She left her mother occupied in front of the TV with her tea and cookies, and she dialed Mike's phone. He didn't answer, likely because he wasn't in his car where he kept the phone she dialed. She left a message. "I'll do it," she said. She hung up and told her mother she was going out for a bit.

In the car, she thought about her parents. They hadn't been the fairytale story people told about their parents meeting and falling in love, living happily ever after. No, Jan and John didn't find each other until later in life, and they were both already fairly damaged when that occurred. Mona's mom was physically abused by her father as a kid. She was meek and needy, and by the age of thirty-five, she still lived at home with her abusive dad. She met John at the truck stop where she worked as a server. He came in on his way to and from his trucking routes. He was in his late thirties and had never dated. He had social anxiety and battled with depression. He was an awkward man who took up trucking because he didn't like to interact with people much.

Somehow Jan and John found each other in the last hour, and they ended up having Mona. Mona's parents were well past forty by that point. Jan quit serving at the truck stop to stay home with Mona. They moved into John's trailer in the park just outside of town. John was on the road so much, it was often just Mona and her mother, who, though a mother herself now, was still fragile and emotionally sheltered from the abuse she'd endured at the hands of her father. Mona couldn't really recall a time she hadn't been the caregiver for her mother, even when she was a child and before the dementia.

By the time Mona was a teenager, her parents were so much older than her friends' parents, she started to notice more of their deficiencies besides just their age. She loved them regardless of their quirky ways, but as she grew, she saw them for the outsiders they were. She learned from their faults and flaws and somehow came out more normal than even she could have imagined. By the time she was twenty, she was a very self-reliant, assertive woman. She was used to being around older people and often found herself falling into a protective role whenever she was around them.

So this idea of stealing from the nice older man was not something she took lightly. She hated herself for agreeing to it. She hated herself for the position she'd gotten herself stuck in with Michael. In exchange for her "friendship," he gave her an affordable apartment over The Grind so she could finally get her mother out of the trailer court after John died. The apartment was clean, and more importantly, it meant Mona could still go to work and take care of her mother, but she hated relying on Michael. She wanted to get out from under his thumb. She wouldn't be doing this if she didn't want more than anything to move her mother to a good care facility so she wouldn't have to worry about her anymore.

Still, Mona felt ill. She wished life wasn't so cruel to her. It was one thing to steal from Michael, but it was a whole different thing to take thousands of dollars from George. He had nothing to do with the horrible cards she'd been dealt. She knew all of this, but Michael had boxed her in; she simply had no other choice.

Chapter 46

After Michael got the message from Mona, he was giddy. He was like a small child. He immediately began figuring out where he was going to invest some of the money and started looking at property listings in the Caribbean. He knew this wasn't going to be enough to get him everything he wanted, but it was a start, and if he could invest wisely, he'd be on his way. Hell, if everything went smoothly, maybe he and Mona could keep this little scam going. He'd definitely have his eyes and ears alert for their next possible victim.

The main thing was he was free from the Olson hold. He would be more successful than them and they were going to regret the day they fired him. That was going to be the best day of Mike's life.

***

A week later, he called Mona to check in with her.

"How are things going with Altman?" he asked. He was getting worried. It'd been awhile since they'd talked.

"They're going," she said curtly.

"Can I get more specifics than that?"

"Don't be crude, Michael."

"No, I don't mean...I just want to know how much longer, do you think?"

"I said I'd call you when it was done."

"Is there a problem?"

"No."

"Mona, you're not really saying much. Is everything going okay?"

"Michael, I'm working on it, okay?"

"I know but are we talking a week? A month? Do you think the geezer's suspicious of us?"

"Don't call him that."

"Jesus, Mon…just tell me what the hell's going on. I got bills to pay."

"I said I'd call you, and that's what I meant. Goodbye, Michael."

The silence hit Mike's ear like a slap to his face. He was used to Mona's feisty moods, but sometimes she knew how to make his fuses run hot. Women were so frustrating; Michael had no idea why he bothered with not one, but two of them. The two combined, though, didn't equate to how awful it had been to work with Paul. He'd take Mona over his brother any day of the week. At least she had more balls than him.

He tried to relax. If this plan was going to work, he had to have some patience. He didn't need to worry about Mona. He had all the faith in the world in her. She'd get it done, he was sure of it.

***

Just like he suspected, a few days later, Mona called him to say she had the info they needed. He drove to a small bank he knew about that was a good twenty minutes away, and he grabbed some forms from the lobby in order to open an account. He walked out feeling like a new man. It was such an easy scam, he scolded himself for not thinking of it sooner.

The cherry on the cake was that he told Mona he didn't want to take down the information over the phone. "You know," he said, "in case they get the phone records. That's hard evidence." So he made up another excuse to tell his wife about how the renter at the cabin was having some freezing pipe issues that he needed to go take a look at, like he knew anything about plumbing. His wife was so used to him going to Duluth under the guise of maintenance on his properties, or handling work matters with The Grind, she never questioned him anymore. Besides, she was too exhausted from taking care of their three young kids to even care.

He checked in at the hotel and almost didn't get his lakeside patio room. Things were starting to pick up as the weather started getting a little nicer. Michael hadn't even thought to book a room in advance—it was a Tuesday for Christ's sake. Except, the guy at the counter told him there was a big conference in town, so they were almost at capacity.

"What do I need to do to get my room?" Mike asked. He once again reminded himself that sometimes he needed patience to get the things he wanted.

The receptionist made a few clicks on his computer and said, "If you can come back in an hour, I can have your room."

"Perfect," Mike said.

He had an hour to kill, and he knew exactly what he'd do during that time. He called Mona from the car. She didn't answer so he left her a message.

"Hey, baby. I'm running an errand. Meet me at the lodge in like two hours."

Mike was feeling so amazing, he headed to a jewelry store. Why not reward Mona for the dirty work he'd had her do? It could not be easy seducing a man like that Altman character.

He picked out a pair of diamond earrings and had the clerk wrap them. She was going to flip when she saw them. Mike could hardly wait.

He returned a while later and found his room was ready. He waited with boyhood anticipation for Mona. He flipped on the TV and looked out at the lake, waiting for her to arrive. He checked his watch several times. She was running late. He started to worry about her. He went to his car and grabbed his flip phone out of the glove box and dialed her cell.

"What do you want?" she said. Her voice sounded off. He heard wind howling through the cell phone.

"What do you mean? Where are you?"

"I'm not doing this Michael. I'm done. It's over."

"What? Mona, what are you…where are you?"

The familiar sound of Mona hanging up on him pulsed in Mike's ear. He dialed her back, one time after another but she didn't pick up. In his rage, he threw the phone onto the street and stomped on it until it broke into several pieces of plastic, then he kicked the pieces with his foot and slid them into a storm drain at the curb. He got back into the car and drove.

Chapter 47

Mona sat in the shadows on the edge of the banks at Knife River. The melt had created a swift stream that flowed down the banks at a good speed. It churned and spit up white foam as water hit the jagged rocks violently. After she'd listened to the voicemail George had left her a few more times, she tucked the phone into her coat pocket and threw a loose twig into the raging water, watching it being carried away. Her tears and self-pity drowned out the awareness that a black SUV had parked and was shining its headlights on her.

When a figure approached her from behind, she didn't turn. She just said, "This is where he did it, you know?"

"I do know. How do you think I knew where to find you?" Michael said.

"He parked his semi in the lot and just stepped right off this bank and let his pain and suffering wash away. Just like that. He used to bring me here sometimes when I was little. He said the noise of the rapids calmed him. I guess he's pretty damn calm now."

"It was selfish, remember? You said it yourself." He sat down next to her.

"I think I understand him now. I've been selfish too. I've done things that I'm not proud of because I was only thinking of myself. What about that poor man? I had no right." Her head shook from side to side. The wind made her brown curls whip and cover her face.

"George Altman? He's going to be just fine. Do you know how many people have money stolen from them? Besides, the bank will likely cover the losses." Mike tried to get her to look at him. She jerked away.

"It's not about the money! He cared about me. I could tell."

"I care about you too, Mona."

She stood up and took a step closer to the edge of the bubbling river and peered down. A large sheet of ice close to the banks broke off and was immediately carried away. Mona felt Michael scurry behind her. "I want to be as brave as my father."

"Mona, come on." He put his hand on the back of her shoulder. "Let's go back to the hotel and discuss this. I have something special for you." She pulled away, inching herself closer to the lip of the river.

"Leave me alone, Michael! I told you it was over! I'm not going through with it." She stepped on a twig, which cracked in half, and just as she thought maybe she could really do it, Michael's hand yanked her back toward him.

"It's too late for that," he said. His tone had changed, and the grip he had on her hand was biting and no longer endearing.

She tried to get him to release his grip, but he only held it tighter. He tugged on her hand and moved her back toward the safety wire that was meant to keep people from slipping into the water. She made one last attempt to free herself. She could still do it. She could jump. Couldn't she? No. She didn't think she could. She was a failure. She'd let George Altman down. She'd let her mother down.

She'd let herself down. Then something clicked as they made their way back to the parking lot, and they stopped next to Mike's SUV.

"Maybe it's not too late," she said. "Maybe I can go back to him and beg and plead, tell him that I made a horrible mistake. Maybe he'll take me back."

Michael moved closer to her face. "Take you back? What are you talking about?"

"I'm going to tear up the information. I can still fix this."

"No. You're not tearing anything up. Are you..." Michael paused. "You're in love with him, aren't you?"

Mona stayed silent. Michael's expression turned from angry to something much more sinister. His face pulled tight, and he began to breathe out of his nose like a raging bull. He didn't say anything else except, "Get in the damn car, Mona." He pulled the passenger door open and pushed her in. She went because she was still thinking about how she could fix things with George.

Chapter 48

During the drive back to the hotel, Mona stayed quiet. It was okay by Mike. He was overcome with emotions that needed sorting out himself. His insides burned with fire. He felt anger and sadness and betrayal. He and Mona were supposed to be a team on this. She was supposed to be part of his team, not George Altman's. They were going to get some easy money and then…well, who knew what then, but Mike had thought one day Mona would want him for more than just his expensive gifts and good ideas. Christ, he'd given her everything: a job, a place to live, his love. She was nothing without him, except trailer trash. Why couldn't she see that?

And he was worried. He'd gotten himself into something here, and he wasn't prepared to go to jail for a girl who didn't love him back. He needed to convince her to change her mind. He thought he knew how, too. The ace in his back pocket was the little box of rocks sitting on the hotel dresser.

Mike parked in the hotel parking lot. "I have something for you," he said. "Come inside. We'll sit and order some room service, talk this through and then after… Well, let's just say, I think you'll come to your senses."

Mona didn't respond, so he took it as a yes. He took her hand and they went into the hotel and walked through the lobby. There was a decent amount of people around, and to the average eye, they probably appeared like a young couple in love. Well, at least one of them was in love.

They got back to the room, and he slipped his jacket off. Mona left hers on, but she released her bag onto the floor. "Take your coat off and relax," he said.

She sat down on the couch. She had a far away look in her eyes.

Mike sat down next to her and put his hand on her knee. "Mon, baby, listen."

"I'm not your baby."

"I'm just trying to help you. We've already gotten away with this. He may not even realize it was you. If you go back and admit it, he's gonna call the cops, sure as shit."

"That's a chance I'm willing to take. I need to make this right. I was a complete idiot for letting you manipulate me. I'm done, Michael. I don't care if I have to go back to the trailer park. I'm done."

"Manipulate? That's what you think this was? This is the thanks I get for everything I've done for you? You spoiled brat! And to think I was going to give you these." He got up and picked up the box with the diamond earrings in them.

Mona stood up. "I don't want your stuff, Michael! I never did!"

"Just give me the damn information you took from George Altman's place, and you can have them."

"You aren't listening to me. I said I don't want them!" She stood up and made a move toward the door.

Michael grabbed her arm and pulled her to him. "You don't know what you want, Mon. You've lost your flipping mind. What's going on with you tonight? You aren't stepping foot out this door until you give me the paperwork."

"Michael, just let me go. I said I don't need you anymore."

"Maybe not, but I still need you."

"Maybe I should call your wife and tell her you said that. I bet she'd be very interested to know that."

"You wouldn't."

"Let me go and I won't. Just go home to your kids and pretend none of this happened. You're better than this, Michael."

That was the last straw. How dare she say that to him? How dare she! Michael dropped the box with the diamonds on the floor. He faced Mona and let all of his rage gather. Mona looked at him with pity. It was the same look Paul gave him that day on the sidewalk after he'd screwed up the deal in Lowertown. He knew now he couldn't trust Mona. She was going to expose him to his wife, or worse yet, get him arrested. He needed this money. He needed to think.

There was a brief moment of hesitation because as much as he didn't want to admit it, he loved her. Almost as if she was hearing his thoughts, she said to him in a calm and soft tone, almost mocking him, "I don't love you, Michael."

He felt something inside of himself snap. Maybe he wasn't all that different from his father, after all. That was the thought he had as he reached for Mona and wrapped his hands around her neck and squeezed. As he did, he let her words sink in, what he hadn't wanted to believe until now. She didn't love him. She'd been using him. She wasn't on his team. Nobody was, not even his own father. He felt his pulse quicken and with it, his hands harnessed all of the frustration he'd felt in the last few weeks, all of the stress of losing his job, fretting about the theft, dealing with Mona. The release felt great. He looked in her eyes one last time as they sort of rolled back in the sockets. He continued to squeeze until she felt too heavy to hold upright anymore. When Mona's body dropped to the floor and landed next to the jewelry box with a thud, Michael Olson felt conflicted. He was suddenly lighter, like he'd just released an anchor into the water, and at the same time, he was empty. He hadn't meant to hurt Mona. He loved her. He only wanted her to love him back, to be on his team. He wanted someone to believe in him, just one time.

He fell to his knees and cried over Mona's lifeless body.

Chapter 49
Present Time

George sat with Ella, still in her hospital bed, but sitting up and getting stronger each day. She was being released today. They were just waiting for the doctor to come in for the final approval to leave.

"I've got a rental car. I can take you back to your house and get you settled, then I'll probably head back to Duluth," he told her.

"Dad...you can stay with me, you know?"

"I have to tell you something, honey. I may have kicked your, uh, roommate out." He'd been avoiding this conversation until the last possible minute. He watched her face closely, not sure how she'd react.

She processed what he said and then started to laugh. "Thanks. I'd been trying to figure out what to do with his sorry ass for weeks. You did me a favor."

"Oh, thank God. I was worried you were going to be mad."

"Relieved is more appropriate. You were right about him. He's not the guy for me."

Now George laughed. "No, he really isn't the guy for you."

"I think I just liked him because he was an artist, like you. I thought I'd try someone who wasn't a scientist."

"I'm no artist."

"Yes, you are."

"I'm not sure I want to be lumped into the same category as Jeff," he said. Ella giggled again. It was so great hearing her laugh. George had tried to keep things as light as possible for the last few days as she recovered. They'd been avoiding the elephant in the room, but now it was weighing on him. He was running out of time, and he needed to make sure he didn't make another mistake, not with his daughter anyway.

They were silent for a minute. George was still sitting in the chair next to Ella's bed. He'd grown very attached to that chair, but he was glad Ella was going home. Maybe she was right, maybe he should stay with her for a while, just to make sure she was truly okay. She still might need some help. That would also give him some time to figure out what to say to her. He checked his watch.

As he did, Ella grabbed his hand. He sharply turned toward her, "Are you okay?" He was about to push the emergency call button, but then he saw tears rolling down her face.

"Dad, I'm sorry," she said through the crying jag. "I'm sorry we fought. I was just so angry with you, but it wasn't that, I realized. I was confused and mostly just still missing Mom, but I know you wouldn't hurt anyone. I just didn't know how to talk to you about it all. I...just... thank you for being here for me. I don't know what I would have done if I'd have come to in this bed without you here."

"It was my fault. I was being stubborn. I should have told you everything right up front. I was scared of what you'd think of me because I knew it was wrong. I'm sorry."

"It wasn't wrong. Besides, look at me. I chose Jeff." She laughed through the tears. George squeezed her hand. There was a knock at the door. The doctor stood there with a clipboard, reviewing Ella's chart one final time. She grabbed a tissue and blew her nose and wiped her tears. George stood up and shook the doctor's hand.

"Well, Miss Altman. Everything looks good. Make sure you're still taking things easy for a while. You're going to be sore. Let's see you back next week for a follow up, and then we'll see about getting you back to work, okay?"

"Thank you, Doctor Pilstrom."

"You're welcome. Take care, now. Both of you."

After the doctor left, Ella got out of the bed and went to the bathroom to change into her clothes when George's cell rang.

"Hello?"

"Hey, it's Nancy. We got him. Michael Olson's in custody."

"You got him! How?"

"He and Mona were on the security tape walking into the hotel together the night of her death. Olson had a ground level room with a patio door going out to the lake. The next morning he left the hotel alone, with something small clutched under his arm. I got a warrant, and we searched his home and found it. It was Mona's purse. I had a hunch he couldn't let go of her and kept something as a souvenir. Inside the bag was a pair of diamond earrings wrapped in gift-wrap still. I think he was bribing or blackmailing her to do his dirty work. She must have put up a fight, and he probably got scared she'd squeal on him. Anyway, when we found him, he had a one-way ticket to the Bahamas in his wallet. I think he was waiting to leave because he thought he'd thrown me on a different trail."

"Good work, Detective."

"I couldn't have done it without your help." There was a pause. "How's Ella?"

"She's going home."

"Good news all around then."

"Yes. Very good news. Thank you, Nancy."

"I'll be in touch, okay?"

"I'd like that."

George hung up and another weight lifted off of him. It wasn't as heavy as the one he'd felt when Ella was in the coma, but it was still a burden he was happy to set down.

"Was that the detective?" Ella asked, coming out of the bathroom.

"Yes. She's got someone in custody for Mona's killing."

"Who?"

"You won't believe it. He was my realtor. I felt something off with him when I first met him. I had no idea it was that off though."

"How did she get herself messed up with him, do ya think?"

"I don't know. She never mentioned him."

"She must not have had a dad like you to come and kick out the loser."

"No. She didn't." George recalled her telling him about her own father as they sat on plastic buckets on the frozen lake. That felt like a whole lifetime ago now, and for Mona it was. Sadness and anger mixed and boiled in the pit of George's stomach, but he had to let it go now. Michael Olson would be punished, and he couldn't save Mona. It was too late.

"I feel sorry for her. It's tragic," Ella said.

"It is."

She looped her arm around George. He took her bag, and they walked slowly out of the hospital together.

Chapter 50

Nancy gave notice to the Duluth PD after she finished up Mona Clark's case. She went home that day and started packing up some of her things. She opened her closet and dug deep into the recesses and pulled out a small shoebox. Clutching it in her arms like it was a fragile newborn baby, she took it to the bed and sat down. She gently set the box down in front of her and slipped the lid off. She pulled out a photograph of her father. Her detective eyes bore into the picture for a long time.

The next day, Nancy drove to the yellow cabin to say goodbye to George. He was there packing up his things too.

"What are you going to do now?" she asked him.

"I'm going to take Ella on that tropical vacation Melinda wanted us to go on. The sun and rest will do us both good, I think."

"That sounds nice. I'm on my way to talk with Mona's mother. I wanted to stop to tell you goodbye, but I was also wondering…"

George gave her a curious look.

She went on, "I'd like to buy the painting of Lake Superior from you, I mean, if it's for sale."

"What? You don't want that."

"I do actually. I'm leaving here, too. I thought it would be the perfect thing for me to remember this Godforsaken town by…and you. Besides, I meant it when I said I think you have a gift. I really love that painting."

George pulled it out of the stack of things he had piled once again near the cabin entrance. "It's yours." He handed it to her. "No charge. Now, had you arrested me, it would have cost you a lot of money. But under the circumstances, I'd like you to have it." They laughed. Then George said, "Have you decided to go be with your husband, or what's your plan?"

"I've been thinking a lot about that. I know the first thing I have to do is go to Sacramento and at least be straight with Roger and see where that goes. And then, since I'm going to be in California, I have something else I need to figure out." She paused. "I think I told you that my father was murdered. What I didn't tell you is that in a lot of ways, this case brought up stuff that I haven't wanted to face for a very long time. I was young when my dad was killed, and at the time, I thought he was the most perfect human who'd ever walked the earth. Then, when he died, well of course, then he became a deity to me. He was on such a higher plane than anyone else, I couldn't even touch him up there.

"But now, I'm starting to come to grips with the fact that maybe he wasn't the guy I thought he was all along. Seeing you and Ella together made me put myself into her shoes. Maybe my dad had flaws too. I mean, you don't get shot in your kitchen for no reason, after all. But maybe, just maybe it's okay to know that he may have made some mistakes, but that doesn't mean I can't still love him.

"I've been carrying around this shoebox with some of his things in it since I left home. I always take it and bury it in the back of my closet because I didn't want to see things. I didn't want to look at them. Do you know, I've never tried to solve my father's murder? I was too scared. I was scared to see him as a real person. Ella was scared too. She just wanted you to tell her it was all going to be all right."

George nodded at this assessment.

"Anyway," Nancy continued, "in the shoebox, there's a photograph. It's a picture of my dad with his arm around a woman. Only, I've never seen this particular person before in my life. My mother claimed to have never seen her before either. The date on the picture was just a few months prior to my dad's death. On the back of the photo is a message written in pen. It says, 'With love always, Roseanne.'

"I'm not sure what I might find with that limited information, but I think I need to finally try. Not because I want to catch the perp and lock him or her in jail necessarily, but because it's time to take my father off that shelf so high up in my closet. I need to get to know the man that was my flesh and blood, for good or bad, flaws and all. Maybe if I can finally put it all behind me, maybe I can open myself up a little more, let other people in a little easier, knowing that just because they've made mistakes doesn't make them a murder suspect, or a bad husband."

George walked over to where Nancy had been pacing as she revealed her secrets to him. He said, "You've been helping everyone else find peace for so long, it's time you find it for yourself. You deserve to be happy."

He moved closer to her and they stood together in front of the small window, looking out over Lake Superior. "If there's one thing I've learned as a detective, it's that everybody is hiding something. We all have skeletons. It's trying to weed out whether or not they've damaged you enough to turn you into something worse underneath it all, that's the part I can usually figure out. But I'll admit, you definitely challenged my skills…Mr. Altman."

"George."

She nodded. "My mom always said it's the quiet ones you gotta look out for, and moms are usually right. I'm glad she was wrong this time…George."

"Me too." He smiled at her, then said, "Actually, I have a favor to ask of you. I know it's probably not standard procedure, but I was wondering if I might be allowed to go and talk with Mona's mother."

Nancy thought on it for a second. She'd wanted to be the one to tell Jan Clark that she could rest easy now that Michael Olson was behind bars, but George had protected her throughout this whole ordeal. It was obvious it meant something to him as well, and it would probably be good for him to connect with her; they both cared about Mona, after all. Nancy had never even met her. It was hard for her to give up the control, but this was a new Nancy. She needed to let go sometimes. "I think Jan Clark would like to talk to you," she said finally. "She isn't completely coherent, but I'm sure she'll understand some of what you tell her."

They said their final goodbyes and Nancy took her painting and headed home to finish packing. She surveyed Duluth again on her drive. Everything happened for a reason, but as much as she'd hated this town, without it, she'd have never figured out all of this stuff about herself. Still, she was more or less happy to be leaving. She was just happy for the first time in a long time.

Chapter 51

After Nancy left, George went back to cleaning out the fridge. He was thinking about everything he'd been through since Melinda had passed. It was now coming up on April but it felt like Mel had been gone for so much longer than six months. After she died, he wasn't sure how he would go on without her. If there was one thing these crazy couple of months had taught him, it was that if he could survive through all of the things thrown his way as of late, he could keep on doing it.

As George swept jars and packages of old food he'd stacked on the counter from the fridge, he came to the bottle of sleeping pills. He picked it up and shook it, contemplating the little pills once again. He tossed them into the trash bin along with the food waste. He didn't want to die now. He couldn't leave his daughter. She needed him as much as he needed her.

George was looking forward to getting to know the adult Ella had become better. It was time for them to work on their poor communication skills, to break past the barriers that they'd both put up. If he could open up to his daughter more, and she could do the same to him, maybe they could figure out how to make their relationship stronger. Maybe the detective was right, it was perhaps what Ella needed in order to push ahead in finding a good life partner, in order to achieve happiness in more than just her profession.

As for him, he'd already experienced happiness in his life; anything else was just an added bonus. That's what all of this had taught him. It was a hard lesson, but it was a learned one. He was pleased Nancy had asked him for the painting of the lake. Maybe it was the boost he needed to continue to hone his skills with the brush. Maybe he'd take some canvases with him on his trip and try to paint the ocean next, maybe even some palm trees.

***

Once he finished cleaning out the kitchen, he took a break and got in his Prius to go see Mona's mother. It took a while for him to explain who he was at the check-in desk. He probably should have asked Nancy to call ahead, but they eventually approved him for a short visit. Since he wasn't friend or family, a staff member had to be present, but George didn't fuss at that, and they showed him in to Jan's room.

She was seated in a straight-backed chair in front of the television. The volume was beyond loud. Jan barely looked away from the screen when George and the attendant entered.

"Hi, Mrs. Clark. I'm George Altman. I was a friend of Mona's."

She nodded.

"Do you mind if I turn the TV down so we can talk for a minute?"

Another nod.

While George worked the remote controls, the staff member brought over another chair for him. He sat down facing Jan, blocking the screen from her view.

"I have some good news for you. They've caught the man who…" he paused and choked back some emotion he wasn't expecting, "killed Mona."

Jan's eyes searched George's face. "Who are you?" she asked.

"I was a friend of your daughter. My name is George."

"You the one who was helping her open an art gallery?"

"No. I'm just a painter."

"It was her dream. Did you know that?"

"I believe it. She seemed to really love art."

"She did. She's dead now though. Did you know that?" Jan asked, searching George's face for answers again.

"Yes. I know. Detective Simmons wanted me to tell you that she caught the man who did it."

"I knew she would. Don't tell me his name. I don't think I want to know it."

"I understand."

"Why, though? Mona was a good kid."

"I'm not entirely sure why," George confessed to her. He'd been wrestling with this question himself.

Jan touched his hand, causing him to come out of his own hazy thoughts. Her eyes were clearer when she spoke again, "I think he wanted to be the one to help her with her dream, but Mona was too strong for him. She wanted to accomplish it on her own. That man was no good for her; he was holding her back. I didn't meet him, but I knew it. I could tell from what Mona told me about him. He wasn't right."

George took that all in, trying to make sense of it. Before he could, Jan was talking again. "I can tell you're a better man. I want you to be the one to help her with her dream."

"She's gone, Mrs. Clark."

"It's not too late."

"I don't understand."

"You need to open her art gallery. In St. Paul. She wanted it to be in St. Paul. She was collecting paintings. I want you to take them and hang them in St. Paul. Would you do that for me?"

George thought for a second. He had plenty of money still. It wasn't a bad idea. When he got home from his trip… "I would love to do that for you."

Jan squeezed his hand. "Can you name the gallery in Mona's honor?"

"Yes. I think that's a very good idea."

"I do too."

George squeezed Jan's hand now too. She didn't seem as confused as Nancy had made her out to be. She seemed to know exactly what she was talking about. George was feeling good about this idea. A warmth radiated between him and Mona's mother, and they both just sat quietly for a minute taking it in.

After he left, he headed back to the cabin to finish his packing. He noticed on the drive he felt lighter, more relaxed than he had in a very long time, maybe even since his last week of work. This idea of opening an art gallery was intriguing. He wasn't necessarily jumping off the moving train of life by tackling this new venture put forth my Mona's mother; instead he was moving along with it, still waiting for the right stop. Maybe the gallery would be a perfect destination. He really needed something good to come out of this mess. Whether he wanted to or not, he was moving on, and the new George was finally okay with that. He was even looking forward to it.

ABOUT THE AUTHOR

Jody Wenner is a Twin Cities native who began
writing for her high school paper and completed a
degree from the University of Minnesota in
Communications. Journalistic writing was set aside
when she realized how much fun it was to do her
own world building. When she's not reading or
writing, you will find her crafting up a storm.

Made in the USA
Lexington, KY
03 July 2016